Mark Kauffman

LAUREL BRETT, a refugee from the 1960s, was born in Manhattan in the middle of the last century. Her passionate interest in the arts and social justice led her to a PhD and a long career as a community college professor. She expanded her award-winning dissertation on Thomas Pynchon's work into a groundbreaking analysis, *Disquiet on the Western Front: World War II and Postmodern Fiction,* which was published by Cambridge Scholars. She lives in Port Jefferson, New York. *The Schrödinger Girl* is her debut novel.

the schrödinger girl

the schrödinger girl

laurel brett

KAYLIE JONES BOOKS

Published by Akashic Books
©2020 Laurel Brett

ISBN: 978-1-61775-729-7
Library of Congress Control Number: 2019935335
First printing

Kaylie Jones Books
www.kayliejonesbooks.com

Akashic Books
Brooklyn, New York, USA
Ballydehob, Co. Cork, Ireland
Twitter: @AkashicBooks
Facebook: AkashicBooks
E-mail: info@akashicbooks.com
Website: www.akashicbooks.com

Also Available from Kaylie Jones Books

Cornelius Sky by Timothy Brandoff
Starve the Vulture by Jason Carney
City Mouse by Stacey Lender
Death of a Rainmaker by Laurie Loewenstein
Unmentionables by Laurie Loewenstein
Like This Afternoon Forever by Jaime Manrique
Little Beasts by Matthew McGevna
Some Go Hungry by J. Patrick Redmond
Inconvenient Daughter by Lauren J. Sharkey
The Year of Needy Girls by Patricia A. Smith
The Love Book by Nina Solomon
The Devil's Song by Lauren Stahl
All Waiting Is Long by Barbara J. Taylor
Sing in the Morning, Cry at Night by Barbara J. Taylor
Flying Jenny by Theasa Tuohy

From Oddities/Kaylie Jones Books

Angel of the Underground by David Andreas
Foamers by Justin Kassab
Strays by Justin Kassab
We Are All Crew by Bill Landauer
The Underdog Parade by Michael Mihaley
The Kaleidoscope Sisters by Ronnie K. Stephens

For Mia and David

*The most beautiful thing we can
experience is the mysterious.
It is the source of all true art and science.*
—Albert Einstein

CHAPTER ONE

I DIDN'T REALLY GET THE SIXTIES or all the sixties worship that went on around me. I was tired of paisley and cartoonish graphics. I would go to my grave convinced that green and blue and orange and pink don't go together, whatever anyone said.

I didn't want to have to take a side about Vietnam and make up my mind about whether our government was right and righteous, mistaken, or even worse, just conning us. I left that to other people.

Everyone bad-mouthed the fifties, and I could see why. Sure, the blacklist was awful. And I hadn't much liked Eisenhower, either. But I liked the neatness of those times—the notion that our routines could save us from the savagery of the war we had just lived through, that they could contain us with their boundaries. That's why I had studied behavioral psychology and made it my life's work—it made people fit into predictable patterns.

And I didn't get the music. I didn't even like Elvis. What was rock and roll? A few chords and a simple beat? My dad had built an impressive collection of jazz records, and had heard many of the greats in person too: Duke Ellington and Count Basie when my dad ventured up to Harlem, and he'd loved Billie Holiday. Before the

war he'd even heard the young Charlie Parker play, and
I knew from the way he talked about him that if my dad
had lived, he'd have loved to see where Parker went.
When the war ended in 1945, and things went back to
normal, nothing went back to normal for me. I was a
fifteen-year-old kid, my dad had been killed in combat,
and I held onto the culture he left me.

That included baseball and the memories of all the
games we saw together. The Yankees meant hope and redemption, but now there was no redemption on the field.
Last season, the summer of 1966, was the worst season
in Yankees history. We came in last place. I had had my
hopes up this year when they won their opening game on
Monday, but then they lost on Wednesday, and now on
Friday they were losing again. I was already panicking,
afraid the team was heading for last place a second time,
even with Whitey Ford and Mickey Mantle still on the
field.

Before this year's opening game, the end of March
had brought freakishly cold conditions and snow, which
hadn't improved my mood, and the management of
the Yankees had traded Maris back in December. The
old gods were gone—Babe Ruth, Lou Gehrig, and
Joe DiMaggio—and Ford and Mantle weren't coming
through for us anymore. No great players were waiting in
the wings to save us, and the Yanks were taking down my
life with them. Baseball had always been the only thing
I was truly passionate about, and spring always meant
baseball.

The game kept me going after my dad died when I
was thirteen. Trading cards was my hobby then, and I
often skipped afternoon classes to sit in the stands. Now

I sat in a dive bar on the Upper West Side nursing my second Rheingold. If I'd known they didn't serve Ballantine here, the Yanks' beer, I would have found a different joint. Rheingold sponsored the Mets, the newfangled team that couldn't make up for the Giants and Dodgers leaving New York. In the few years the Mets had been around they had finished last or next to last. I could find no solace in baseball, and if it wasn't in baseball it wasn't anywhere.

I found myself staring at the picture behind the bar of the last Miss Rheingold, a Hitchcock blonde elected by twenty-three million votes in 1964, just before the contest ended. Nearby a table of gals was watching the game too, and one or two of them eyed me with interest. The four made an interesting collection—two resembled fifties good girls in their sweater sets, and the other two, London "birds," were decked out in the recent British street style— stick-straight hair and mini-length print shifts. A blonde caught my eye and smiled with her fashionably pale lips. I thought of approaching her, but I was in a real slump too, so I nursed my beer alone. Absolutely nothing felt right when the Yankees were losing.

Jeez. Strike out for Mantle. Disgusted, I left the bar. I didn't watch the Yankees to see them lose. I carried a beat-up briefcase with notes for a book on an experiment I had been running on super-unmotivated rats that I had bred to procrastinate, and now the rats in my lab wouldn't run the maze I had set up. I really identified with those rats. I'm a research psychologist and teacher, and I was looking for something that would motivate the rats, but now I realized that I hated the experiment. In the mood I was in, I decided that the animals could just be dispirited for life, and I dumped the satchel in a trash can I passed on the way from the bar to Columbus Circle. I knew I'd regret the loss of the leather case, but I was in the mood to make a grand gesture.

Instead of spending a dreary afternoon in the New York Public Library scouring periodicals for my rat experiment, I was now free to walk to my favorite paperback bookstore, Bookmasters on Columbus Circle. I had never seen a space so overflowing with soft-covered books. I pointedly ignored the psychology section and headed to science to peruse books on quantum physics, which I studied as a hobby. For the hundredth time I wondered why I'd chosen to study psychology and not physics. It must have been that girl—buxom, with the darkest eyes I'd ever seen—in science class, who told me that deep down I was really a people person. I wondered where she was now.

I selected a volume with two stunning Egyptian cats on the cover representing Schrödinger's cat experiment. At one point Schrödinger had found quantum physics silly and had imagined a thought problem in which a cat is penned up in a metal box with a very small amount of a radioactive substance. The probability that the substance will decay is equal to the probability that it won't. Should it decay, the decaying atom will immediately smash a device containing poison gas that will kill the cat. If it doesn't decay, the cat will live. While the cat is still in its box, in theory the equation that describes the entire system includes a dead cat and a live cat. The indeterminacy that is our state of not-knowing, that begins with the decaying atom and includes the fate of the cat, can only be resolved by opening the box and observing the cat directly when it is clearly alive or dead.

Poor Schrödinger! Instead of dissuading people from the complementarity hypothesis, the idea that light is both a particle and wave, they took his little allegory, simple as a children's book really, as a perfect representation of the concept. That's the way things work. Schrödinger's satiric fable became the emblematic parable of quantum physics, also known as quantum mechanics, and his cats had been appearing everywhere ever since—on book covers, in conversation, and in jokes and cartoons. Here they were on a populist account of "the new physics," which was really not new anymore.

I began earnestly reading the Schrödinger chapter in the text when a crowd of shoppers entered. Despite the morning's beautiful weather, the skies had suddenly opened with a sun shower, the rain falling in such profusion that droves of laughing, rushing, pushing people entered to escape getting soaked. The weatherman had not predicted rain.

Aisles became so full that as more bedraggled pedestrians crowded in, the mood became convivial. A fiftyish woman in a dampened gray hat asked what I was reading, and I showed her the cats and began talking about quantum physics until she waved and headed off to gardening or cooking or maybe it was classic literature. A younger woman, alone, asked me for a recommendation for her teenager who liked biology. "*The Voyage of the Beagle*," I replied. I wondered if the child would be thankful for the Darwin.

I saw that there were other copies of the Schrödinger book on the shelves. I decided that if anyone else picked up the book I'd ask him to lunch for the fun of talking to another science lover. The randomness of the possible meeting appealed to me.

Ten minutes passed with no takers. There were no serious browsers, just people who had discovered that the science section was one of the less crowded. I glanced over to the children's aisle where a mom was reading one of the Alice books to two tiny girls who seemed too young to appreciate it. Just close enough for me to eavesdrop, I heard her reading from the chapter called "Down the Rabbit-Hole":

Alice was beginning to get very tired of sitting by her sister on the bank, and of having nothing to do: once or twice she had peeped into the book her sister was reading, but it had no pictures or conversations in it, "and what is the use of a book," thought Alice, "without pictures or conversation?"

So she was considering in her own mind, (as well as she could, for the hot day made her feel very sleepy and stupid,) whether the pleasure of making a daisy-chain would be worth the trouble of getting up and picking the daisies, when suddenly a white rabbit with pink eyes ran close by her.

There was nothing so very remarkable in that; nor did Alice think it so very much out of the way to hear the Rabbit say to itself, "Oh dear! Oh dear! I shall be too late!" (when she thought it over afterward, it occurred to her that she ought to have wondered at this, but at the time it all seemed quite natural); but when the Rabbit actually took a watch out of its waistcoat-pocket,

and looked at it, and then hurried on, Alice
started to her feet, for it flashed across her mind
that she had never before seen a rabbit with ei-
ther a waistcoat-pocket, or a watch to take out
of it, and, burning with curiosity, she ran across
the field after it, and was just in time to see it pop
down a large rabbit-hole under the hedge.

The mom read in a lively manner so I kept listening and realized that I had never read Lewis Carroll and
thought I might like to. His quirky world was unexpected, mysterious, and more fun than the one I lived in
where the Yanks were now a losing team and rats suddenly bored me.

I looked back at the book rack and saw that the physics text, with its cover of the two Egyptian cats, spines
pressed together, black and gold, with their fancy tails,
was being held aloft by someone in a yellow rain slicker
with the hood up. I couldn't ascertain any notion of the
person, except it was someone prescient enough to know
it was going to rain. Wow! Perhaps something unexpected
would enter my life.

I muttered excuse me's as I elbowed my way through
until I was peering down at the reading figure who barely
reached my chin.

"Pardon me," I said, "but are you interested in quantum physics?"

Slowly the hooded head lifted. Emerald eyes gazed up
at me, and the hood fell back to reveal clouds of auburn
hair. "Yes, of course. Yes. Yes, I am."

"Oh," I said, barely a syllable. The sound was really
just an expiration of air.

"Hm?" she inquired.

"Would you like to have lunch with me? I promised myself I would offer lunch to anyone who picked up this book." I showed her that I had the same book in my hand, the same enigmatic cats staring out of the cover. I was nervous, though I couldn't imagine why. My heart appeared to have sped up, and it seemed that something momentous was happening. I really wanted her to say yes.

"That doesn't sound like something I could refuse," she said, and then she giggled, and I saw she was very young—perhaps sixteen. Not more. I had the silly thought that she had materialized straight out of *Alice in Wonderland.*

"Where shall we go?" she asked. "The automat? That's where I go. I love putting the change in the slot, opening the little door, and taking out my fruit salad topped with a fresh fig. I never had a fresh fig until I went to the automat. They're so different from dried figs. Don't you think?"

"Oh yes, of course." I don't think I'd ever really eaten a fresh fig, but the moment felt charmed, a bubble that could burst. "Lunch is on me," I said. "That was my plan, whoever picked up the book."

"It's your choice, then."

"We shouldn't go too far. It's still raining."

"I don't care," she laughed, pointing to her hood.

"Are you nervous about going to lunch with a stranger?" I asked her.

"Not a scientist," she answered somewhat wryly.

"How did you know it was going to rain?" I asked, gesturing toward her rain slicker. There were beads of rain clinging to strands of hair that had escaped the hood.

She shrugged and said, "I have to buy this book."

"Allow me," I offered.

She shook her head. "That wouldn't be right. No, no, thank you. Lunch? Okay. But I'll buy the book."

"I'll buy my copy too," I said, though I already had a library of books on the subject. Buying the same book she was about to buy might continue the connection.

The register line was long, rain being an excellent advertisement for the pleasures of books. As we waited, me standing right behind the yellow-slickered girl, I tried to think of where we should go. That question hadn't been part of my calculations. I was imagining a man with an attaché case or a retired gent with a bow tie or even a plump gray-haired grandmotherly sort who was interested in all manner of things. Eighth Avenue was pretty dreary, with only a pharmacy, an upscale fashion boutique, and this huge bookstore on the block. The Huntington Hartford building with its alabaster arabesque facade was the only interesting architectural detail to relieve the monotony. We'd have to walk over to Seventh.

The downpour had just stopped. Although the afternoon sky had returned to blue, an atmospheric breathlessness suggested it might rain again so we settled on a small, nearby coffee shop. The entrance was crowded by a prim mother and her two toddlers just coming out. I noticed that one wore his lunch on his face, spaghetti by the look of it. The girl from the bookstore, the Schrödinger girl I was calling her in my mind, made eye contact with the child whose mother was rushing him through the open door. I assume the girl from the bookstore was making faces at the toddler because he was giggling.

The café was crowded. It was past lunch hour, but
the shower had shepherded in people caught in the rain.
A harried waitress who'd had a busier afternoon than
usual showed us to the one empty table in the back. The
Schrödinger girl deftly negotiated the feet and bags on the
floor—the trophies of afternoon shopping trips—while
my size-ten feet had more difficulty wending through the
clogged and zigzagging space. The round, worn wooden
table had seen better days but, with the bentwood chairs,
gave the space a European atmosphere. It wasn't the worst
place we could have ended up. The girl hung her slicker
on a close-by hook. She was dressed fashionably—fishnet
stockings, miniskirt, and a turquoise sleeveless silk blouse
with white polka dots that made her sophisticated and
kittenish at the same time. She took the far seat with her
back to the mirror. "I don't like to see myself," she explained, while I took the near seat so I had no choice but
to notice myself in the mirrored wall when I looked up
suddenly without thinking.

I caught my reflection and saw a rather tall, regular-
featured, brown-haired man of thirty-seven. I was
clean-shaven and my hair was just long enough to not
be military. I had been told I had a pleasant smile, but
I wasn't smiling at myself in the mirror. I also saw my
glasses glinting in the bright lights of the little eatery.
Inwardly, I sighed. I had been self-conscious since childhood about the thick lenses, and I had heard all the usual
comments, "four-eyes" always the favorite.

I could see her miasma of auburn hair in the mirror
too. When I studied the girl I found a face that was full of
possibilities. Her features were small and precise. She had
bright, intelligent eyes that suggested mystery when set in

a pale face that was punctuated by the wild profusion of hair. She was speaking.

"My name is Daphne. Yours?"

"Garrett."

"Family name?" she asked.

"Yes. It was my father's. Why did you ask that?"

"Was?" she asked.

"He didn't come home from World War II."

"I'm so sorry." Her voice was surprisingly low for her age. She was speaking very quietly. "So you're not a Junior anymore then."

"No. I guess not. I was once."

"Did you mind?" she queried.

"What? Being called Junior? I guess I did, but I went to pieces when he died."

She was nodding sympathetically. When was I going to get over the loss of my father? Doing the math she asked, "Did you fight in Korea?"

I shook my head. "Student deferment," I answered.

The encounter was not going as I had expected. When I had decided to ask to lunch any bookstore patron who picked up my book, I imagined the diversion of discovering another mind. But we weren't talking about science. We weren't exploring ideas. Instead, this girl was finding out about me.

"I asked if it was a family name because I've never met anyone named Garrett before, not that it doesn't sound like a real name. It just sounds like the kind of name people in New England pass down for generations, creating little Garrett variations."

"It sort of is," I agreed, thinking of our old Boston family. My father had been the black sheep and run away to New York where he married my mother, a barmaid from a big New York Irish family.

My mother's family worshipped the Yankees, but my dad never lost his fondness for his old team. Whenever the Red Sox played, my dad would lecture me about character and loyalty while we watched the team lose. He implied that it was vulgar to need to win, though I had never learned that lesson. I wondered what he would have made of the Yankees in defeat. I could imagine him telling me that now I had no choice but to develop character. I thought I'd wait it out until the Yanks started winning again.

Changing the subject I said, "Well, I've actually never met anyone named Daphne either."

"It's from a myth," she said. "Ovid."

"I'm not much of a classicist."

Just then the busy waitress appeared to take our order.

"I haven't finished the menu," Daphne said, but she settled on grilled cheese with tomato on rye. Just as we'd bought the same books, I ordered the same. We were quiet as the waitress brought us our water in gold plastic glasses filled with almost more water and ice cubes than the glasses could hold. When she put the glasses in front of us, Daphne's spilled a bit, and she quickly snatched her bag away so the book wouldn't get wet. After the waitress's mumbled apology, Daphne spoke again in a formal way: "Garrett, I have something to ask you."

I caught sight of my restless self in the mirror. I got uncomfortable when things got personal. I wanted to talk about Schrödinger. She had been smart to sit against the mirror so she wouldn't have to catch disconcerting glimpses of herself. Her eyes met mine directly.

"I want you to take me home with you."

I was sipping my water. I immediately choked on an ice cube and endured a flurry of coughing. Other diners glanced over, worried, and I heard someone say, "Put your arms over your head." I did and finally stopped choking. I carefully took a very small swallow of water. The sip stayed down. I was okay.

When I was myself again she said, "I've done that millions of times—choke, I mean. Ha ha. I've never seen someone coughing because someone asked him a question. It was like you were in a movie."

I avoided her big question, but she put her hands in her lap in such a studied way that I was afraid she was going to ask again. I didn't want to hear her ask herself home with me a second time, so I plunged in: "No. Absolutely not. No. Why would you ask me that? You're a child. And you don't know me. I could be a mass murderer."

"I'll take my chances," she said, jutting her chin out to indicate her determination. She seemed more childlike than ever.

"I'm not taking you up on that proposition, ever," I said, in what I hoped was a decided way. "I don't date children. Do your parents know you're going around offering yourself to men?"

"You can say that," she pouted, "but I'm not a child." Her cheeks were turning red, from irritation, I presumed. Her high coloring made her look even prettier than she had before, but she still appeared girlish. "It's none of your business what my parents know, and promise me you'll never speak to them."

"You are a child under the law, and you are a child

to me. How many men have you asked before me? You could get yourself in a lot of trouble. But no. I'll respect our friendship and not approach your parents."

"One before," she admitted. "He was outside the Museum of Modern Art holding a huge blue plastic question mark. He said he was protesting the art mafia. I couldn't quite come right out and say that I wanted to go home with him, but I hinted a lot, and stood around for hours until I had to go home." Her eyes reflected her defeat. "Why did you ask me to lunch, then?" she asked.

"I told you. I wanted to find a random person to talk to about quantum physics. I wasn't having a good day, and I wanted something unexpected to happen."

"What hadn't been going well?"

"The Yankees."

"Yeah, they lost," she said. "I just heard someone at another table say it."

"Tell me about it. They're going to come in last again. I can feel it."

At that she burst out laughing so hard that now *she* almost choked on her water. "You just look so sad," she explained, "that it's funny. It's just baseball."

"The Yankees held me together during the war and for many seasons after that when I couldn't take any more loss—" I stopped. The Yankees were beside the point of her outlandish proposition. "Why are you offering yourself to random men?"

"Because I hate the suburbs where I live. I hate the lawns. I hate the people. I hate being a teenager. I hate high school. I hate proms. I hate—"

"I get it," I interrupted. "You're ready to grow up. But

that's not the way. Have some patience. You could ruin your life."

"I don't care. It's just too awful. Maybe I *want* to ruin my life. Do drugs. Live in the streets. Have some life instead of no life."

There was real pathos in her face. I had forgotten how much the young suffer. We envy them, all that time they have in front of them, but their time hangs heavy. They have so many hours, so many hurdles to clear, before they can call their lives their own. No one has figured out a way to escape childhood without growing up. She wanted to skip a few hurdles and race into the future on the arm of an adult. She wanted to have freedom without ceding her imagination. I couldn't blame her for that, though I couldn't imagine her plan working.

It certainly wasn't going to work with me.

The restaurant began clearing out. The waitress asked if there was anything else. I ordered coffee, and so did the Schrödinger girl. We wanted to talk some more. We had the restaurant to ourselves.

"What about your parents?" I asked.

"I'm not talking about them. I'm not talking about the suburbs. I'm not talking about bourgeois life."

Daphne made me laugh with that comment, but since I wasn't going to accept her proposition, it was time to think about getting her home. To my surprise, I discovered I was taking an interest in this girl; I found myself feeling protective. The idea of her throwing herself at random men in the city bothered me. I wanted to know she was safe. We agreed to walk the twenty-five blocks south to Penn Station so she could catch the train to Long Island.

The streets had been washed clean by the rain. The sidewalks hadn't completely dried, and were still darkened by the shower, and the air smelled of damp concrete. The day had cooled so that it was almost pleasant strolling to the train. We didn't hurry. Her schedule showed that in rush hour there were many trains she could catch. We tried to carry on a conversation, but our heights made it difficult, she being a head shorter than I.

I was straining to listen when she said, "Garrett, you are a mystery. We didn't talk about you at all. What do you do? Do you live in the city?"

"We did talk about me. What we didn't talk about is quantum physics. I live in New Paltz and teach at the college. I often come to the city for the day. I grew up here."

"I'm not sure I'd want to live in New Paltz anyway," she said peevishly, a small frown playing at the corners of her mouth, her lips the perfect rosebud shape. "I was seeking an urban abode."

"I bet you were."

"What do you teach? Physics?"

"No, I teach psychology. Behavioral psychology. And I do research."

"Rats and all that? Wow. That's kind of creepy."

I'd heard that before. I wanted to explain behaviorism to her, to convince her that it wasn't creepy. I had a standard lecture that I gave first-year psych students. They came into psychology thinking they would be talking about egos and complexes and serial killers, and instead they were met by mazes and rat experiments. I had patented my spiel to entice them into experimental psych. I almost launched into it on the spot.

We were nearing the station. The rain hadn't washed

away the graffiti peace signs spray-painted on all the buildings near it. I was disappointed that my little self-wager—to talk about physics to the first person who picked up the Schrödinger book—hadn't worked out, but Daphne had made our encounter engaging and improbable and very memorable. I began to have very unfamiliar feelings. I wanted to protect the girl from herself.

"Promise me you won't throw yourself at any men before we can talk again."

"I don't think I want to promise that," Daphne said, pouting.

"Promise anyway," I insisted.

"Till when?"

"Two weeks?"

"Two weeks—two thirty p.m. at the luncheonette," she said.

And then she ran down the stairs and disappeared into the station. She hadn't promised, and we hadn't talked about Schrödinger, and I hadn't really discovered anything about her except her eagerness to grow up.

CHAPTER TWO

ALL I COULD THINK ABOUT FOR TWO WEEKS was the Schrödinger girl standing in the bookstore in her yellow rain slicker holding aloft the book with the two cats on the cover. Would she come or not? Would I see her again? She was every student I wanted to influence, every young person I wanted to bring under the umbrella of some kind of wisdom.

Our fates had been entangled by chance.

I prepared for our meeting just as I prepared for my classes. I took my notes at a desk in my small house. I could sit at the desk and oversee the garden that was filled with very early spring blooms—snowdrops, crocuses, and the earliest daffodils. Just last week looking out the same window I had noticed that the ground was barren. *Nature is always in flux,* I thought. I didn't usually make much of spring flowers, but there they were. And then I concentrated on the ideas I'd bring along to my lunch with Daphne.

My work boiled down to saving my thoughts on index cards. Inside my head I heard a voice making fun of me. *What a pedant you are,* I imagined my friend Jerry saying, just as he had so many times before. We'd been in graduate school together after college, and we were each other's best man at the weddings of our short-lived marriages.

Jerry became a clinician, as he called it. He'd moved away from academic psychology and gotten training at a Freudian institute. He ran a thriving practice in New York City, psychoanalyzing the rich and getting rich himself, while I toiled away in experimental psych.

I was searching for truth, for knowledge, for something our discipline could solidly build on. Science was not just speculation. I wanted psychology to take its place along with physics, so we might talk about what we know and what we can prove. Why shouldn't people be defined by natural laws?

The cards for my rendezvous with Daphne read as follows.

Index card one:

April 1967: Discuss Schrödinger. Important points to consider: the cat is dead/alive until we open the box and see. Cat is in a dual state that challenges the old idea of the law of the excluded middle— that something cannot be both A and not A at the same time—it can! The cat in Schrödinger's thought experiment! Until the box is opened, that is. Then the cat is either alive or dead. Discuss relevance to quantum physics. Ask how she thinks it's relevant to life.

Index card two:

April 1967: Discuss Heisenberg's momentum of an electron. Explain velocity and momentum. Ask

her to imagine how this idea affects our under-
standing of reality. Can we know anything fully?
If we know the position of an electron and not the
velocity, can we know anything about its trajectory?
Ask her to think about all we cannot know.

Index card three:

April 1967: Talk about the observer effect—the
idea that we influence the phenomena we observe.
We affect things just by observing them. Invite her
to discuss this concept.

Index card four:

April 1967: Behaviorism. Answer to depth psy-
chology—to Freud.
James B. Watson—Psychology should only con-
cern itself with observable events.
Pavlov—Conditioned reflexes. Reflexes become
associated (conditioned) to new stimuli that are
systematically paired with the old ones.
Skinner—All behavior is shaped by rewards and
punishments.

These were the important ideas I wanted us to discuss—
the ideas in the Schrödinger book, of course, but also my
convictions about psychology. I wanted her to understand the concept that it's pointless to talk about things
we can't observe, like how we feel and how other people feel and how meaningless an idea like consciousness
is, though everyone talks about consciousness as if it is

real. In my world of behavioral psychology we shouldn't think about our dreams. They can't be measured. Something was fraying for me—one minute I wanted to read Lewis Carroll and the next explain James Watson. I had always felt safe in Watson's world, but this new malaise was threatening my complacency.

In the experimental clique in my psychology department, for example, no one would find it interesting that I imagined Daphne lying on her bed reading the science book. I conjured her waiting to have a conversation with me. I had believed that behavioral psychology was all anyone needed to save his or her life, and I was clinging to those ideas. I wanted to save her life—metaphorically speaking, of course. She seemed determined to throw it away.

She was already in the restaurant at two thirty when I walked in. She had seated herself in the same chair against the mirror. Her auburn hair surrounded her like a halo. Her head was buried in the book. I could see the familiar cover in her left hand. She didn't know I'd come in until I was seated right in front of her. The emerald eyes peered at me with recognition and expectation.

"Hi," I said, and laid my book on the table. I took the index cards out of my breast pocket and laid them on the table too. She regarded me quizzically.

"You brought notes?"

"It's just a habit of mine," I explained, as I launched into my discussion of quantum physics, behaviorism, Heisenberg, Skinner, all of them, until she interrupted.

"Whoa, I thought this was going to be a discussion, not a lecture. I loved the book. I like the idea of the world as probability—the idea that the reality we are in is just one of an infinity of possibilities and that the one we're in exists by chance. I really want to understand what reality is. I sometimes wonder if we live parallel lives in alternate realities. Maybe the cat could be alive in one reality and dead in another that exist side by side at the same time."

Daphne was precocious. I found that I didn't want to talk about quantum physics after all—I wanted her to understand behaviorism. She had called my discipline creepy, and I wanted to change her mind. I couldn't bear the thought that she might find me creepy too, an old fuddy-duddy who refused her adventurous and indecent proposal. I led the conversation away from Schrödinger and Heisenberg and toward the lecture I had prepared on the index cards. I concluded by saying, "And what about conditioned reflexes?" I glanced at myself in the mirror and saw how foolish and needy I appeared, but I couldn't stop myself. Some random Beatles song played in the background. I was too old to follow the Beatles, but Daphne was softly singing along, "*Turn off your mind, relax, and float downstream, it isn't dying . . .*

"*Revolver,*" she informed me. "The last Beatles album to come out."

I was probably supposed to say something about the Beatles here, but I had nothing to offer. I stared at an index card to escape the feeling that she was making fun of me. Then I put the index cards back in my pocket but still charged on: "Operant conditioning describes the way we acquire behaviors, through rewards and punishments. Skinner emphasizes the consequences of behavior. I study these. I am beginning to think that John Watson mischaracterizes science, which is often about unobservable phenomena, and measurable events are used to test hypotheses about things we can't directly see."

The waitress saved me from my own pedantry. Daphne ordered the same grilled cheese. I ordered ham and Swiss on rye.

Daphne asked, "How do you reconcile the observer effect with your ideas of behaviorism? Doesn't the uncertainty of the quantum world challenge your tidy worldview?"

I had to think for a minute. I began to answer that we couldn't generalize from atoms to people, but something in her countenance stopped me. I needed her approval more than she needed mine, a condition that destabilized me.

She interrupted my thoughts: "Garrett, I did keep the promise. No more men—at least not in the past two weeks. I haven't decided whether or not I'm still looking." Then she commanded, "Give me the index cards. They're silly in your pocket." The flirtatiousness in her manner suggested that she still liked me.

I handed them over, feeling suddenly naked. I didn't know if I should admonish her for her continuing interest in me. In a manner of speaking I was old enough to be her father. I wanted to point that out to her, but I suspected my comment would do no good. She was determined to make more of our encounter than I wanted her to. I was determined to avoid any suggestion of a sexual attraction. Daphne was a child. I insisted on that in my mind. We finished our sandwiches, and I paid the bill. We didn't linger over coffee. My discomfort prompted me to begin to tell her I needed to be somewhere else, when she said, "Let's go for an ice cream cone. We can find a Good Humor truck near Central Park."

Of course, I acquiesced. We wandered over to the park, which was filled with kids on roller skates, people walking dogs, au pairs escorting their little charges through the greenery, kids climbing rocks, older folks sitting on benches, and lovers intertwined in very public embraces. A long-haired kid was sitting on the grass strumming a guitar, singing, "*Well, it's one, two, three, what are we fighting for? Well, I don't give a damn, next stop is Vietnam* . . ." Signs of opposition to the Vietnam War were growing.

"Country Joe and the Fish. The song, I mean. I wish spring would hurry up," Daphne said.

"A common enough sentiment," I answered, slightly aloof.

She got a brown bonnet—a cone with vanilla ice cream and a hard chocolate coating. I didn't usually eat ice cream, but I followed her lead and ordered an ice cream pop. It was surprisingly delicious. I walked her to the subway and watched her descend. She turned around for an instant, her pale face and green eyes giving nothing away. Her auburn halo illuminated her. I wanly waved. *I'll never see her again*, I thought.

CHAPTER THREE

SIX WEEKS PASSED, and Daphne began to feel like a phantom. At first, I thought of her many times each day. Why was I so obsessed with this girl? When I had handed her my index cards at our last meeting I included the card I gave out at conferences and to publishers, encouraging her to contact me. She had nodded, and handed back my cards, saying, "You can have these back now that you're not going to be hiding behind them." She didn't give me her phone number or ask me to call. I waited for her, and sometimes I saw her in my dreams. I felt foolish caring so much about a random encounter with a young girl, and I found myself surreptitiously staring at every auburn-haired young woman who walked into my classroom.

I resigned myself to not seeing her again, when one day, checking my mail after the spring semester had ended, I reached into my cubby in the busy mailroom of the psychology department. Professors' names, arranged in alphabetical order, made my box first; my nameplate, *Adams*, above the box. I pulled out the usual department memos and reminders, a few very tardy student papers that would not receive consideration, publishers' text-book advertisements, and a postcard. I took the mail to my office. I scanned the lame-duck memos and found nothing important. I filed the publishers' detritus in the circular file, for once making my trash can basketball shot with ease. I glanced at the names on the student papers and finally got to the postcard. On the front was a picture of the statue of Columbus that stands in the middle of Columbus Circle. I read somewhere that all geographical distances from New York City are measured starting there. When I turned the card over the first thing I noticed was how it was addressed. It read: *Garrett Adams, PhD, not Jr., Behavioral Psychology, Psychology Department, New Paltz College, New Paltz, New York.*

Okay. Of course I immediately knew it was from Daphne. Her handwriting, spidery and artistic, indicated that she'd spent long hours perfecting the slant and formation of the letters. She used a purple fine-point marker. Her message was simple. The card read: *Bored, lonely, need diversion. I have a book for you. Meet me at the luncheonette at our time, Friday, June 16.* I noticed that she had not included a return address.

My pique at Daphne's absence passed immediately. Although our meeting was only a week away, inspired by her singing along to the Beatles in the coffee shop, I visited the record store in New Paltz where I bought Beatles records and those of Bob Dylan, also in preparation for our get-together. The last time we'd arranged to meet I had tried to bring her into my world with all my note cards; this time I thought I'd try to enter hers. Since radio stations only played hit singles and bits of albums, I had to buy complete albums to learn the music.

I knew nothing about Daphne's music. I know it sounds strange but I never listened to Buddy Holly or Elvis Presley or Chuck Berry. My father had loved music, and I learned

to love it with him. Music was Bing Crosby, Benny Good-
man, and Glenn Miller. Sometimes when my mom and I
felt blue we listened to "Sing, Sing, Sing" and "Moonlight
Serenade." My father had been a bit of a ne'er-do-well,
and my mother had had a lot to put up with, but when
we'd listen to his records I could tell she missed him too.
I had almost felt disloyal in the record store, especially
when I purchased Sgt. Pepper's Lonely Hearts Club Band,
which I knew was being touted as the greatest album of
all time. I hadn't made it past the surrealistic album cover
before my meeting with Daphne.

This time I got to the café before she arrived. Our
usual table was empty, and I had a momentary impulse to
take her seat so I could escape the mirror and self scrutiny.
I stood by her chair, but finally I left the choice place for
her. She was late. By two forty-five I decided she wasn't
coming, and then, suddenly, in a flash of activity, like a
hummingbird, she glittered near me. Before I could completely register her presence she hurried past, knocking
into my chair, taking her seat against the mirror. She
looked just like herself—her hair disheveled and free. We
nodded at each other. I let her begin.

"You inspired me," she said in a rush of words, hanging her coat on the hook by the table. "I started reading
psychology—Watson and Skinner, but Freud, Jung, and
William James too. I don't think I'm a behaviorist. All the
things you're not supposed to talk about? That's what I
want to talk about. The self. And how a self is made. And
what we feel. Don't you want to talk about them?"

"I'm more interested in what we do and how we're
taught to do it."

She didn't seem to register what I said, but went on:

"Anyway, I brought you this book. You'll probably hate it." She put a paperback on the table. "I really liked it," she underscored.

The title read *The Divided Self: An Existential Study in Sanity and Madness*. It was by R.D. Laing, a British psychoanalyst who had very political theories about psychosis. I had read a brief review of it in a psychology journal, but hadn't gotten around to reading the actual text.

"That is very thoughtful of you," I said.

"Don't worry," she replied, "I still have my own copy. We can talk about it the next time we meet."

Is she this confident about everything?

The waitress approached, smiling as if she remembered us. When Daphne was about to order, the waitress asked, "Grilled cheese?" and Daphne nodded. I ordered a classic New York Reuben.

We ate quickly. We didn't talk about intellectual matters. She talked about learning how to water paint, a new pastime. She held up her hands, which were a bit stained by color.

"I thought watercolors were water soluble," I said.

"They mostly are, but sometimes they leave a trace behind." The tips of her fingers were a subtle aquamarine.

"What is your favorite subject?"

"The sea. I am from Long Island after all. I love all the beautiful watery places."

I began putting words to the song that had just miraculously come on the radio, eerily echoing what she was saying. It's funny how these coincidences often happen. I didn't have a bad voice, just a bit deeper than the Beatles' tenors, but I could manage, "*But of all these friends and lovers there is no one compares with you . . . and these places lose their meaning when I think of love as something new."*

"*Rubber Soul?* Did you buy it and listen?" The expression of delight on her face and the lilt in her voice as she asked me this was thanks enough.

"Yes. I've been listening to the Beatles." As I said this I realized that I really liked the group. I may have begun listening to them as a way to share Daphne's world, but with repeated listening I'd become a fan. Doing a little research had revealed that even Leonard Bernstein made admiring comments about them, though maybe this shouldn't have mattered to me. "*In my life I love you more,*" I concluded the song. I didn't feel romantic love for the pint-sized philosopher in front of me, but she was my guide out of the past I'd been living in, right down to her stained fingers. "How do you do your seascapes?" I asked.

"Pale. Lilac and turquoise."

"I have a friend who runs an art gallery. They had an exhibit of watercolors that I read about in the *Times*. The gallery is only about a block from here. Let's go."

The West 50s hosted a gaggle of galleries, and we could visit several. I knew a woman, Caroline, who worked at the Forester Gallery. She was actually someone my friend Jerry had introduced me to. Caroline and I had gone on one lackluster blind date and then decided to pursue only friendship, but neither of us had called the other since then.

My Schrödinger girl promptly got up from the table and lifted her plum-colored crocheted shoulder purse from the hook. The rich shade enhanced the red glints in her hair and the deeper emerald glints in her eyes.

We walked several blocks. I had to slow my pace to allow Daphne to keep up. I had forgotten how small she was. She trailed me by a few steps no matter how much I slowed down. When we arrived at the gallery, and I held the door for her, I could see that the sun and heat had reddened her cheeks. She presented a canvas of jewel hues: emerald eyes, auburn hair, purple purse, and reddening cheeks.

Caroline saw me immediately. In contrast to Daphne, she wore elegant black. Her slim-cut, mid-thigh minidress showed her endless slender legs. Her black hair was twisted into a casual updo, held in place by a sterling silver hair ornament. Caroline, a woman at her peak, appeared to be working hard to stave off a creeping disappointment in life. Our one date had revealed that we were fundamentally mismatched. Caroline tried too hard, laughing at all my jokes, telling stories in a rush of forced intimacy, whereas I didn't try hard enough. I was detached and impassive. *What was Jerry thinking?* I had wondered. Or maybe I resisted connecting to anyone. I carried around the failure of my early marriage, and I hung onto things too long.

I surprised myself at my happiness at seeing Caroline. She strode across the gallery, took my right hand, and in a musical contralto voice said, "How great to see you! And this is . . . ?"

Daphne glanced up, and I could hear Caroline's loud intake of air. She stared at Daphne with an inscrutable expression. Did she think Daphne was too young for me? Well, of course she was. Did she assume we were dating? I had thought Caroline and my decision not to date was mutual. Now I could see Caroline was holding her breath, and I wasn't so sure.

"This is Daphne, a young friend," I answered. "And Daphne, this is Caroline, another friend. Is the Katagosha exhibit still here?" Daphne's description of her watercolors had reminded me of the paintings of this Japanese artist who painted nature scenes in dreamlike pastels, straddling the East-West divide.

"No," Caroline said. "We've hung a new show. Galen Green. Have you heard of him?"

Of course I had. He was a big deal. I had seen his photographs on the cover of *Art News* several times over the years.

"I've heard of him too," said Daphne. Her cheeks had kept their ruddy glow.

Green's work lined the walls: portraits, still lifes, some landscapes. We perused the back wall of the small gallery, where they had hung the larger paintings. We faced a canvas that was about four feet tall by three feet wide, large and commanding. We approached it, and stopped cold. Daphne let out a loud yelp of extreme dismay, and I could feel her fingers digging into my arm.

In front of us was a very appealing nude. Although the painting was somewhat abstract, Green had left enough shape to the features of the young woman to reveal that she exactly resembled Daphne: same heart-shaped face, small, straight nose, and profusion of auburn hair, though the strands draped in tiny plaits, not like the riot of tresses of the girl beside me. The nude in the painting startled me with both her beauty and her complete resemblance to the girl beside me. This explained Caroline's odd glance. She must have recognized Daphne immediately.

Daphne wailed, "Garrett, I swear, I did not sit for that portrait, and I have never met Galen Green!" The artist had named his painting *Daphne in Salmon and Green,* punning on his own name I supposed. Daphne kept insisting, "I don't know the girl in the painting." Then she asked, "How can she look just like me and have my name too?"

CHAPTER FOUR

WE BOTH STARED AT THE CANVAS. I wasn't comfortable staring at the naked girl who so resembled Daphne, but I couldn't take my eyes away. The figure reclined on a red divan near a well-set table in a room with peach walls. A small meal awaited, laid out on an apricot tablecloth, served on pale celadon green plates. On each of two plates were what appeared to be a serving of salmon and haricots verts. Everything had been painted in warm tones except the plates and the green beans. The artist had rendered the model's skin a pink alabaster and her breasts with rosy areolas. Although some of the detail of the painting had been sacrificed to the abstraction of Green's work, I couldn't escape the resemblance of the subject to Daphne or the power of the portrait. Galen Green had created a remarkably successful painting.

Daphne hadn't relaxed her grip on my arm. Several other gallery patrons sneaked surreptitious glances at the Daphne beside me and the girl in the painting, their eyes confirming what she and I saw. I could feel her discomfort growing.

I turned to her and asked, "Would you like me to ask Caroline about the painting?"

She nodded.

Caroline stood at the front of the gallery to greet incoming visitors. When I approached her, she said in an almost natural voice, "Your young friend is so lovely in her portrait. Green has captured her."

"But she insists that she never sat for the portrait. She feels quite upset, actually. And mystified."

"How can that possibly be?" Caroline asked. "Not only is the girl in the portrait her identical twin, but they share the same name."

"I know. But she is so adamant."

I asked Caroline a few questions. Yes, she had hung the paintings. The gallery had been planning a show with Galen for quite a while. He had so much new work. She confirmed that *Daphne in Salmon and Green* was the last canvas; it had been completed just a week or so before the show opened, brought down after the rest of the collection.

"It's good, don't you think?" she said. "Matisse through the lens of abstract expressionism."

"I do think it's good," I answered. I asked her about Galen's model.

"I don't know anything about her," she said.

"Do you think that's her real name?"

"It could be," she mused. "But in the history of painting there have been many other Daphnes. Pollaiuolo, Trevisani, Tiepolo, Albani, and Waterhouse each have a Daphne painting, for example. And, of course, the most famous is Bernini's sculpture."

I forgave Caroline for showing off a little. Not only was she trying to get her bearings in an unusual situation, the memory of our date seemed to have added to her unease. I didn't recognize any of the artists' names, and I didn't think I had ever seen those works. My mother liked to take me to museums and galleries as a day out, but I had never made a study of art. I did remember that in April when I'd met Daphne, she mentioned a myth concerning her name.

"I saw Galen when he came to inspect his show," Caroline volunteered. "He didn't say anything about this painting or its model."

"So you have never seen the girl in the painting?" I asked.

"No, never." She shook her head no for emphasis. "Although I would swear that I have seen her today."

"Maybe I should talk to Galen Green because my Daphne is so upset. Could you put me in touch with him?"

"I'm sorry, but I can't do that," she replied gently but firmly. "I'd risk my job. We protect our artists."

"Of course. Excuse me, Caroline." I turned away from her to go find Daphne, but she was no longer standing where I'd left her, in front of the painting. I shouldn't have expected her to be—the portrait was very unsettling to her. I began to survey the space, but she was nowhere to be seen. She had effectively vanished.

I went out to the street, but after looking as far as I could in both directions I could find no trace of her. She had had too much of a head start. I walked all the way back to the bookstore at Columbus Circle, but there was no sign of her there either. I even checked back at our café, but our table stood empty.

I sat down and ordered a coffee to figure out my next move. I worried about Daphne having to get home by herself in such a state of agitation, but I satisfied myself with the knowledge that she must have taken the Long

Island Railroad many times. After waiting for forty-five minutes, I drove home, but even the picturesque Hudson River failed to distract me or calm my agitation.

If someone had asked me, I wouldn't have been able to say why I believed Daphne, yet I did. That girl was not acting. I did not believe she had been the model for the painting, although I had never seen two people more alike. Caroline had seen it immediately too, and reached the simple conclusion that we were looking at the same girl. I couldn't agree because of Daphne's reaction. I cataloged many possible explanations—that Daphne had a lost twin, that she had amnesia, or simply that she had a doppelgänger. Her embarrassment and anguish, as well as her mysterious departure, left me troubled and exhausted as I drove north. It was like a mystery from an old Hollywood movie, a Hitchcock, or *Laura*.

When I finally arrived home I fell into bed and into a dreamless sleep.

I woke up the next morning in a more resolute mood. I decided that I would find Galen Green on my own. Of course, the possibility existed that Daphne had posed for the portrait and had just been too embarrassed to say. She may have suffered from some psychological or neurological condition, or this painting might be a portrait of some random auburn-haired girl who happened to bear an extraordinary resemblance to Daphne; perhaps Galen just happened to name his painting *Daphne* in reference to the myth. As I had contemplated the night before, Daphne could have also had a twin she hadn't told me about, or even one she didn't know about. If that was the case, the painting could be named for her, or the twin could have been adopted separately, or . . . I was spinning out possibilities. Now I had even more reason to be captivated by the teenager I'd met.

I visited the college library to find out all I could about Galen Green and his model. I thumbed through all the recent periodicals and newspapers, and the only fact I was able to glean was that Galen Green not only painted, he taught art at Sarah Lawrence College. It was an easy ride from New Paltz, just an hour and half down the Taconic. Since it was summer, I had no classes, though I had called the school and discovered that Green was teaching a special studio class that summer. From the words of the art department secretary, I gathered that being admitted into the class was quite a coup. The secretary told me the room and building where the ten a.m. class met.

Monday morning, when I arrived at Sarah Lawrence, even in my agitated state I was delighted by the charm of the small campus. The Tudor architecture gave the impression of a bucolic English village, in Surrey, perhaps. The school had the reputation of being the most expensive in the country.

Signs directed me to Bates, the gracious Tudor structure that housed the painting studios, among other things. I walked past a circle of protesters, young women who sat in a ring with signs that read, *Hey, hey, hey, LBJ, how many kids did you kill today?*

They must be here every day, even in summer—any day classes meet, I concluded. Now that was dedication. I still sat on the fence about Vietnam and was continually surprised by the vehemence of the war's opponents.

Inside the building, I found the large studio. There

were canvases everywhere, and a small knot of students gathered around a posing model. I saw with a start that the model was Daphne. She reclined on a couch like the one in the painting, only this one was green velvet. Her rosy skin, pink frock, and glinting red hair contrasted strongly with the deep, verdant fabric. The natural light caught all the electric highlights in her hair.

I recognized Green from a *Life* spread I'd seen on him. He stood in front of the class in a studied attire, mannered, down to the robin's-egg-blue scarf that he had knotted at his throat. His leonine head was large and imposing, with thick masses of gray hair worn longer than was usual for men in their fifties. There was a romantic, almost Byronic look to him. When he moved over to one of the young artists to instruct her, I saw that he walked with a limp, and upon further investigation I saw that he was clubfooted with one very large black platform shoe, the match for an ordinary one.

Clearly, he had painted Daphne. I didn't expect that. I had believed her performance at the Forester Gallery. Both her shock and her dismay had seemed genuine. I felt betrayed and duped. No one noticed me. The professor was intent on his teaching duties, and Daphne was concentrating on holding her pose. Finally, she looked up, and with a startled expression called out, "Garrett, what are you doing here? It's so nice to see you."

"You know me, right?" I asked, just making sure.

"Of course I do," she replied, staring at me as if I had three heads. "But what are you doing here?"

"Looking for you," I admitted.

"Really?"

I had just seen her three days before, and yet it felt

as if an eternity had passed. The two separate realities—
Daphne claiming she had never met Galen Green and
running out of the gallery in dismay, and this scene of a
model in front of Green and his students—just did not
fit together at all. I felt almost dizzy at the incongruity.
I wouldn't have been able to explain it, but even though
she seemed to be Daphne, she also seemed to be someone else. I didn't feel the same way around her as I did
with my Schrödinger girl. *So this is Capgras syndrome,*
I thought, when someone seems like an impostor. I had
studied it, but I had never experienced it. She appeared to
be a totally different person. Her hair was twisted into a
sleek chignon at the nape of her neck, perhaps so students
could sketch her creamy shoulders. I missed her wild, free
mane.

"You are ogling me strangely, Garrett. Don't you recognize me?"

Of course I did. I would have picked her out as Daphne
anywhere, but she was so different from the girl I thought
I knew. Perhaps it was the influence of Galen Green.

"Of course I recognize you," I answered. "Ogling
you? Isn't everyone in here staring at you?" She didn't
blush at all. "Let's go talk," I suggested.

"Sure," she said, "but I can't leave the class in the
lurch."

"Go," the artist said. "We've done enough for the day.
They have plenty to work with." He stretched out a large
paw and said, "I'm Galen. You must be Garrett. Daphne
told me about you." He was a commanding man who controlled the situation and at the same time suggested that
he only had everyone else's interests at heart. I wouldn't
go so far as to say he was sinister, but I didn't trust him.

"Should we go to the cafeteria here or the coffee shop in town?" I imagined sitting across from her while she ate a grilled cheese sandwich. Or maybe not. I didn't think this elegant girl would order grilled cheese.

"Don't be silly," she replied. "We'll go to Galen's house, a very cozy home conducive to a chat." She walked over to the artist and spoke to him quietly for a moment, kissed him on the cheek, and then returned. She walked behind a screen and emerged dressed in a pale-blue summer dress and heeled sandals. Galen casually waved as we exited the studio together.

We climbed into my car, with Daphne giving directions. Galen lived in a large stone house that stood out among the wooden and brick homes of the area. It was a fitting residence for an artist; its stone facade and manicured gardens evoked Provence.

As we entered we were flooded with a riot of sunlight from massive windows. The house was decorated in an eclectic style and the living room was elegant, striking, and cozy all at the same time. She sat on a bittersweet-orange sofa, not the red divan of the portrait, and I faced her on a paisley chair. The light emphasized the warm tones of her skin.

"So," I said.

"Don't be so serious," she countered. "Garrett, nothing is wrong."

"Are you sure?" I queried.

"Of course I am." She sat perfectly composed, with good posture, comfortable in her surroundings. "I'll be back in a few minutes," she said. "Make yourself at home."

She came back fifteen minutes later carrying a large, heavy tray.

"Let me help you with that," I said, rising. She allowed me to relieve her of the tray, which I set down on a large, tufted leather ottoman between us. On a red lacquered tray of Chinese design, she had placed a white china teapot, two white mugs, a plate of sliced apples, a wheel of brie, and some beautifully arranged sesame crackers.

"I couldn't fit the milk and sugar. How do you take your tea?"

"Plain will be fine," I said. And I added after a pause, "I wanted to find out about a girl in a portrait I saw at the Forester Gallery."

"Ah, you've seen it then," she said, appearing pleased.

"Of course. You were with me."

"What do you mean?" she asked, genuinely puzzled. "I haven't seen you since our first meeting, but I have thought of you so many times. Especially when I see the Schrödinger book or think about physics. If you'd taken me up on my proposal I wouldn't have met Galen."

I don't know what I'd expected, but the circumstances were growing ever more strange. Either this girl had amnesia, was a great actress, or someone else had been with me at the Forester Gallery.

"Let me get this straight: the painting is of you?"

"Of course."

"I saw the resemblance immediately. I must admit I was surprised."

"Of course you were." She giggled, reminding me of the adolescent I had met just two months before. "Me too! Can you believe it? I'm a muse."

"You're sure we didn't meet up on Friday and go to the gallery together?"

"Are you okay?" she asked. "No, I was in Boston last weekend with Galen. He gave a lecture at the Museum of Fine Arts. They have a restaurant there with tables among the paintings. We had dinner there yesterday and came back just last night."

I wanted to say something, but what could I say? *Prove it?*

She was ahead of me. She crossed the room to reach a small cream-colored antique desk. Sitting right on top was a photograph that she retrieved.

"This is from Friday," she said, and held out a black-and-white Polaroid image of herself in the Public Garden with the sign for the swan boats behind her. Someone had written *Daphne, Boston Public Garden, 6/16/67.* This was the same day I was with the other Daphne at the Forester Gallery.

The other Daphne? What was I thinking? Had I accepted the strange idea that these two Daphnes were really two different girls? That couldn't be right. The photograph and its date were very odd, though. Clearly the girl couldn't be in two places at the same time. I was certain of that physical principle. The snapshot wouldn't have been definitive proof in a court of law, but Daphne, this Daphne, couldn't have known that I would be coming to Sarah Lawrence, so why would she have a snapshot ready and dated to perpetrate a hoax? She had nothing to gain from me. Obviously, these girls weren't unknown twins or random doubles because this Daphne had known me on sight. My head was reeling. For the moment, I could only conclude that Daphne existed as both one and two people. I couldn't help but notice the similarities to the Schrödinger experiment. Only a cosmic coincidence would bring this girl to me while we were both reading the popularized physics book with the two beautiful cats on its cover.

My conclusions seemed logical, but insane. I knew that most disinterested bystanders would have said that Daphne was acting out an elaborate ruse, but my gut told me that both girls were sincere—that I was dealing with a phenomenon I didn't yet understand. I'll admit I was spooked, and the little hairs along my forearms were standing on end as I suppressed a shiver. I tried to keep steady in the face of my own confusion. I shifted my attention to her current life. That she would be posing for a famous painter in his fifties surprised and unsettled me, almost as much as the bigger mystery surrounding her.

"When did he paint the picture?" I asked.

"He began it the day after we met and finished it a month later, just in time for the show at the Forester."

"That was fast work," I remarked. She didn't reply. Nothing was making sense. How could all this happen so fast? "Will you be returning to Long Island today?" I continued my interrogation.

"No, Garrett," she answered quietly. "I live here now, with Galen. Surely you guessed that."

Surely I had, but I didn't want to believe it. "How did this happen?"

She laughed merrily. "We met by chance at lunch in the Russian Tea Room. I went back to the city the day after we met, on the Saturday, and decided to take myself to the Russian Tea Room because I'd read about it. I was planning to go the day I met you, but I decided to have lunch with you instead. It's right near that Bookmasters. I was going to go but I stopped in to buy a book first, and there you were."

There I was. She told me this story of sitting at one of the cherry-red leather banquettes. She had ordered chicken Kiev. Practically everyone does there, unless they order borscht or salmon. Galen told her that she was beautiful and asked her to his table just before the food arrived. Daphne was thrilled to meet him. She followed art and knew who he was. He was eating borscht, and she voiced an observation about the sour cream floating like boats on a red pond, slowly dissolving into creamy pink water. Charmed, he followed up on her nautical imagery; he asked her to go sail a toy boat on the pond by the boathouse in Central Park. I concluded that he was a smooth customer. That was a far cry from the dinky coffee shop we went to, or the ice cream truck in the park. But I had taken her to the art gallery, I reminded myself. *Wait a minute. Why was I becoming competitive with Green?* I didn't like the old fart romancing Daphne. That was it.

She told me that the two spent a perfect spring afternoon launching their toy boats and regaling each other with stories of their lives. She also engaged him with her precocious and passionate ideas about literature, psychology, and physics. He talked about his painting and his travels.

I understood that when Daphne met Galen she already knew what she wanted—she wanted to be whisked out of her life by an older man. For god's sake, she had asked me! He said that all he wanted was a model, so when her parents, busy, harried, distant, and puzzled by their odd and brainy daughter, met the famous Galen, they were happy to have Daphne pose for him. Things had just evolved from there. She was appropriately reticent about their intimate life. She had ventured to Sarah Lawrence on weekends to pose for her portrait, and when she finished her finals and Regents exams, she had moved to Bronxville full-time. She had only been there for a week.

"But Daphne," I said at the end of her story, "you're just a kid, and he's a dirty old man. Your parents can't possibly be okay with this. And what about your future? This is crazy. Will you get married?"

"First of all, I am not a kid. I am sixteen." She said this as if she had said that she was thirty. "My future is all arranged. I'm completing my GED degree and will start Sarah Lawrence in September. I want to study art history. As for getting married, now that's crazy. I'm too young for that. Trust me, Garrett, I am very happy. No one is taking advantage of anyone."

I could tell she was remembering the day she had asked me to be her rescuer. Her paramour? It all smacked of Europe in an earlier century. Or *Lolita*, that Nabokov novel that had become all the rage, which I had never gotten around to reading.

I remembered that moment too, and I would still make the same decision. If her parents had agreed to this situation, there really wasn't anything for me to say. It was all so Elvis and Priscilla, but Elvis had always claimed that the girl he'd met in Germany lived with him platonically until past her eighteenth birthday. I had no way of knowing that wasn't true here too.

Daphne had announced her desire to be plucked out of her life the day we'd met, and the next day she had been. That much was clear. But it wasn't clear who the Schrödinger girl was. I had gone over the prosaic ex-

planations for these girls in my head, but none fit. The
fact that Galen's Daphne knew me kept upending logical
deductions about identical twins. And the photograph
proved she was somewhere else when I knew she'd been
with me, destroying the sensible conclusion that she was
one girl. As a behaviorist I wanted a neat and simple explanation for all phenomena.

When I was a boy, the day my father died on a field in
Italy, I spoke at length to his apparition, who sat down on
my bed and told me I needed to be the man of the house
now and look after my mother. Why do they always tell
young boys that? It's a burden they can never fulfill. But
he told me other things too, like how to endure pain and
be open to life. I don't think I learned that lesson at all,
and maybe that's why I chose behaviorism, to encase the
world in its neat wrappings. But I never abandoned the
memory of that meeting, of seeing him in his uniform,
and I never denied its reality either. Maybe the Schrödinger
girls and my father's visit were like those 3-D glasses you
wear at the movies, and once in a while we suddenly see
a new dimension that was there all along. Maybe.

CHAPTER FIVE

I NEEDED TIME TO PROCESS MY TRIP to Bronxville. My brain reeled from the cognitive problems posed by the two Daphnes. They were so different, yet so alike. I decided to name the second girl, the model, Galen's Daphne, just to keep the two personae straight. If the girl(s) were to be believed, what was happening was impossible. Both Daphnes had lunched with me, but only one Daphne had accompanied me to the Forester Gallery. And the great artist painted only one Daphne. And despite the similarities to his experiment, there was only one cat in the box in Schrödinger's experiment. How could there be two Daphnes?

I couldn't make any sense of the conflicting evidence. I thought about the paradox constantly, especially now that summer left me at my leisure. I imagined the fall, when Daphne might be sitting in one of my classes. I always taught the intro psych course, and I pictured her in the first row of the lecture hall, or in the small seminar room, sitting at the table in the upper division course on research methods. I envisioned her in my house, pouring tea from a beautiful teapot. Or eating grilled cheese in the little restaurant near campus. She haunted my dreams as well. Auburn-haired teenagers appeared out of nowhere.

After just a week, by Friday, I knew I needed to talk to someone else about her.

I called Jerry, and we agreed to meet the next day, though he had one condition.

"So," he said, "this is a kind of professional meeting?" I averred that it was.

"Well," he replied, "I need some kind of fee, then. You know Freud insisted that therapy isn't really worth anything to the patient unless he pays for it."

"How serendipitous for therapists," I murmured.

"None of that," he asserted, his humor and confidence obvious, even across telephone wires.

"Okay," I conceded. "what is your fee?"

"You couldn't afford my fee. But I'll settle for you buying me a deli lunch."

"Carnegie Deli?" I asked. They served huge, over-stuffed Jewish deli sandwiches and had the convenience of being on the West Side near Jerry's apartment.

"No, *bubbeleh*," Jerry replied with the Yiddish endearment he liked to use, "I think we need to get away from the Upper West Side. I'll meet you at Katz's Deli at two. I want to avoid the lunch mania. On weekends it's unbearable."

Katz's Deli ruled the Lower East Side on Houston Street, pronounced House-ton Street. If you said it the way you do when talking about Texas, people knew you were a tourist. Actors from the Yiddish theater in its heyday had congregated there, and during World War II, when all the sons of the owners were in the service fighting, they had a slogan, *Send a salami to your boy in the army*, making the deli a venerable New York institution.

On that Saturday afternoon, the streets of the Lower

East Side were bustling with shoppers of all ethnicities drawn by open-air tables of clothes and accessories and by shops offering deep discounts.

Jerry was already seated when I arrived. He was a wiry man, small and quick, with a head of black curls and startling blue eyes, all of which he put to good use in his pursuit of women. He stayed fit by playing racquetball three times a week. He had grown up playing handball in this neighborhood. When we met as undergraduates at Cornell, our New York City roots were one of the commonalities that initially drew us to each other. Of course, half the school was from the city. We also shared our major and sat together in many of our psychology courses. Now his expensive Lacoste shirts said money. There was very little left of the old firebrand who had gone on freedom marches in the South, sitting at the back of the bus, though his beliefs hadn't changed.

We chatted in an easy way until the waiter served our lunches. All the waiters at Katz's were about a thousand years old and acted like they were doing us a favor by allowing us to eat in their restaurant. Jerry had ordered pastrami on rye, Katz's specialty that arrived with a huge pickle, and *kasha varnishkes*. Mine was a corned-beef sandwich, a pickle, and a knish. We slathered on the bright yellow mustard in unison. He drank a celery tonic, and I a cream soda, which both came in brown bottles. Later on, he had a Bloody Mary, but I just nursed my cream soda.

He peppered his conversation with Yiddishisms more than he usually did. I knew what he was doing; he was inviting me into the Jewish culture that had spawned psychoanalysis, so I would leave behind my ingrained WASP reticence and midcentury American male stoicism. My normal detached rationalism would not help me open up to Jerry. I needed to leave my disdain for self-revelation behind. I concluded that he must be an effective therapist.

As we began to eat, I ventured, "Well, I met her—" when he interjected, "No, first we eat. Then we talk."

He ordered coffee and cheesecake to finish the meal, but I had only coffee. I couldn't imagine where he had room in his wiry frame for all that food. The cheesecake would have sunk like a stone in my stomach. Maybe I was just nervous.

"Where to now?" I asked, as I saw him motion for the bill and I retrieved my wallet. I had thought to talk there, but even after the lunch crunch, the colorful patrons engaged in boisterous conversation as well as serious eating made a focused conversation a challenge. I glanced around as people laughed, told stories, and gestured vigorously. The mustard glistened on the overstuffed sandwiches and the ancient waiters shuffled between tables. Although the place had once been the stomping grounds of mostly Eastern European Jews, it now teemed with people of all descriptions—Indians, African Americans, Chinese Americans, WASPS, and, of course, Jews. The huge trays the waiters carried and the constant noise of them entering and exiting the kitchen didn't create the intimacy we needed. But this had been Jerry's neighborhood, and he knew of a small coffee shop a few blocks away. I followed him out of Katz's to a quiet corner table. We ordered more coffee, and he began.

"So what seems to be the problem?" He sipped his coffee. "There's a girl?"

"I met her in April."

His eyes showed no judgment, just interest. I told the story of our encounters, straining to remember every detail. I stressed my protective instincts toward Daphne. My other focus concerned the confusion I felt from this ontological dilemma I had uncovered and how crazy I knew I sounded with this bizarre experience that defied ordinary reality. The situation that this girl presented was just impossible! Jerry didn't react to the weirdness of the events. He showed no emotion as he listened to me. He considered for a moment, and then spoke.

"Hmm. Let me ask you this: does Helena come into all this in any way?"

Helena was my ex-wife whom I rarely talked about with anyone, though Jerry was an exception. But I still didn't like *him* bringing her up.

"Helena? What does she have to do with this?"

"Don't play dumb."

Helena and I had gotten married because she was pregnant. It happened in college when we were both twenty. Neither of us had had any plans to marry at that point, but you just didn't leave a girl pregnant then. It simply was not the right thing to do.

She was a slim, pale young woman with long, flat, flaxen hair. She played the flute and wanted to be a professional musician. She was studying music education at Ithaca College, in the same town as Cornell, because her parents insisted that she have a "backup" career as a teacher. She was a companionable, easygoing girl. Her pale eyes often seemed to be observing something far away. We got along fine, but it was no grand passion. I could have done worse, though both of us saw the pregnancy as putting a monkey wrench in all our plans. We were, however, both determined to finish college after the baby was born.

It was a very difficult pregnancy, and the baby was stillborn, the umbilical cord wrapped tightly around her neck. Even though neither of us had wanted a baby, we were both in shock. Unsurprisingly, Helena took it especially hard and left school to live with her folks for a while. When she returned, both of us saw that all there was between us was sadness, and together we decided to split up. We never said a cross word to each other.

"You think my feelings for Daphne are related to Helena? To Amy?" Helena had insisted that we name the child.

"Don't you?"

"No. I hadn't thought about Amy at all. I met Daphne in the most random manner. She's fun to talk to. Jeez. Freudians make something of everything." I felt very uncomfortable and regretted my decision to talk to Jerry. This was not what I wanted to discuss.

He said, "I know you don't like going over this ground, but you did say you had a fatherly interest in Daphne. You also admitted that you are now obsessed with her."

"Them," I interjected, but he ignored me.

"You had a stillborn daughter sixteen years ago, and you have never been able to have another serious relationship. And you're sure none of this is related?"

When put that way, I could see he had a point, but I pretended he didn't. "Can we come back to this?" I requested.

"Okay. So you want to talk about this girl. How old did you say she was?"

"Sixteen."

"Why did you call me?" he asked mildly. "You don't think she's part of some conspiracy, do you?"

Since the 888-page Warren Commission Report concluded that a lone shooter killed Kennedy, conspiracy theories abounded. I recognized Jerry's strategy. He was working to rule out the possibility that I was paranoid and delusional.

"No, Jerry. I just wanted to know if you think both Daphnes could be the same person, and if they are, is it more likely that she has a split personality, some kind of amnesia, or that she's a pathological liar? Or are they twins? I wish there were reliable records of all the twins born in 1951. All those twin studies we learned about relied on volunteers. And then of course there's the myth."

I had researched the myth of Daphne, which actually was the myth of Daphne and Apollo, in an old Encyclopaedia Britannica that my mother had given me.

"Myth?" Jerry queried.

"Yeah. By Ovid. You know. Apollo and Daphne? Daphne mentioned it and Caroline alluded to it because of her name. I just read a summary. It doesn't seem very relevant. It's about Daphne being chased by Apollo and turning into a laurel tree. Do you think Galen Green is Apollo?"

Jerry ignored the question. "Caroline?"

"You know, Caroline. The one you introduced me to. She works at the gallery where we saw the Daphne painting by Green. Remember? Let's not go off on that tangent."

He mumbled something about Jungians and their childlike interest in myth and the lack of clinical relevance. So much for the myth. He concluded, "Occam's razor, kid—the simplest explanation first—which is that, of course, it's the same person. I can't say why she is doing this or whether or not she knows she's spinning out the idea that she is two people. I can't make a clinical judgment about someone I have never met."

"Okay," I acknowledged, downcast. "I just want you to talk me through the possibilities."

"And you don't want to talk about your own situation at all? Surely you see that would be more fruitful, because I really can't say anything about the girl, Daphne, but we can talk about you, right?" He paused, and I did not respond.

So he continued, "I think you have summarized the possibilities, but you don't have enough information for me to begin to say anything else, except to be careful. Things can get messy very fast with a few of those things you're talking about. Compulsive lying and multiple personality disorder are two things you should definitely stay away from. You probably should avoid this girl. She might be destructive."

"I hear you," I said, though I had no intention of following his advice, despite having no way of knowing when I might see Daphne again. I didn't plan on going back to Bronxville anytime soon, and the way the first Daphne, the Ur-Daphne, had run out of the gallery left me no indication of when we might meet up again.

"There's one more thing," I suddenly remembered. "When I met Daphne the second time she wondered if we might be living other lives in parallel worlds."

"Oh boy. What claptrap! It's the kind of thing teenagers like to think about. Ha ha. I remember a *Twilight Zone*

episode about that. One about an astronaut, two astronauts, actually, who each got misplaced in the other's
reality. But that's fiction, Garrett. Science fiction." Jerry
paused. "I didn't figure you for a metaphysical guy. With
you it was always what you could see or what you could
hear and what you could measure."

"Things change."

Jerry brought me back to the particulars of my own
life: "You should work through your feelings of sadness
and loss about Helena and Amy. I've only been telling
you this for years. Processing these emotions will help
you resolve your obsession with Daphne. Trust me."

"I wouldn't say obsession, Jerry."

"Why don't you try to speak to her parents? They
know how many daughters they have."

"I'm not sure they do. They could live a parallel existence too. Besides, that would be a kind of betrayal.
I promised Daphne I wouldn't. And I won't break that
promise."

"*Oy vey*. It's worse than I thought." But he said this
very gently and I saw only friendship and concern in his
blue eyes. "Are you sure you really want to get to the bottom of this? Because I'm not sure you're really thinking
clearly."

"Look, Jerry. Even the most unlikely possibility, if it
becomes real, is more present than statistical probability.
We swim in a sea of improbable events. After all, there is
only the most minute probability that we would be born
or that the universe would even exist."

"That's true," he said, "but people go crazy every
day."

I had nothing to say to that, so we left it there with

questions hanging in the air. Jerry must have been very used to that.

I had parked my car in a garage downtown, but I walked Jerry to the subway. Before parting, I said, "Next time, we talk about you. I monopolized the entire discussion."

"You bought the sandwiches," he replied, though his eyes still expressed doubt; he clearly didn't buy my story. Still, Jerry had always been a friend, and he didn't press me now. As he turned away, he called, "See you later, kid," over his shoulder. "I'm here if you need me."

CHAPTER SIX

I LEFT THE CITY IMMEDIATELY and drove straight home. *Well, that didn't help at all.* I had no idea of my next move. The first question I had to answer was whether or not to tell Daphne, my Daphne, that she had a doppelgänger. I realized that I could have told the second Daphne, Galen's Daphne, that she was a dead ringer for another girl, or even more to the point, that she *was* another girl, but I hadn't. What could I have said beyond explaining that in my world she had gone to the Forester Gallery with me and had been shocked at her own portrait?

I became very preoccupied with my thoughts about Daphne. I read every article I could about Galen's paintings and was rewarded by learning the name of the town on Long Island his model was from, though no more details about her. She had not given me her phone number, and I still had no number for Ur-Daphne. I could have pressed the young model, but then I would have had to tip my hand about my belief that there were two of her, and I imagined the conversation getting sticky.

I read the Laing book Ur-Daphne had given me at the coffee shop. He distinguished between the sane person who was ontologically secure, someone comfortable in his own skin, and someone insecure who had been confused by displaying inauthentic behavior and reactions and had never felt fully alive. That person was often perceived as crazy and devolved into schizophrenia. At thirty-seven I was past the age of a first schizophrenic break, and I certainly didn't feel crazy. No one at school seemed to notice anything wrong, though I had detected a smoky concern in Jerry's blue eyes when I talked about Daphne. Maybe I was going crazy. Maybe I had always been crazy. The realest moments of my life were those I could never tell anyone else about, like when my father's apparition came to me just after he died. I felt real when I was with Daphne too.

I watched *Twilight Zone* episodes hoping for answers and finally even caught the one Jerry mentioned, featuring two identical astronauts existing in different dimensions. Science fiction played like reality to me. I hadn't concerned myself with abnormal psych since school, and I certainly hadn't been interested in Laing and his new sixties approach. He implied that sanity had a social component and was part of a social agreement. Was it possible that I had found a sane spot outside the social agreement? My own little pocket of sanity?

I kept these thoughts to myself for the next several weeks, but in the middle of July I heard from Daphne again. It was a slow summer, and I had spent it reading everything I could about multiple personality disorder, Capgras syndrome, separating twins, anything that would shed light on the two girls. Now I had nothing to do after ditching my research in a dumpster. The Yankees were still playing badly, heading for last place again, and I hadn't found anything but Daphne to interest me.

I was sitting at my desk at school composing syllabi

for the upcoming semester when the department secretary knocked and said she was transferring a call to my extension. When I picked up the receiver I heard the familiar voice.

"Hi, Garrett! What's new?"

"Hello, Daphne," I casually replied. "What's new with you?"

"Not much. I'm not doing much this summer."

"Which courses are you taking next year?" I asked, to be polite.

"American history, advanced trig, and physics. I'm bored," she pouted. I could almost hear it over the phone. "And I miss you," she added. "Can you meet tomorrow?"

"I would love to. The usual place?"

"No. I need to do some research. Meet me at the New York Public Library. I'll meet you outside by the lions."

"Two thirty?" I asked.

"Why not?"

"See you," I said, just as she hung up.

The next day I approached Bryant Park near the appointed time. The trees stood forth in an exuberance of green that made me exuberant too. I was singing, "*I need to laugh, and when the sun is out, I've got something I can laugh about. I feel good in a special way. I'm in love and it's a sunny day. Good day sunshine . . .*" The Beatles again.

I walked around to the front of the library. Just then I saw Daphne leaning against the lion on the left, near the entrance to the library, waiting for me as promised. She was defiantly smoking a cigarette. She wore jeans and a combat jacket that she later told me had been purchased at an Army-Navy surplus store in St. Mark's Square. Her auburn hair was pulled tight into an austere braid that she wore over one shoulder. Her high, laced brown boots were too warm for July. As she smoked, I could see that her fingers were beginning to sport nicotine stains.

"Isn't it a beautiful day?" I began. Truth be told though, it was hot and humid. But strolling with her just made me happy.

"Uh-huh," she said in an abstracted way. "Do you want a smoke?"

"No. I don't smoke. And you shouldn't either. When did you start?"

But then she snapped out of her sullen mood. She glanced at one of the trees flanking the building. "The tree reminds me of Walt Whitman. *Uttering joyous leaves.* That's how he described it. Perfect, don't you think?"

"I do," I said, but there was still something different about this smoking girl. And I had never seen Daphne sullen. "What were you researching?" I asked, ever the professor.

"Oh, just something I'm interested in."

I didn't understand her evasion.

"Where shall we go?" I asked.

"Let's walk through Times Square. I love Times Square."

"You do? Times Square is just for tourists."

"Then I'm a tourist," she said, lighting up another cigarette. "I like the crowds. I like to feel anonymous."

Times Square, which was just two avenues away, was a bit disreputable. Panhandlers, working girls, girlie shows, and porn shops existed alongside overpriced tourist memorabilia stores. Of course, as we neared it we started to see the neon of the Broadway marquees. I could see how she might like all the excitement.

As we walked through Times Square, Daphne stopped cold.

"What is it?" I asked. People were surging around her, and she was holding up pedestrian traffic.

Wordlessly she pointed to a storefront sign that read: *Army Recruitment Office.* The recruiting posters plastered to the building were marked by scrawled comments like *Fuck you* and *Go to Hell.* She took note of everything and finally said, "I had no idea a recruitment center was here." She paused. "Have you ever been to a recruitment office?"

"No, I haven't, though I did have to register for the draft on my eighteenth birthday. Everyone does."

"What happened?"

"What do you mean?"

"Did you go into the service?"

"I was the right age for Korea, but I got a school deferment. I told you that the first day we met. Don't you remember? By the time I got out of school after my PhD I was too old to be drafted. Then the war ended, but Vietnam hadn't started up yet."

"Uh-huh," she said in a way that managed to imply disapproval. "This is what I do now. In my spare time."

"What?"

"Draft counseling."

"Really? You? A high school kid?"

"We tell them to register. It's against the law not to, but we tell them to leave their address blank. Can you imagine if everyone did that? They couldn't draft anyone if they couldn't find them."

She said this with the peculiar logic of adolescents

who exist in a world where hoping makes dreams come true.

Neither Schrödinger girl had ever said anything about Vietnam. I hadn't either. At college the war was a constant companion. Kids organized protests, boycotted classes, and handed out flyers on a regular basis. I hadn't declared myself either a hawk or a dove. Enrollment kept growing. As long as college attendance earned a draft deferment, the ranks of young male college students would continue to swell. I didn't want any of my students to go off to fight and be killed, but I hadn't confronted the issue of the war. I had left it to the Harvard think tank that was behind it to figure all that out. I braced myself, because Daphne was clearly going to challenge me.

"You're not a hawk, are you?" Her face registered anxiety and the beginning of disgust. Her upset was clearly worry for the purity of my convictions. The disgust was . . . I have no idea. I desperately wanted her to approve of me, so I began feeling a little anxious.

Times Square is very noisy, always. In midday, it was a cacophony of car horns, traffic, sirens, and crowd noises. "Let's go somewhere quiet," I suggested, eager for the tête-à-tête that defined my relationship with Daphne.

"I don't think there is anywhere quiet in Times Square," she said, but something else was up. "Let's go into the recruiting office."

"Why would we go there?"

"I'll show you." And she rushed in before I could stop her.

The office had a predictable American flag, a big desk with chairs for army personnel in uniform, and rows of chairs for young guys who wandered in off the street.

Although lots of college kids were against the war, there were many young men who still were itching to serve their country in Southeast Asia, and many poor white, Hispanic, and black kids who just needed a decent gig.

Daphne stood with her back to the recruiters and faced the three or four young men who were patiently waiting, scattered throughout the two rows of folding chairs. She raised her voice and shouted, "Guys, this is an illegal war! Kids are being killed! Don't be part of that!"

This was more than draft counseling; Daphne was actually disrupting the recruiting center, and the army personnel appeared ready to arrest her, or worse. She was oblivious to the threat, warming to her message, but I felt that I needed to get her out of there. The sergeant in charge rose from his chair and approached Daphne. I was afraid he was going to drag her off. But then he thought better of it and approached me. "Mister," he said, "you'd better get your daughter out of here. She's causing a disturbance." I thought he wanted to throttle her. His uniform and dour expression had me cowed, yet Daphne acted completely unperturbed. She renewed her entreaty to the guys in the chairs until they started heckling her. They were definitely hawks.

"Leave us the hell alone," one said.

"Who cares what you think? Go home to your mama," said another.

I took her by the arm and forcefully pulled her out into the street. I was in no mood to be polite. "What do you think you're doing? You could have gotten into real trouble."

"Who gives a shit, Garrett? Didn't you hear me? Kids are being napalmed. Kids are being killed! Shouldn't we do something? Shouldn't *you*?" Her emerald eyes flashed. "I'm not afraid of that sergeant. I don't give a flying fuck what they do to me."

"Calm down," I said.

"There's no time to be calm," she answered.

I managed to steer her to a small hole-in-the-wall pizza joint. I ordered us slices and Cokes. "Now sit down and behave yourself," I said.

She took out her cigarettes and very pointedly lit one up.

"I don't want cigarette smoke with my lunch," I told her. "Could you please put that out?"

She did.

"You don't really believe that domino theory crap, do you?"

The domino theory was the idea that once one country fell—that is, became Communist—another would follow and all of Southeast Asia would fall like dominoes. This idea was the professed cornerstone of our Vietnam War policy, thought up by the Ivy League think tank Kennedy had brought with him that was still on board for Johnson.

"What do you think is going on?" I asked in a level, noncommittal tone. I wasn't a college professor for nothing.

"I think Vietnam is fighting for self-determination and we should just back the fuck away. We are killing American soldiers and local civilians on the news every night. How are you okay with that?"

"When did you start saying fuck all the time?"

My problem with adopting Daphne's position was that it would mean repudiating a lot of the ideas I'd grown up with, especially the idea that we could trust our government to take care of us. Because my dad had been killed in World War II, I had a strong belief in fighting and valor—the only way I could bear it. I was afraid of betraying him and of the abyss that would open up if I entertained the possibility that our government was a mouthpiece for corporate interests, as the doves insisted. I was still on the fence. Teaching had brought me face to face with committed doves every day, but I was still reluctant to wholeheartedly embrace their ideology.

The pizza came and Daphne settled down a bit.

"How did this new conviction come about?" I asked her.

"I tried to have a pen pal in Vietnam. I got him at school. Rick Lopez. He had to fight because he only has a green card. How unfair is that? After his first letter he stopped writing back. And then I met Terry Collins, a guy who dropped out of the University of Ohio. He was in SDS, Students for a Democratic Society, at a rally the day after I met you, and he started a chapter in the next town. He rents a big house with some other guys his age where we all hang out and smoke grass."

"But you're only sixteen, what about your parents?"

"They're too dumb to know what's going on."

"Is he your boyfriend?"

"No. But we fuck sometimes."

"And . . . that's okay with you?"

"I don't know," she said, allowing the chink in her bravado to show. "I started going to the high school in the next town, where Terry's house is. A few months ago. I changed schools."

"Why?"

"Just because. Because I couldn't stand my friends. Because I wanted to devote all my time to movement work."

"What about Schrödinger? And R.D. Laing? And Walt Whitman? Didn't you tell me that you want to understand reality?"

"I can't be bothered with all that crap. I have to act."

"But you're still going to school, right?"

"Yeah, but I feel stupid. Selfish."

"That's what you're supposed to do. You're a kid. You're supposed to study."

"Aren't I supposed to stop people from killing Vietnamese kids?"

"Did you want to talk about the war, or shock me by smoking cigarettes in front of me and saying fuck?"

"I don't know. Did you hear? The sergeant called you my father."

"Yeah. I'm old enough to be, but I'm not, though when you act stupid I have to act like one. A father, I mean."

As usual, Daphne refused to talk about parents. "I don't want a father. I want an ally."

"I think you need a father."

"My father was in the OSS during the war. You know. Codes. Spy stuff. He was very young. And he believed in that war and won't say anything against the government now. I wish you would see things as I do, like your students do."

"Some of them," I corrected. "Go home. Move out of Terry's house. You're living with him, right? Do something productive with your summer. The world will still be here when you grow up a bit."

"Spoken like a grandfather to a little girl. Fuck that. I like living at Terry's. I like being an emancipated minor. I have this summer job living with a family in the Hamptons and being their au pair. But they went to Europe for the week, so I have some time off."

"That sounds fine. Just don't be so impatient to grow up."

"Garrett!"

"What?"

"You know that's the crap adults always say." Then her mood changed and her countenance softened. "I like your longer hair. And I like that you were singing the Beatles. You *do* think about the war, right? If you really think about it, I just don't believe you will be on the fence anymore. It's vile. In fact, that's what I was researching. The war. Not Schrödinger. Not physics. Not poetry. You'll think about it?"

"Absolutely. Speaking about something else, I didn't know when I'd see you again. Not after you ran out of the Forester Gallery."

"What the fuck are you talking about?"

"The Galen Green portrait?"

Her eyebrows met in a picture of puzzlement, and she gently shook her head. No, she did not know what I was talking about. Then she glanced down at her watch, a large-faced man's wristwatch, her father's, Terry's, or maybe even Rick Lopez's. "Fuck," she said. "I have no idea what the fuck you're talking about. I never went to any gallery with you, and I have no idea what portrait you're talking about. The last time I saw you, you brought those stupid index cards. But I'm going to miss my train. Terry has an organizing meeting I have to help him with. I just wanted to check in with you. It's a good thing we're so near Penn Station." She hurried out, barely taking the time to wave goodbye.

"Wait!" I shouted after her. "You do know me from
the bookstore, right? You did buy the Schrödinger book?"

"Of course," she called back over her shoulder without breaking her stride.

Wow. I would have bet the bank that I had just met
another Daphne. That foulmouthed urchin didn't resem-
ble either of the two Daphnes, apart from being exactly
the same. The contradiction was dizzying. What was happening? The girl was like a hydra, sprouting existences
like the monster sprouted heads. If I was right, there were
enormous questions opening up before me, questions
about her nature and the mechanics of her life. And questions about reality, which just didn't work this way. *And
something is happening here, but you don't know what
it is, do you, Mr. Adams?* Since I had no idea what was
going on, I had no idea how Daphne's life worked.

Here's what I knew: all these girls had met and formed
some kind of bond with me, though they seemed to have
no idea of each other. Each was Daphne; each was different. I had no proof of my new suspicions about this
new Daphne, but I was going to have to find out, and
I was afraid that if I really understood the Schrödinger
girls everything in the world would start to be different.
Or it was still possible that she was a fraud, or that I was
crazy? Is definitive evidence about reality ever available?

C HAPTER SEVEN

ALL THE PICAYUNE DETAILS that go into planning a semester started to drive me crazy. Creating new courses and researching new texts published that year was a time-consuming process, and this summer I had little interest in my job. I wanted to analyze the Schrödinger mystery full time, not that I really had much to go on.

I finally submitted book requests for the fall 1967 semester to our department secretary. When I left the social science building I noticed the hydrangeas burgeoning with their riotous mophead blooms of blue, pink, and purple. As a natural litmus test announcing the pH of the soil just by their color, they had always fascinated me. Back home, I pulled my ten-year-old T-bird, my one extravagance, into the driveway of the old house I rented.

Stepping up my efforts to understand these girls, I dedicated my small study to sorting out the Daphne data. I took down my framed van Gogh reproductions, *Starry Night* and *Pear Tree in Blossom,* without thinking and stood them on the floor facing the far wall of the room to free up the wall space for my investigation.

All my meetings with the Daphnes, those auburn-haired adolescents, those Schrödinger girls, swirled in my head, so I began with a time line. I taped paper to the wall and gathered up my markers—I used black for the dates, red for the settings, and blue for the descriptions of Daphne.

After I finished the time line I added the snapshot of Galen's Daphne standing by the swan boats in Boston. When she had handed me the photo I put it in my jacket pocket instead of giving it back. Since the time stamp on the snapshot exactly matched the time I had been at the gallery in front of the portrait with Daphne, I reasoned that I had proof, of a sort, that there were two Daphnes. I had worked on enough twin studies in grad school to know that sometimes twins were separated and adopted and knew nothing of each other, but the girl in Bronxville knew me and had shared experiences with my original Daphne. So did the girl at the recruiting office. All three claimed to be the girl from the bookstore. And although physics suggested that an alternate Daphne could theoretically exist, no one expected a second or third girl to actually show up. I remembered my first meeting with Ur-Daphne and her explanation of Ovid's myth. Maybe I was Apollo, and my gaze was splitting the girls apart. Instead of being transformed into a tree, each new incarnation just began a new life, a kind of tree, right? With each Daphne one of its branches? Now I was just being fanciful, I thought. Maybe Jerry was right when he called Jung myth, and the collective unconscious clinically irrelevant.

The time line didn't divulge much, but maybe another reading of the R.D. Laing book Daphne had given me could help. I flopped down into the brown chenille chair that served as my reading spot. A floor lamp and a small side table were the only furniture in the room apart from a small wooden desk. I'd left Daphne's gift on the table by the chair.

Laing didn't provide any clues to understanding my multiplying girl, but he seemed to be talking directly to me. Meeting these Daphnes had me imagining a reality constructed in an entirely different way than ordinary reality. Instinct told me that these were not twins or triplets, and that the girl in Bronxville and the girl in Times Square were not acting. I had to admit to myself that I believed that the girl in the bookstore was now three girls. She had split into another self. One girl had run off with Galen Green, one had returned to her parents and was still in high school, and one had emancipated herself and lived in a student house with an SDS organizer. As outlandish as it might seem to Jerry, this is what I believed.

What if I *was* mentally ill? Laing's main idea was that the mentally ill are not insane, just differently sane, a radical notion. My mind protested. What about the guy in the loony bin thinking he was Napoleon? Was he just differently sane too? I wasn't comfortable with Laing's conclusions, as I had spent my entire academic life avoiding just this rhetoric. It was exactly his way of thinking that had led me to behaviorism where we didn't have to consider these questions. Didn't people think Copernicus was crazy? And Semmelweis had gone crazy knowing the truth that germs caused childbed fever and having to watch so many women die. *Slow down,* I thought. I had to guard against grandiosity now. I knew that was a symptom of paranoia. *No, you are not in the company of Copernicus or Semmelweis,* I reprimanded myself.

I was certain of one thing: I wouldn't find out who Daphne was from a book. Feeling agitated because I was getting nowhere, I decided to retrace my steps and return to the Bookmasters where I had first met her. I might find a clue there. Driving down along Storm King, a hilly, curving highway, I glimpsed striking vistas of the green world, orchards and the stalwart river, glistening blue in the late-July sunshine. I arrived in the afternoon, and the store was almost empty. The day was too beautiful for book browsing. I walked down the science aisle, but then I swerved toward classics. I stood facing several different translations of Ovid's *Metamorphoses*. I chose the one with the nicest font.

As I left the store, on a whim I stopped at a nearby phone booth. The huge, ratty White Pages hung down. I leafed through the book until I found the listing for the Forester Gallery. Caroline answered. After the normal greetings I said, "Hey, are you willing to have dinner with me tonight? I know it's short notice. I was a bit distant last time. Would you give me another chance?" I wanted to ask her about the Daphne painting.

"Hmm. Would I be willing? Not the best line ever, Garrett," she joked. "Let's see. I assume you're paying," she said in a lighthearted way. I assured her that I was. "Well, then, sure. What's a girl got to lose? Where?"

I suggested the Russian Tea Room. I had wanted to go since Daphne said that she and Galen had met there. I was stalking an apparition. But the legendary restaurant also had its own glamorous appeal; it was very near the gallery. I hoped I'd be able to afford something on the menu.

"I'll meet you at seven," I said, giving her time to finish up. "I'll make a reservation. If there's a problem, I'll call you back."

"Sounds good to me."

I was lucky that day because my change held out long

enough to make the arrangements from the pay phone. I headed to the usual coffee shop to kill some time; I could sit and read the Ovid. I saw our usual waitress. She asked, "Where's your redheaded friend?" in her soft Caribbean accent.

I half hoped that the Schrödinger girl would be sitting at our table eating a grilled cheese sandwich, but of course she wasn't. This time I was able to sit against the mirror so I would not be plagued by the random views of myself, a lanky fellow with medium-brown hair, now in a Beatles cut, wearing his new granny glasses. I didn't want to be embarrassed by glimpsing my own earnestness.

The encyclopedia entry I had read had summarized Ovid's tale faithfully. Apollo ridicules Cupid as the lesser archer, so Cupid takes revenge by shooting Apollo with a golden arrow and Daphne with a lead one, causing Apollo to fall deeply in love with the nymph. He pursues her, but she flees and begs her father, the river god, to protect her. He does, by turning her into a laurel tree. That much I already knew, but the summary did not communicate the intensity of Apollo's desire for her, or the pathos of Daphne's desire to escape him and remain devoted to Artemis, a virgin goddess. Although I couldn't see much relevance, I realized that all Ovid's stories described metamorphoses. There was a connection there.

My plan was to talk about the myth with Caroline over dinner. I had never been to the Russian Tea Room. My mother wasn't the type to spend money frivolously, and I had never considered taking a date to such an expensive restaurant. As I walked under the red marquee in front of the building, I was relieved that I'd worn a sport coat that morning, as I did every day if I was going in to school. Being inside the restaurant felt like being in a Russian jewel box. Everything was red. The deep red banquettes curved around tables. I'd heard that there was a huge bear-shaped aquarium one floor up.

I had been seated for only five minutes when Caroline arrived. As she walked toward the table I watched other diners regarding her appreciatively. She wore another little black dress. Her straight black hair was down over her shoulders, and long, dangling gold earrings peeked through. She smiled broadly when she saw me.

"Garrett," she said, extending her hand to clasp mine.

"You look really well," I said. "So good to see you. Sit down, please." She sat near me on the banquette. I could smell her subtle perfume.

She noted that. "Mitsouko," she said. "I always wear it."

We ordered vodka tonics and pored over the menu. She ordered the duck, and I ordered the salmon, thinking of Galen's painting, the warm tones of the salmon on the plate in front of the reclining girl. The prices were as bad as I'd feared, but I had cashed my paycheck before leaving New Paltz, and now that we were sitting there, I decided that expense be damned. We sipped our drinks.

"This is a surprise," she began. "I thought we had agreed to be just friends. Or have I misunderstood?" For a beautiful woman, Caroline was surprisingly direct.

"No, you haven't," I assured her. "I can't imagine what was wrong with me."

This time, she didn't rush in to help carry the conversation. She waited.

"Well, I'm not going to make that mistake tonight," I said.

She smiled at that. Her eyes were such a light brown that they shone tawny and golden in the soft light of the restaurant. I ordered us a second drink.

We made small talk. I liked her voice for reasons I couldn't quite place. Something seemed familiar about it. We hadn't ordered appetizers; the waiter brought our entrees just as she was saying, "I come from Indiana, but my mother was a Russian girl from Pittsburgh. I guess I should feel at home here."

"And your dad?" I asked.

"Regulation American. From a farming family, but he worked for local government. I'm named for my great-grandmother and my grandmother. Caroline was my father's grandmother's name, and Tanya was my mother's mother. So I'm Caroline Tanya Andrews."

Just then she took her first bite of duck. The vodkas were working. Something was uncoiling inside me, and I realized that I was having a good time, though my Schrödinger mystery hovered. I had wanted to talk about Daphne, but now I didn't want to ruin our second date.

We ate our food until Caroline took a breath and said, "I feel like there's an elephant in the room with us. Do you want to talk about that girl you brought to the gallery and Galen's painting of her? You ran out of the gallery to find her, didn't you?"

She was saving me again. I averred that what she said was true. "There are things I want to talk to you about, but this is just so lovely." I surprised myself by saying, "I wish it could wait till tomorrow."

"That can be arranged," she said. Her almond-shaped eyes tilted up as she smiled. She had worn red lipstick that by chance matched the banquettes exactly. Her white skin did make her appear Russian, a woman from northern climes. "Tomorrow just happens to be my day off. You're free for the summer, right?"

"As free as a bird."

"So it's settled."

I told her about my father, lost in the war. And just a little about Helena. I didn't mention Amy. I admitted that there hadn't been anyone serious since then. She told me she'd come east with her high school sweetheart. They both needed to get out of Indiana. He'd gone to Amherst and became an actor. She'd gone to Smith and studied art history. They'd moved in together for a year or two, until he announced that he was gay, and eventually she had drifted to New York, as he had. She hadn't had anyone serious in her life in the eight years since the break-up.

"It was hard for me to get used to New York after Boston, where we moved after graduation, but now I wouldn't live anywhere else." So that was it—the familiar sound of Boston in her voice that she'd picked up living there, the sound of my father.

"Are you a Red Sox or a Yankees fan?" I asked.

"Cubs," she said. "I'm a masochist."

We shared some fancy dessert and then exited into the clear summer evening. The silver moon was a waxing crescent, and its bow shape made me think of Artemis the hunter, and Daphne, her acolyte, and the laurel tree she became. "Do you have someplace to stay tonight?" she asked. "Or do you want to stay with me?"

"I haven't actually made any plans," I admitted.

"You're coming home with me," she said, as she artfully hailed a taxi. "The cab ride's on me. I live in the

Village." As we clambered into the cab she told the driver, "Forty-nine Barrow Street."

How was it possible that Caroline lived on my favorite street in New York City? As a grad student at NYU I often wandered over to Barrow Street to walk around. The buildings were mostly old-fashioned redbrick, and the short street felt like a planned square. The biggest building had been built at the beginning of the century as affordable housing for the poor, but now the entire area was very expensive. I couldn't imagine how Caroline could afford to live there on a gallery income.

I had my answer the minute she unlocked her door. She was saying something about how lucky she had been that this apartment had just fallen into her lap. Her apartment was a twelve-by-twelve-foot square white box with a small bathroom tucked in back. Her kitchen was a hot plate, a mini refrigerator, and a small toaster oven, all stacked on a baker's rack. I guessed the bathroom sink served as a kitchen sink. There were built-ins all around the room for books, her clock, a few pictures, her jewelry box, and other personal items. She stored her clothes behind a built-in door. She had two chairs and a small settee with a tiny round glass table between them. I didn't see a bed anywhere. I was about to sit down on one of the small bentwood chairs when she lined them up against the wall. She moved the settee and the table also, so I rose and lined up my chair with the rest of the furniture. The central space of the room was empty, and she walked over to the center of the wall facing the door, pulled on a handle, and pulled down her bed. I didn't know anyone still used Murphy beds. I was amazed that she did this every day, moving the furniture back and forth. "I like to come home to a living room," she explained.

This meant there was no couch to sleep on. She didn't even have floor space I could use. Staying with Caroline meant sleeping in her bed. Once the bed was down there was just room to walk around it to reach the little kitchen wall or bathroom, but not much else. Caroline was smiling. She loved her apartment.

As I was getting my bearings, she slipped out of her dress. She hadn't been wearing a bra. She was a slender woman, and she stood before me with small, firm breasts and lacy underwear. She walked over to the glass table and dropped her earrings in a colorful blown-glass bowl, and then walked around the bed to where I was standing and started unbuttoning my shirt.

"I can do that," I said, and as I did, she pulled me onto the bed.

Starlight entered from a row of high windows. She had opened the white shutters, so the night became part of the décor. When my clothes were off she stretched out her arms for them and laid them on the settee.

The bed appointments were pale too. I was lost in a sea of white—the sheets, the walls, and her beautiful white body and long fair limbs. Her skin was cool and smooth as a stone, and we made love in a white blur of desire and delight, neither taking over the other. She came as if she was singing, but then she started to cry.

"I'm so sorry," she said. "It's not that I'm sad. It's just that it's been a long time since anyone went that deep inside me—emotionally, I mean—and the sadness, I guess it just lives buried in me. I didn't mean to ruin it. It was so lovely."

I kissed her raven hair and stroked one of her long beautiful arms. "Oh, sweetie. It's all right. It really is. I know exactly how you feel. It's been a long time for me too. Nothing is ruined."

I fell immediately asleep from the heavy meal, the vodkas, and our lovemaking. I awoke to sun streaming through the high windows because Caroline had left the shutters open the night before. I had only to turn my head to see my new beautiful naked woman, long and sultry like a Modigliani, doing the impossible: making scrambled eggs on her baker's-rack kitchen. She was humming "Good Day Sunshine." An electric coffee machine and two white mugs were lined up on the lower shelf of the rack.

"Good morning, sleepy head," she called out. "Use the bathroom and come to breakfast."

We ate eggs and drank our mugs of coffee sitting cross-legged on the bed. Thankfully the bed was low to the ground because the floor was the only place to put the coffee.

"Now we get dressed and you tell me about Daphne," she said brightly.

When we were dressed, and the bed was put away, we sat facing each other in the small chairs.

"Ah, where to begin," I said. I wasn't ready to share the bizarre, seemingly supernatural aspects of the case. I wanted to keep that to myself. "I want to start with the past paintings of the myth. The ones you talked about when I came to the gallery in June. Are any at the Met?"

"No. I think that they might have some etchings that are not for public viewing. We could see them with my credentials, but I'd need more notice to arrange it. What we could do is go to the Met, go to the gift shop, and find a book with most of the pictures I want to show you. Painting the Daphne-and-Apollo myth was very popular during the baroque period."

"Why was that?" I asked.

"I guess they were fascinated by the themes of sexuality and escape. They liked the idea of metamorphosis. And also, it was a great challenge to show a girl turning into a tree. I think they might have been competing with each other."

I found Caroline's talk about art engaging, yet her information didn't bring me closer to understanding my Schrödinger girls. Still, it was the only lead I had.

"Okay. But what does the myth have to do with anything? What's this all about, Garrett?"

I had to tell her something. "You remember the girl in the gallery? You remember her running away when she saw the painting?" I heard myself say. So like the mythic Daphne, my Daphne was running away, except instead of becoming a tree, she had become another Daphne. Perhaps this was metamorphosis in the age of Schrödinger. I did not say this.

I watched Caroline place the details and then answer, "Yes. I remember her and the painting of her."

"That's just it. She claims it's not a painting of her. That she never sat for it. That she doesn't even know Galen Green."

"Yeah. I sort of gathered something like that. Do you believe her?"

"I went to see the girl who posed for the picture, and it was still Daphne, but it was a different Daphne. Well, she started as the same Daphne, but she grew into a second Daphne. And she's the one who sat for the portrait."

"You're not making any sense. I can barely follow what you're saying. Do you mean that you believe people can split apart and become two?"

I sighed and avoided meeting Caroline's gaze. I did believe it. To my best understanding of the situation, an alternate reality had been born, probably at the Russian Tea Room when Daphne met Galen. I had no idea about the mechanism of that or what happened to the Ur-Daphne at that moment. It was all beyond me. I guess that's what made me seem crazy, believing in something I had no process to describe. In a way it was like the myth. Just as the nymph's encounter with Apollo had changed her form, so had Daphne's encounter with Galen Green. Was I saying that women are shaped by the men they encounter? I hoped not. That seemed a very old-fashioned idea.

My theory was that one Daphne had joined Galen for lunch, one Daphne had either eaten her usual bagged lunch and remained behind, or remained at her own table eating a solitary lunch at the Russian Tea Room, and the third was at a rally. I'd heard something about ideas of alternate realities, but I had no idea of the logistics of things, of where the matter that made a new Daphne might have come from. But I was getting very nuts-and-bolts about a bigger mystery. I also suspected that these realities shouldn't exist side by side, that I shouldn't be able to travel so easily between them, but obviously I could. Or it seemed like I could when I was with the different Daphnes. But now I was getting myself confused.

"I'm not sure what I believe, Caroline," I said, "but something's going on. I need to find out what it is."

She nodded. "And the myth? Why are we interested in Ovid?"

"Because Daphne is. She told me that she was named after a myth. I want to know about the myth and the imagery of the myth. Like Galen's painting, for example."

"Okay. Fair enough," she said in- a noncommittal way. Then she added, "There's talk around the gallery that Green has created an entire series of Daphne paintings that capture different moments of the myth. The one we hung is perhaps the least explicit reference. Of course, I haven't seen any of the others. I'm just going by what I've heard. These are all very recent paintings, apparently painted very quickly. Your young friend is quite the muse."

"I guess he was inspired by her name."

"And her youth," she said slyly. "Lots of painters have been inspired by that myth."

I nodded. Those were the painters I planned to devote the day to.

On a day off from work, jeans replaced the gallery uniform for Caroline. My jacket was certainly annoying on such a warm day, but I refused her suggestion of leaving it at her apartment. In the museum gift shop, she picked up a big heavy volume that was too expensive for my budget, so we found a spot on the floor hidden by displays and studied many baroque renderings of the myth. The one I liked best showed just one of the nymph's hands starting to turn into leaves as Apollo almost catches her. I grew tired before Caroline did, and suggested lunch.

We found a table in the cafeteria. She put a salad on my tray, and I had a turkey sandwich. We opted for iced teas.

"So. Learn anything?" she asked.

"Yeah. I learned that you, Caroline Andrews, know a shitload about art."

"I do. You know, I've often thought that the famous Klimt, *The Kiss,* is an Apollo-Daphne portrait. You've seen that, haven't you? All the gold? Art nouveau?"

I vaguely knew the painting, but I'd have to see it again to understand what she was talking about. She plucked a postcard from her purse and handed it to me. It was Klimt's *The Kiss.*

Noticing my surprise, she said with a laugh, "I bought it while you were in the men's room."

A tall male figure embraces a small female figure, surrounded by a shower of gold and black. They seem to be leaning toward each other, but I couldn't see any reference to the myth. This woman wasn't fleeing.

Then she took the card but tilted it toward me. "Look here," she pointed. "The man wears a crown of laurel leaves, and the woman's hair is growing flowers. See here at the bottom of the painting—vines grow up her legs. She's wearing a floral dress, yes, that's true, but these vines seem to a have a life of their own. And the woman swoons, maybe in resistance to his advances."

I could see what she meant, and when I finally looked carefully at the painting my heart leaped. The swooning woman had almost auburn hair, and she was small and delicate, like my Daphne.

"Listening to you talk about art is wonderful," I murmured, quite shaken.

"Is it helpful?"

"Maybe."

"We didn't talk about Galen Green's painting."

"It doesn't seem to have the elements of the myth in it, except that the girl's name is Daphne."

"Perhaps," Caroline said. "But think about it. The girl is very young. She is being swallowed up by her surroundings. Her table is sprouting green plates and green beans. The vegetable world is approaching."

"That sounds a bit far-fetched. And anyway, there's no Apollo in the painting."

"Maybe," she conceded. "But how about this— maybe Galen is Apollo, watching her, and maybe he has captured her on the canvas."

I felt a pang when she said this. Had Galen hunted Daphne? Something didn't quite fit. She had been the huntress at our encounter, not the other way around. But Galen didn't know that. Or maybe his pursuit was the painter's eye, an unconscious encroachment.

"And there's nothing more you can tell me about the girl or your interest in her?"

"Not right now." I was hesitant to appear too crazy to Caroline right after we'd been to bed together. I didn't want her closing the door on me already.

She had something else on her mind. "I told Jerry after our last disastrous date that we wouldn't be seeing each other again—"

"How do you know Jerry?" I cut in. "Did he come into the gallery? You're just the kind of girl he'd want for himself."

"I was his patient," she said, showing some embarrassment for the first time. "We liked each other, sure, but dating is way against the rules. He told me he had a friend for me."

I didn't know why, but Jerry's involvement in our relationship annoyed me. It felt like meddling, even if he had been right that we would make a good pair.

"What I am asking," she continued, "is that you tell him about us. Maybe because he was my therapist I don't like keeping secrets from him, but I don't want to call him either. It just feels too professional."

There was no denying the fact that there was now an *us*. Sometimes it happens like that. From just one night, we were a couple. We both knew it, so there was no reason to pretend otherwise.

"Sure, I'll call him," I assured her. And we finished our lunch.

CHAPTER EIGHT

CAROLINE AND I HELD HANDS as we walked through the cavernous lobby of the museum and lingered on its long flight of stone steps leading down to Fifth Avenue. Hippies, in colored bandannas and tie-dyed T-shirts that copied the style that was coming out of San Francisco, sat around in groups, playing guitars and laughing.

I was tempted to ask her if she wanted to return to her apartment to spend the afternoon in bed, but she mentioned she had some errands to run on her one day off. I spontaneously decided to visit Jerry to tell him about Caroline and me.

I turned and studied the imposing building behind us, with its huge banners announcing current exhibitions: *In the Presence of Kings: Treasures from the Collections of the Metropolitan Museum of Art*, and *Russian Scenes and Costume Design for Ballet, Opera, and Theater*. Caroline noticed my wistful expression, squeezed my hand, and said, "We'll come back," and then scampered away down the stairs.

Before she reached the bottom, she turned and called up to me: "Garrett, I have a strange feeling. Just be careful with this Daphne business. Don't fall down the rabbit-hole." She paused, waiting for my response, so I nodded, and she walked south on Fifth Avenue.

I lingered, remembering days spent with my mother at the museum during the war. We were both acutely aware of my father's absence, and we found some solace in these great works of art, especially the statues from antiquity with their solid presence. But that was a long time ago. At the foot of the stairs I tossed some coins into the open violin case of a young guy playing Vivaldi. Then I walked to a pay phone to call Jerry.

He offered his usual greeting. "Hi, *bubbeleh.*" He added, "In town?"

"As a matter of fact, I am."

"Come on over. Today is the kind of afternoon when patients cancel. They just can't bear to be inside. They even pay for the session for the chance to play hooky."

I made my usual comment: "Ah, you guys have it made. You get paid for not working."

Jerry had a large apartment in a brownstone on West 89th Street, just off Central Park West. He lived on one of those streets that let you think you were in Paris. When I buzzed he came to the door immediately.

"Hi, kiddo. Follow me."

I followed him into his consulting room. He had furnished it like Freud's: big desk, bookshelves and shelves with statuary, a large comfortable chair, a second small chair, and a daybed covered by an Oriental rug, just like Freud had on his couch. Jerry took psychoanalysis literally. He also had a large wooden desk with a beautiful silver-and-glass decanter, and two little shot glasses. I was sure Freud didn't have a decanter on *his* desk, but then again, Jerry didn't have Freud's cigars. I should have remembered the bottle of Scotch I always brought when I visited him. The rare times he visited me in New Paltz, he brought a six-pack of Heineken.

I felt like a patient in this setting. Why had Jerry brought me in here? I found out immediately. He seated himself in the comfortable large, black leather chair. I took the small chair covered in green velvet. "So, Garrett. I've been worried about you. I haven't heard from you since our odd conversation after lunch at Katz's." He waited, expecting me to say something, but I waited too. All of this felt uncomfortable. Finally he said, "Still having those unusual thoughts? Still fixated on that girl? Daphne, isn't it?"

His question put me in a quandary. If I answered him honestly, he would see me as a patient and turn our meeting into a therapy session. But if I lied, I would be worried that there really was something wrong with me, necessitating deception. I tried to straddle the question.

"I think about her sometimes. I've seen her again . . . but fixated? No. I am definitely not fixated." Too bad he wasn't into cigars because it would ease the tension if he lit one up.

"Hm. And what does 'I think about her sometimes' mean?"

"It means I think about her sometimes. Jerry, I came to talk about something quite different. Let's go into the living room. This chair is not comfortable, and I feel at a disadvantage."

But he wasn't letting go of the reins. "Why is that, kid?"

"Jerry, stop playing Freud. We're friends."

But he still didn't move. I wondered if he was genuinely worried about me. "Have you ever had any other strange experiences?"

I don't know what made me let down my guard, perhaps there was something magical about the setting, but I told him about the visitation from my dad. I had never told anyone else. "One night during the war my father came and sat on my bed. He was wearing his pilot's uniform, including the cap. He was so happy to see me, and of course I was thrilled to see him. I missed him so much. 'You're a big boy now,' he said. 'Remember the things I taught you. Remember that it's okay to lose and that character is everything. Never be afraid to be yourself. And take care of your mom.' The next day when we got the telegram from the war office we found out that when I saw him sitting on my bed he was already dead."

I could see Jerry processing my story, at a loss about what to say. Then he said, "I don't want to be dismissive, but you know that this was probably a dream." To his credit his voice was even and nonjudgmental.

"And the timing?" I asked.

"Probably coincidence."

I nodded. I was sure I'd seen my father—that his spirit had come to say goodbye—but I wasn't going to tell Jerry that. Talking to Jerry, I realized that I had most likely become a behaviorist in response to this mystifying experience that had created questions I wanted to avoid.

Then I volunteered, "I came to tell you that I'm seeing Caroline. I think she might be it for me. She wanted you to know."

He grinned. "Great news, *bubbeleh*. I thought you two would hit it off. I couldn't understand what happened last time."

"I guess I wasn't ready."

Before I left, I walked over to his shelves and lifted up a creamy marble reproduction. I held the Bernini rendering of Apollo and Daphne. Their two faces were achingly beautiful. The god stood just behind her as her outstretched arms ended in leafy clusters. "Great statue," I said.

"The image of transformation," he replied. "What we're after here."

"What about the fact that she's a tree?"

"Yeah. There is that," he laughed. "Norman O. Brown thinks it's the image of neurosis. Yeats thinks stability. There's a lot to work with."

So he does like myth, I thought.

Caroline's discussion of Galen's portrait of Daphne made me long to see it again, and long to see the girl who'd inspired it. Driving up the Bronx River Parkway, I decided to stop by Bronxville; I had to drive by there on my way home. Impulsively, I stopped in front of Galen's stone house and parked my car on the street. I turned off the ignition but didn't get out. I was nervous. I had no plan for what to say, no index cards, and no conversation to continue. I had no way to explain my visit, but I climbed out anyway and shut the door.

A young woman in khakis and a sweatshirt answered my knock. "I'm a friend of Daphne's," I said. "And Galen's," I added, though it wasn't true.

"I'm house sitting," she explained. "They're in England for a show. I'm a painting student at the college."

I thought I might have seen her at the morning painting class where I'd found Daphne posing. This girl was cute and chubby, with honey-brown hair in a pixie cut and some freckles scattered across her nose and cheeks. She had tied a batik cloth in bright blue around her head so the ends hung down. I could see that her sweatshirt bore remains of painting sessions. Judging by the stains, I deduced that she liked a bright palette.

"And you are . . . ?" I inquired.

"Jane."

"Jane, I'm Garrett. I don't suppose Galen hung a portrait of Daphne at home, did he? I saw it at the Forester Gallery, and I'd love to see it again, as long as I'm here."

"Sure. I can show you that. You hungry? I just made some chili. I would love someone to eat with."

We went into the kitchen, which was like an old farm kitchen with butcher-block counters and wainscotted cabinets. She set the table with heavy crockery dishes decorated with roosters, the icon of Provence. She put two bottles of Coke on the table. Her chili was delicious, and we ate in a companionable silence until we'd almost finished, and we got to gossiping.

"So, you know Daphne and Galen?"

"I know Daphne," I said.

"How do you know her?"

"It's complicated."

She accepted that. "Galen is a great painting teacher, you know. I can't imagine learning from anyone else. But it was really surprising to us when he brought such a young woman home. It felt kind of nineteenth century, to tell you the truth, like Renoir with his last model. Of course, we all had a crush on Galen. He told us to call him that. There aren't any boys here at Sarah Lawrence, so I guess we thought this girl, Daphne, was poaching."

This surprised me. He was a burly man in his fifties

with a clubfoot and a limp. I didn't think he'd be such a prize to girls. But what did I know of the desires of young women? I had been completely flummoxed when Daphne had propositioned me. "So, he's a good guy?" I asked.

"Most of the time. Sometimes he just asks us to do the impossible and bristles with impatience when we can't. He's not the kind of guy you describe as kind. But he's fair. And he wants us to succeed. That's what you really want in a teacher. He seems nice to Daphne, if that's what you mean. Though he can be impatient with her too, I've noticed."

"Daphne. Do you like her?" Now that I was gossiping, I couldn't stop.

"She's young. She pretty. She's his muse. We all want to be her, I suppose." Jane laughed. "She's okay. She's nice enough to me. A friend of mine is in an art history class with her, and she says that Daphne is really smart. At least that's something. But I shouldn't say bad things about her. She lives here."

"Are they a couple?" I asked.

"Yes. No. Maybe so? How would I know? But we probably shouldn't be gossiping about them either."

I admitted that she was right because I saw that she really couldn't answer my question. She smoked a cigarette as she finished her Coke and announced that it was time to visit the painting.

The studio was a one-story addition at the back of the house. Green had built it with a vaulted ceiling and skylights to maximize the light. Finished and half-finished canvases filled a lot of the space, and we carefully threaded our way between them, as they stood at least three deep against the walls, a drawing table, and the chairs. She knew just where in the room the Daphne paintings were. Green had done many studies of her—some nude, some clothed—that explored different moments of the myth. I thought of Caroline, who would have loved to see them. She was right in saying the rest of the series were more explicitly about the Ovid myth than the painting Ur-Daphne and I had seen at the Forester Gallery. In one, the young girl had actually become a tree, trailing telltale strands of beautiful auburn hair intertwined with leaves. Then I saw the painting I'd seen in the gallery. Yes, I could appreciate what Caroline had said, that even in this abstract, less literal canvas, Galen Green was interpreting the myth of Apollo and Daphne. In this rendering, Daphne hadn't become a tree, but she sat oddly still within the scene that included the startlingly green plates and beans. The swift nymph, Daphne, had grown still among the dishes. Perhaps the same thing had occurred in the Russian Tea Room when Daphne had joined Galen eating salmon and green beans.

I glanced away from the painting and asked Jane, "Does Galen talk to you about what he's doing with myth in his work?"

"Yeah, sometimes. He's very big on myth and on Joseph Campbell, who teaches at Sarah Lawrence too, and on Jung as a way to get to our subconscious associations. He loves Mark Rothko, who uses myth. And Jackson Pollock. Galen says that myth is just part of abstract expressionism. Of course, Galen's work isn't that abstract. He borrows from other painters. Cézanne and Matisse, to name two. In his work the figurative elements are fading into abstract expressionism. Do you know what I mean? Are you a painter?"

I laughed. "No, I'm a psych professor at New Paltz, but there sure has been a lot of art in my life lately. I do understand what you mean. Do you like these paintings?"

"I think they're breathtaking, and they've influenced me. I am neorealistic, which as you can imagine isn't very popular. No one wants to see realistic paintings. But Galen has shown me how to give them a mythic quality. He said I could use his studio. Over there is a painting I've been working on." She pointed to the opposite corner, and we carefully stepped between the canvases on the floor to get to it. She had painted a simplified white horse with a phantom rider. The bridle was red and blue, and the rider wore a bright blue skirt, maybe denim, with a scarlet blouse. Her skin was translucent, which gave her a phantom appearance. Jane had used a stencil to write, *THE IMPERIAL ANIMAL*, in striking red block letters. And in fact there was a strangely mythic quality to the work.

"I call the series 'Mythic Americana.' I use red, white, and blue in all of them."

"What are they about?" I asked, though I suspected her answer.

"Colonialism. The Vietnam War. How fucked up the US is."

"I really like this piece, Jane. It's powerful."

"That's what Galen says. I'm glad you like it. How about we go out and you buy me a beer?" I must have appeared skeptical because she said, "Don't worry. I'm way over eighteen."

She directed me to a bar in Yonkers because she pronounced all the local bars in Bronxville too snooty and expensive. The bar was kind of a dive, but it redeemed itself with a large pool table. We got two glasses of the beer on tap and started a game. I didn't embarrass myself because Jerry and I had spent many disreputable hours unwinding from our studies in bars with pool tables. As it happened, Jane was pretty good too.

While playing, our attentions were diverted by some unpleasantness at the bar. Two large long-haired guys were harassing a kid in uniform, hurling the usual taunts at him. "How does it feel to kill babies?" they asked. "What do you do to the women? You like killing?"

Despite his youth, the kid had a weary air, as if he'd heard it all before. "I'm on leave from Fort Lee," he patiently explained. "I haven't even been over there yet. Man, I got drafted. You guys might get drafted too. I think the war is shit."

But that didn't stop them. Finally, the bartender asked the hecklers to leave. We bought the kid a beer.

"I flunked out of New Paltz," he said. "I had a 1.4 GPA and they wouldn't let me stay. Mostly, I just couldn't make it to class. So here I am."

I thought it best to keep the fact that I taught at New Paltz to myself. I knew I would remember him the next time I assigned my grades. He watched as we finished our game. It was a squeaker, but I won. Then the soldier challenged Jane to a game and promised to drive her home, so I left. I still had an hour-and-a-half trip ahead of me. The last thing I heard as I walked out was Jane's voice saying, "I hate the war too, man. Sorry you have to go."

When I got home, the late hour didn't keep me from my study. I felt like I'd returned to a different universe than the one I'd left. In two days my life had transformed, but one thing hadn't changed: I was still committed to solving the Daphne mystery that remained for me as compelling as ever, even with Caroline in my life now. I'd left the markers on the desk near the time line. Freehand, I added the visit to Galen's house with the date, and I added a bit of Jane's description of Daphne.

I absentmindedly reached into the pocket of my sport jacket, which I'd carried in from the car, and found the Klimt postcard that Caroline had surreptitiously left for me. She had also left me a postcard of the Bernini. I wondered if she remembered the statue from Jerry's office. The photograph did not diminish its beauty. I taped the two postcards above the time line and jotted down all the information to date. I was as puzzled as ever.

I was inspired to go find the Schrödinger book I'd left on the night table by my bed. I had a pair of scissors in the desk drawer and I cut out the two cats from its cover and taped them next to our first meeting at the bookstore. Art, myth, and science presided over the mystery together. Are they really different?

CHAPTER NINE

CAROLINE AND I WERE FORCED TO WAIT ten days to see each other again. She worked six days a week, so she had to use days from two different weeks to come up and see me in New Paltz. I would have been happy to meet her in the city, but she insisted on visiting my home. That left me ten days to think about Daphne. Being an academic by both profession and temperament, research in a library promised solutions to me.

When I wanted to spend time in a library I would cross the small bridge that spanned the Hudson between New Paltz and Poughkeepsie and work from books at the Vassar library. It had twice as many volumes, and its library had Gothic architecture, wood everywhere, and stained-glass windows. I felt like I was worshipping in a cathedral.

I sat in a carrel that I had piled with books from the stacks. I wanted to discover everything that science had to say about my Schrödinger girls. I was surprised to learn that as early as 1957 there were ideas in physics about the multiverse, also called the Many-Worlds Interpretation. However, from the articles I read, there was no hint that any scientists were walking around meeting their own Daphnes. I couldn't find any mention of someone prismatically splitting into multiple, yet simultaneous incarnations.

I wondered what Jerry would have said if I'd tried to discuss the scientific aspects of the case with him. I imagined him leaning hard on the idea that without evidence, these weren't really scientific theories.

I had to admit to myself that I didn't have much to go on: just the single snapshot that seemed to prove that one Daphne was in Boston when one was in New York, with me. But as I'd realized early on, the snapshot could be hoax. I had to accept the possibility that Daphne was creating this entire drama.

If Galen had taken Daphne to Boston in the middle of June, perhaps I could find some reference to that in a newspaper article. After all, Galen Green was a celebrity. I asked the librarian for the microfilm for the Boston newspapers for June. The Vassar library had microfilm for both the *Boston Globe* and the *Boston Herald*.

I loaded the roll for the *Boston Herald* into the reader. I had struck out with the *Globe*, but I got lucky with the *Herald*, finally finding this article: "June 16, 1967: Galen Green at the Boston Museum of Fine Arts." The report noted that one of Galen's paintings, *Hudson Autumn*, had been acquired for the museum's permanent collection, and he'd been present at the museum to mark the occasion. I could see him and Daphne standing before a semiabstract painting of the river and a stylized autumn scene. Unfortunately, the black-and-white newspaper photograph did not do justice to the canvas. His autumn scene must have been spectacularly colorful; I had grown to appreciate Green's palette.

The article revealed that Winslow Homer, Claude

Monet, and John Singer Sargent had also been honored during their lifetimes, but Galen Green's painting was the first work of a living artist in many years to be included in the museum's permanent collection. According to the story, Galen had given a talk on Friday the sixteenth, the same day I was with Daphne at the Forester Gallery. I experienced a shiver up my spine. Here was proof that my idea was not just an idle theory. The caption of the picture even identified Daphne as Green's newest muse. The snapshot she had given me was no hoax. And I had Caroline's recollections to prove that a Daphne was with me in New York on the same day. Could I be crazy when this objective evidence really existed?

The angry girl at the recruiting center could have been merely a separate personality of the first Daphne, even though she seemed so different from the girl in the bookstore and the girl in the coffee shop. Just because there were two Schrödinger girls didn't mean that there were three. The girl I'd met at Bryant Park could have been a manifestation of Daphne's anger and mental confusion; or my belief that she was a new incarnation of Daphne could have been a manifestation of my own confusion.

I didn't think there was anything else in Vassar's library to help me figure out the Daphne mystery. I was sure that library wouldn't collect copies of local Long Island papers, and even if SDS Daphne did exist, she'd just entered a new school, and I was pretty certain Vassar's library wouldn't archive arcane Long Island yearbooks.

Okay. So the girl I'd met in front of the public library lion told me that she'd moved in with an SDS organizer and changed high schools. I came up with a plan to check out her story.

From my office at school I had the department secretary place calls to the schools Daphne claimed to attend. I devised a story about her contacting me while doing research on psychology departments at schools she might choose for college. Guidance counselors aren't usually around for the summer, but I gave it a try and struck gold when the first guidance counselor was in. She was happy to talk to me.

"Oh, you're from New Paltz," Mrs. Winter said. "New Paltz is a safety school for many of our students, though to be honest, I don't really see Daphne attending there. She is an excellent student and wants to study writing and literature. She did really well on the SATs too. Who did you say you were?"

I saw no harm in giving her my real name. "She told me she is interested in psychology when she called. She wanted to know about our program. She seemed so bright and engaged that I must admit I was intrigued, Mrs. Winter. Is she involved with any extracurricular activities at the school?"

"She is the assistant editor of our literary magazine, *Ken*. And she published two poems in the magazine too. We are very proud of her."

"Is she involved with any other activities?"

"She is in the Choraleers, our advanced choir. She sings soprano. As a matter of fact, they sang at a local Summer Fest last week. Daphne sang a small but lovely solo."

I thanked her for her time and asked Ruth, our secretary, to place a call to the guidance department at the high school near the house Terry rented, the one the new Daphne had mentioned. The secretary at that school confirmed that Daphne was a student there; she'd have Jonathan Tyler, her counselor, call me back when he checked in for his messages, which he did on weekdays during the summer.

My suspense mounted steadily until Ruth put his call through to me.

"Jonathan Tyler here, how can I help?"

I introduced myself and asked the same questions I'd asked of Mrs. Winter, explaining that we might be interested in giving Daphne a scholarship to study psychology at New Paltz.

"Yes, Daphne is a student here," Mr. Tyler confirmed. "Who did you say you were?"

"I'm Dr. Adams," I answered, subtly pulling rank. I could almost hear him nodding.

In response to my question about her extracurricular activities, he explained, "Our school is number one in the region, and we take debating seriously here. From what I've gathered through the grapevine, Daphne is brilliant. The debate team adviser has already recruited her, and she was the star of the showcase debate with another highly ranked school. Apparently her ability is going to take our team to another victory."

When I asked Tyler for the date, I got the confirmation I needed—the debate showcase was the same night the first Daphne performed in the Choraleers concert.

Since Daphne couldn't be in two schools at the same time or two places on the Tuesday night in question, these phone calls supported the idea that these girls were really separate people. Perhaps the most logical explanation was that they were triplets, the conclusion to which my mind naturally jumped, but as usual I reminded myself that this conclusion didn't fit the facts of the case. In both instances, these new Daphnes seemed to have just suddenly and recently appeared. None of these three girls had ever mentioned being a twin or a triplet, and in the gallery, my Daphne certainly had no idea of a twin who may have sat for Galen's portrait. If she had, she wouldn't have been so shocked and upset. Even more significant, each Daphne remembered meeting me in the bookstore and joining me at the coffee shop. The evidence would indicate that if they were triplets, then they knew each other. Perhaps the girls played pranks. But no one had mentioned triplets at all—neither of the guidance counselors—and they wouldn't all have the same name. If they didn't know each other and adoptive parents had given them all the same name, they couldn't all know the details of our first meeting. The situation as they presented it to me was that at one point one girl met me in the bookstore, but at another point their experiences diverged. They shared a past, but they traveled different trajectories.

Maybe a new Daphne came into being the same way the original Daphne transformed in response to Apollo's chase? Perhaps she'd stood at the door of the Russian Tea Room, uncertain about whether or not to enter. For a sixteen-year-old girl, crossing the threshold into that glittering world may have been daunting. So, one Daphne had turned back, and another had been born, who went in to lunch and met her future, Galen Green.

The demeanors of the second and third Schrödinger girls suggested that Galen might have shaped his own muse, and Terry his own disciple. That left me to wonder if I had created the original Schrödinger girl from a nondescript teenager wearing a rain slicker. But wasn't

I giving men too much credit? The girls could be distinguished from the destinies they were spinning out. They were their paths, their incarnations a complex locus of personality, proclivity, behavior, and goals. Now I was sounding like a psychologist again.

My work in the library revealed that in 1957 Hugh Everett III postulated the relative state formulation. I wasn't sure yet what that meant, but I knew it had to do with the many-worlds theory, as it came to be known, which said that all possible future histories are real. According to my research, the many-worlds theory asserted the objective reality of the universal wave function and denied the reality of wave function collapse, the idea that probabilities finally become just one reality. In other words, all the Daphnes were real. Before Everett's work, reality had always been viewed as a single unfolding history. But the many-worlds theory, devised to resolve all the paradoxes of quantum theory, imagined an infinity of futures. For Everett, both futures existed simultaneously: one in which Schrödinger's cat was alive and one in which it wasn't.

None of Everett's theory explained why I could see three possibilities, these three girls, at the same time in my universe. As a behavioral psychologist I was ill-equipped to understand or explain the phenomenon I was observing, but I didn't think I was crazy, even if Jerry or Caroline did.

Two days later, I met Caroline at the Poughkeepsie train station. She wore a denim skirt, and her city-white feet were slender in her sandals. She had a large straw bag slung over a shoulder. Before she even reached the car, she shouted, "Oh Garrett, you didn't tell me you had a T-bird. It's gorgeous!"

A woman after my own heart.

I had put the top down on this glorious August morning. We were a bit shy of each other, so I was grateful for the noise of the wind from the car as I navigated the short trip across the river to New Paltz. When we arrived home, nothing escaped Caroline's attention. She admired the porch, the garden now blooming gaily with dahlias—a gift of previous tenants—and she eagerly entered the house. I had already set the table for brunch, and we feasted on salad with mozzarella, red peppers, cherry tomatoes, and green olives. I brought out peach cobbler I had actually made myself with local peaches and my mother's recipe.

"Let's wait till after," Caroline said. "I don't want to get too full."

"After?" But I was just being coy.

We climbed the narrow stairs together so quickly we were both almost breathless when we reached the top step. My bedroom had a brass headboard and a colorful patchwork quilt I had bought at a local fair the first year I got to New Paltz. She folded back the quilt and got out of her clothes as easily as she had the first night in New York. The room was bright with lemon-yellow sunlight. Our bodies were familiar to each other, and we fit together perfectly. Caroline came with her same singing sounds, but instead of crying, she laughed, and her voice sounded like happiness.

Making love had worked up our appetites for the peach cobbler. After she had taken her last bite, she jumped up quickly to look around and lurched out of the dining room ahead of me to enter my small study. She faced the time line, and stopped dead.

"What the hell is this?" she asked, her voice suddenly guarded.

I wasn't sure why she was wary. We had talked about Daphne at the Met, just before we studied all the paintings about the myth. She hadn't seemed at all upset then.

"Caroline," I said as gently as I could, "you knew I was exploring this mystery. You helped me. I don't get your reaction."

"You don't?" she replied with a sardonic edge. "You really don't see how crazy you look?"

There was more to her feelings than her uneasiness at my time line. What was she hiding? Or did I just see mysteries and complexities everywhere?

"Is that why we're dating? So you can explain this Daphne mystery?"

"No. I am not dating you because of Daphne. Maybe at first when I called you, but not once I saw you again."

"But at first. When you called me at the gallery you were thinking about her."

I thought she already understood this. I said nothing. What was there to say?

"Are you interested in her?"

"Not in the way you mean. She is a child, whatever Galen Green thinks. I'd like to punch him in the nose, in fact. It's just that I like the way she surprises me and teaches me about the present—you know, the Beatles and the war. And I have to understand her mystery."

"Her mystery?"

"You know. That Daphne is one person but three people too."

"God, Garrett. I didn't know you really believed that. I thought it was just a great story."

"Come on, Caroline. You saw her run out of the gallery. You of all people know that there are different Daphnes."

She avoided my direct plea for her corroboration and simply said, "I want to get dressed now, and I want get out of here and away from that graph."

Giddy after sex, we had raced downstairs barely dressed. She had worn only my shirt, to my great satisfaction, and I wore only a pair of boxer shorts. Now, as if we were strangers, she didn't want to be uncovered in front of me. We went back upstairs, dressed, came back down without speaking, exited the house, and got into the car. The beauty of the August afternoon now felt like an accusation. I crossed back to the east side of the river and drove north.

To ease the tension I made small talk. "We're going to Rhinebeck," I said. "It's only about a half hour away. I love the Dutch names for places and things. They remind me of when the entire Hudson Valley was Dutch. Did you know that the Dutch settled Albany before the British settled Boston?"

"No, I didn't know that." Her voice was noncommittal.

"Some people think it's why New York is so different from the rest of the country, because the Dutch were so much more liberal. They weren't Puritans."

"What about Santa Fe and St. Augustine? Weren't they settled even before Albany?"

"You have me there, Miss Indiana. I guess I'm just a northeast boy thinking the world revolves around New York and Boston. Point goes to Miss Indiana."

We were trying to have fun. We both knew that a grenade had been thrown into our fragile new relationship. When we got to Rhinebeck Caroline rewarded me by saying, "What a beautiful little town!" I parked the car and steered us toward the Beekman Arms, a staid old inn where they served high tea, not that either of us was hungry. I chose it because it was the last place where anyone would want to make a scene.

At a banquette we each ordered tea and scones that we put in Caroline's bag for later. After the waitress had served us, Caroline insisted that I tell her everything. I started with the rainy day in the bookstore, the mysterious figure in a yellow slicker holding the Schrödinger book, and I ended with leaving the bar after playing pool with Jane.

She had a lot to take in, but for a moment Caroline ignored most of the story and reacted like the art historian she was. "So, you mean you were in Galen Green's studio and you saw an entire Daphne series of paintings? Were they really based on Ovid? Do you think you could take me to see them?"

"I saw them and could probably take you to see them."

After that respite, her attention returned to my relationship with Daphne. "So, if I may summarize," she said, "you believe that you have met three separate girls and that the second two branched off from the first one, that experience and memories diverged."

"Exactly. Actually, the idea that universes branch off like the branches of a tree is part of the multiverse theory."

"Whatever," she said, but her sense of irony got the better of her for a moment. "So the universe, like Daphne, becomes a laurel tree? . . . It's not an idle question," she insisted. "When clues line up so neatly it usually means that the observer is suffering from paranoia and making up patterns. You should know that. You're the psychologist."

"I'm not that kind of psychologist, and just now you're the one who saw the pattern. I'm just telling you what happened."

"That's true," she conceded. "What does Jerry make of all of this?"

"He hasn't quite said, but I can tell it's nothing good. He hinted that I am projecting unresolved conflicts onto ordinary situations. I don't agree. I haven't told him about the last Daphne incarnation at the recruiting center. He wouldn't like that at all. He hates thinking about Vietnam."

"This would sound crazy to almost anyone."

"Yeah, I guess so, except maybe Everett. So, I sound crazy to you? I was hoping you would understand."

"Yeah, it does all sounds crazy, but I do admit that I saw that girl stare at Galen Green's portrait and bolt out of the gallery. You *have* considered the possibility that you are dealing with a mentally ill child or a great actress, haven't you?"

"Sure. But neither of those possibilities explains all the circumstances I have uncovered, most importantly that I can corroborate the fact that on specific dates the girls were in different places. Jerry thinks she's crazy or just plain trouble. He warned me off her, and now he's treating me like I'm crazy too."

"Hmm. Isn't that to be expected, given these circumstances?"

"We've been friends for eighteen years. I wish he would give me the benefit of the doubt. I am trained to observe and analyze human behavior too."

"And he is trained to see neuroses everywhere. Just to be clear, you think it's a better explanation of events to postulate alternate universes that no one has ever really seen and no one can prove exist, than to accept the idea that there is something fishy with this girl?"

"Put like that, I have to admit that I do sound irrational, but I'd have to say yes. I believe that the multiverse theory is a better hypothesis than the idea that Daphne is just a drama queen, a liar, or has multiple personality disorder. I'm standing by my experience."

"What you need to do, if you can manage it, is get at least two of the Daphnes in a room together at the same time. That would help confirm your hypothesis."

"That might not be easy to do. Up until now I have waited for them to contact me."

"Your mental health seems more important than a nicety. Anyway, you did stop in Bronxville to see the second Daphne."

"What if the girls can't exist in the same room together? What if they can't inhabit the same reality?"

"But *you* are in all three realities, Garrett."

"True. But it's the same me."

"You do know that according to quantum theory an object *can* be in two places at the same time."

I didn't know that. "How do you know that?" I asked.

"I did go to Smith, Garrett. I didn't just study art history. I understand a lot of things."

I saw her point. I couldn't obsess about these Daphnes forever. I had a scientist's training, and I could use it.

We finished our tea and then walked through town window-shopping. Rhinebeck had a toy train store, and we both enjoyed the miniature town in the window. Caroline pointed out the theater, and I pointed out the skating rink. The miniature train station was at one end of town and resembled the station in Poughkeepsie. In the real world the commuter train didn't travel as far north as Rhinebeck.

I had planned a surprise for when we returned to New Paltz, but I wasn't sure she'd be in the mood for it now. As we entered the house I said, "I have the new Beatles album, *Sgt. Pepper's Lonely Hearts Club Band*. It's been out for two months, but I haven't heard it yet. I decided that I wanted to listen to it with you after I heard you humming 'Good Day Sunshine' at your apartment. How did an almost contemporary of mine come to the Beatles?" I asked.

"I am in the art world, Garrett. I encounter all sorts of things. And I make it my business to. You have been in your ivory tower too long."

"Touché."

We sat in the living room on the floor. She put her head in my lap as we listened to the album. I had never heard anything like it. We entered a world of marmalade trees and tangerine skies. *Look for the girl with the sun in her eyes, and she's gone.* I knew all about that. It seemed as if Daphne was always disappearing. Then I took John's advice from "Tomorrow Never Knows" and turned off my mind and floated downstream. When the last notes of the really sad "Day in the Life" ended, Caroline exclaimed, "That was amazing!"

We sat quietly together. The afternoon was turning to dusk and the honey light was fading. Out the window we could see streaks of peach and violet. Caroline lifted her head out of my lap and said, "I think I want to go back to the city tonight. Don't read anything into it. I just need to think. I'm sorry."

"You are that upset about Daphne?" I had been kidding myself into thinking that I had already explained everything to her and that she understood. But there was nothing to do now except go along with what she wanted.

"Okay," I said, "whatever you think best. At least let me drive you back to the city so you don't have another two-hour train trip on the same day."

"Nah. That's okay. I like the train. It's soothing. I'll be fine."

She gathered up her things and stuffed them into her straw bag. We checked the schedule and discovered that we didn't have much time to spare if we were going to make the next train. I dropped her at the station, and before she boarded, she turned to me and waved.

I drove home with the T-bird top down under a clear sky lit by a riot of stars.

CHAPTER TEN

THE SUMMER OF 1967 had brought love and hate. In San Francisco hippies celebrated the Summer of Love with the Monterey International Pop Festival, flowers, dreams of communes, and images of love. Over 100,000 tourists converged on the city armed with flowers and hallucinogens. Throughout the rest of the country the long, hot summer brought 159 race riots, some featuring arson and looting.

In the midst of this chaos, I heard nothing from Daphne for nearly a month, and I could detect Caroline's ambivalence in our frequent phone calls. Some days she was warm and confiding, and other days noncommittal and distant. I was tired of waiting for her to resolve her feelings and wanted to see her. One hot mid-August night, I decided to call her with an invitation. "Hey, you," I said when she answered after one ring, "how about dinner Friday? My treat. Any place you want to go."

She didn't respond at first. The silence stretched out uncomfortably. Finally she said, "I don't know, Garrett. I still don't know."

"Don't know what?" I asked, trying to keep the exasperation out of my voice. I was walking a tightrope. I didn't want to let her drift away, but I didn't want to drive her away either.

"I don't know if I want to see you or not." She sighed. "I mean, I do want to see you. I know that. But I also don't want to see you. As long as you're wrapped up in all that Daphne business, I don't think we can move forward, and I get angry with you. That's not really fair. You're not technically doing anything wrong."

"Technically?"

"Okay. You're not doing anything wrong."

"Caroline?"

"Yeah?"

"I love you."

"I love you too, but it doesn't change anything."

This had to be the least romantic exchange of first "I love you"s ever.

"So back to the original question. We can talk about all this Friday night."

She finally agreed. I engaged her in small talk. I asked about the gallery, inquiring after its current show. She talked with animation about a neorealist they were showing. I imagined Jane's work hanging there someday.

That Friday, I arrived at the Italian restaurant that Caroline had chosen. The place was intimate without being crowded. The exposed brick walls and soft taupe leather banquettes were rustic and elegant. I slid onto a bench and appreciated its plush comfort. I ordered a glass of wine, red. I was just starting to buzz with a pleasant anticipation when the waiter approached the table again. I tried to wave him away, having everything I needed for the moment, but he stepped forward and bowed slightly.

"I have a phone call for you," he explained.

It had to be Caroline, and it was.

"I just don't feel up to going out tonight. I have a splitting headache. I spent all day haggling with a customer. I hoped it would get better, but I'm seeing stars." She sounded closed and weary.

"Okay. I'll just pop around with a bottle of aspirin," I suggested.

"No, that's all right. I just need to sleep it off. I'm sorry. I know it's a pain. You drove all the way here, Garrett. Don't be angry."

"No. Of course not," I lied. "You can't help not feeling well."

I really wished Caroline could get over her reservations about me. I hadn't even seen Daphne for a month.

Since I was in the city anyway, I gave Jerry a call. I was pleased that he was still home at eight. "Things were odd the last time we saw each other," I began. He agreed that they were and proposed that we meet up on the Upper West Side. "I was just on my way out," he added.

Jerry's hangout was on Broadway at 112th Street. He loved getting out of his tony neighborhood and venturing fifteen blocks north to Morningside Heights, which he considered more authentic. He liked all the Columbia types he'd meet up with there. The place was an Irish bar where I was in my element too, yet even though I was the Irishman, he was usually the one singing "Danny Boy" at the end of the night.

It took me awhile to get to the bar. I decided not to ride the subway but to move the car so I could get out of the city quickly when I was ready to leave. Uptown I had to circle around for a while before I finally found a parking space on Riverside Drive. By the time I got to the bar it was obvious that Jerry had started without me.

"Garrett, my man!" he said boisterously. He was at a table with a smart blonde—just his type. Someone she knew walked in, and I slid into the chair she vacated. His eyes were glassy. He was feeling no pain. He asked me what I'd drink.

"Beer is fine," I answered, and he headed over to the bartender.

Jerry put the beers on the table roughly so that some of the foam sloshed out over the mugs onto the scarred wood. "Oops. Sorry about that," he said, working hard to avoid slurring.

"I'm having lady problems, Jer. Caroline is really annoyed with me. She's really spooked by Daphne—"

"Both of them," he interrupted, very pleased at his understanding of events and finding humor in my plight.

"Well, actually, there's a third, a radical activist—"

"Three of them? That's crazy!"

This last remark was a little too unrestrained, but it was Friday night, and his raucousness was to be expected. I saw that it would be impossible for us to have a serious conversation. Just then I watched the attractive girl he'd been talking with coming back to our table.

"Why don't you buy a girl a drink?" he said. "We can have a double date."

"Because of Caroline? Remember?"

"Of course," he said, reaching for his beer. "The beauteous Caroline. She was my patient, Garrett. Did I ever tell you that?"

Of course I knew that, and if he weren't plastered, he'd know that I did. He'd also know that he wasn't supposed to be talking about it, especially in public. I'd come to smooth things over and get his advice, but Jerry was one of those people who liked to work hard and party hard, and after all, it was the weekend. I felt discouraged, and I felt alone with all the mysteries of the universe, so I decided to leave early and head up north. Since he had already begun an animated conversation with the blonde, I had to tap him on the shoulder to tell him that I was leaving.

"Really?" he said, clearly crestfallen. "Before you go, do want you want to hear me sing 'Danny Boy'?"

I didn't.

On the way home, I realized I'd have to make sense of things on my own. I decided to take a week to visit my mother, who now lived in Florida. I liked making the drive, and I hadn't been to visit in a while. She had remarried about five years before, and she and her husband, whom she met tending bar, had moved south to open their own Irish pub. The pub was in West Palm Beach, and they had named it Molly Bloom's. I had to laugh when I thought of my sixtyish sapphire-eyed mom reciting bits and pieces of Molly's soliloquy to any customer who asked. They lived in a large house on a man-made lake. My mother always kept a room waiting for me.

I had forgotten how much I hated Florida in the summer, but we had a good visit; my mother was doing well. She got along with her husband, a big Irish guy named Danny Malone, and business was good. She had trained me to tend bar when I was a just a kid, and I enjoyed spending time behind the bar. Sometimes I wanted to talk to her about my dad, but those conversations never went anywhere. She had made her peace with the past and wanted to leave it behind. She had loved him, but by the time he'd gone off to war, their marriage was strained because he found it difficult to settle down and put his shoulder to the grindstone of life. She tried to be brave, but things hadn't been going well when he got the urge to enlist. When he died she was almost felled by guilt. It was nice to see her happy now. My longing for my father was all my own.

I had put Caroline and the Daphnes out of my mind as much as I could during my visit, and I saved my worrying for the drive home. I worried that Galen's Daphne would be furious with me for seeing the other Daphne portraits in Galen's studio. I worried that she would be angry that I knew Jane. I worried that I would never see any of the Daphnes again, and I worried that Caroline would never want to see me again.

The mechanics of the trip home were always the same. I drove nonstop except for brief breaks at truck stops, and I stayed the night at the same motel in St. Pauls, North Carolina.

After the long drive and a night in my own bed, I arrived at my post office box bright and early the next morning. My next stop was my mail cubby at school. I collected an impressive haul of academic detritus and the few important school memos that had trailed in during the summer.

Hidden in the monster pile were two postcards, one from Caroline and one from Daphne. I felt relieved and terrified. I read Caroline's first. On the flip side of a picture of Modigliani's *The Black Dress* she wrote, *I want to cautiously proceed. I tried calling, but no answer. Call me.* Daphne had chosen a postcard of a photograph of an Egyptian sculpture of a cat. Her message read, *I finished*

the book. Meet me August 25th at our place at our time.
It had only been one month since we'd met, but the universe was now a completely different place. I probably should have wondered which Daphne it would be, but I hoped she would be my original Daphne.

It's funny how quickly we can move from despair to elation. I had returned from Florida feeling empty in a way I hadn't known I could be six months earlier, but now it seemed that all might be well because I was going to be seeing both Daphne and Caroline. I wanted to make arrangements to spend a few nights in the city. I tried calling Jerry, but his answering service indicated that, like many New York therapists, he would be away for most of August. He wouldn't have minded me crashing at his pad in his absence, but he had never given me a key. I didn't want to impose on Caroline. I called around and made a reservation for three nights at a discount hotel near Times Square even though I wasn't a tourist. The room would be fine—I wouldn't need much.

I wanted to see Daphne before I saw Caroline. I imagined myself bringing Caroline an answer like a cat carrying a bird in his mouth and laying it at the feet of his mistress. I called her at the gallery and we made quick plans for Saturday. "This is my outing, and my treat," Caroline volunteered. "Be at my place by ten a.m."

"What will I need?"

"Shorts. Swim trunks. Just in case."

"Sure, see you then." We didn't talk much because she had to get back to work.

Although the meet-up at the coffee shop was just a few days away, I decided to take Caroline's advice and try to get Galen's Daphne there as well. SDS Daphne, as I had named her in my mind, could wait for another time. I didn't have Daphne's phone number at Galen's house, but Jane did, and Jane had given me her own number. I called her. She was bubbling over with excitement because a painting of hers had been accepted into a juried show. After I offered my sincere and enthusiastic congratulations, I asked for Daphne's Bronxville number, and I told Jane to let me know how her painting fared.

Daphne answered the phone on the third ring. "Garrett. Hey. How are you?"

"Well. You?"

"Great. We went to England. London is wonderful. And we went to the Lake District. Have you ever been there? Wordsworth lived there. It's the most beautiful place I've been so far."

"How are things in paradise?" I asked.

"What do you mean?"

"Things still good with you and Galen?"

"Why shouldn't they be? How did you get this number?"

"From Jane Pinsky. I stopped by when you two were in England, and I met her. She showed me the entire Daphne series."

"Really? That's so strange. She never mentioned anything about it. You'd think she would have." I decided that Jane had been protecting me. Daphne asked, "What did you think of the series?" Far from being upset, she sounded delighted that I'd seen these paintings.

"Honestly, I thought they were just beautiful. Will they be exhibited together?"

"Galen's working on that. You know, I love studying art. It makes me a better model. Do you know the myth?"

"I actually read the Ovid because of you."

"Good for you. Now what can I do for you?"

"I'm going to be in the city on Friday, and there's someone I'd like you to meet—another young woman, if Galen asks. We'll be at the coffee shop at two thirty, where you and I met. It's important to me, and I think you'd really like her. She's just your age."

"What fun. Galen's been talking about going to the city for some supplies. We have a picnic to go to in Bedford the next day, but Friday sounds good. Galen knows all about you. I think he would like to talk to you. He even mentioned that your names are similar. Count me in. Give me your number so I can call you if I can't come."

I couldn't bring myself to mention the other Daphne. I thought things would work out better if they discovered each other by meeting in person. I didn't want to introduce skepticism, confusion, and suspicion into our uncanny situation.

I feared that the two girls might arrive before I did, so I got to the coffee shop early, but my Daphne, at least I thought that's who it was, was already in her spot. She must have been really hungry, because she already had the grilled cheese sandwich in front of her.

"Garrett!" she squealed.

I sat down. The waitress took my order. I was too nervous to eat so I just ordered lemonade. It was a seasonally hot day. I observed Daphne with a sinking feeling. I didn't think that the girl in front of me was a new iteration, but she seemed very different. She was dressed like a member of the Junior League. Her wild mane of hair had been smoothed into a shining helmet without a hair out of place. She was wearing a strand of expensive pearls.

"Garrett, what's wrong?"

I wasn't sure what to tell her. Should I tell her that I was afraid that we were in the *Invasion of the Body Snatchers* and a pod person had replaced her? I didn't think so.

"Tell me," she commanded, actually sounding more like her old self.

"It's just that I'm not used to seeing you like this, all groomed, wearing pearls. I like to think of you as a fashionable ragamuffin."

She burst out laughing. "Oh, is that all? Well, I don't like seeing me like this either."

"What do you mean?"

"We came into the city today for portraits. My uncle, my dad's brother, is getting married. The family, including my cousins, took pictures together. My mother insisted I get my hair done like this. They set it in the beauty parlor with huge rollers and made me sit under a hair dryer for hours because it takes my hair so long to dry. I hate this get-up, but you should have seen my mother beaming."

"And the pearls?"

"A gift for my sixteenth birthday from my parents. I wanted a guitar. I think they're hideous, but my mother says I'll be grateful for them someday. I feel like I'm an impostor."

"And who are you impersonating?" I asked.

"The good girl you thought I was."

"So you're not a good girl?"

"God, I hope not."

"And you haven't become president of the Young Republican Club or anything like that since I last saw you?"

"No, I don't think so, though my mom has been talking about Vassar."

"You're not interested?"

"No guys. I don't think so."

The cloud lifted. She was my Ur-Daphne. I was very anxious, waiting for Galen and his Daphne to arrive. Every time the door opened I checked out the mirror to see who was entering. So far they were no-shows. I wanted some answers, but I didn't know how much to reveal to my Schrödinger girl.

"You seemed pretty upset when you ran out of the gallery two months ago, the last time I saw you. I was really worried about you."

"I guess I am a bit of a good girl. I got so embarrassed remembering the way I propositioned you, and I couldn't bear seeing myself naked with you next to me. I guess all that bravado was a bit of an act, though I hated to admit it. I was just so mortified I had to run away. Have you found out anything else about the painting or the model?"

"No," I lied. I'm not really sure why, but after Caroline's reaction, I was keeping the particulars of the Schrödinger mystery to myself. Besides, I rationalized, the truth might be too upsetting to a teenager. "I have been studying the myth though," I added. "I find it fascinating that Daphne gets turned into a tree."

"A laurel. I know. I've been reading about the myth. A psychoanalyst said that the laurel tree represents Daphne's paralysis, but I think Ovid is after something else. By becoming a laurel, Daphne gets to stay herself, even if she has to change form. Changing form is trivial. Losing oneself is much more serious. I think the laurel is a symbol of self-actualization. That's Maslow's term." She blushed. "I must sound pompous."

"Not at all. Don't forget, you're talking to an academic." I had studied a bit of Maslow, though the human potential movement was as far from behaviorism as you could get.

"Well, one thing has changed, anyway."

"What's that?" I asked.

"I am not going around offering myself to men like you and that guy with the question mark outside the Museum of Modern of Art. Thank you so much for not taking me up on it."

"Don't mention it," I said sheepishly.

As the hour passed it became clear that Galen's Daphne, the beautiful artist's muse, was not going to show up. I felt bitterly disappointed. Although I had been nervous about what might have happened, I needed some answers. I wondered if a magnetic force was keeping the Daphnes apart.

I was caught up in these thoughts when I heard my young friend say, "So the most interesting part of our physics book was the idea that our universe is only one possibility in an array of many. It is just as likely that vastly different events could have happened or that we'd be very different people. In fact, those people might actually exist in alternate realities."

"That is interesting, but no one can prove anything."

"I know," she sighed. "Promise you won't laugh if I tell you something?"

"I can't 100 percent promise because laughing is a pretty involuntary reflex, but I promise I'll *try* not to laugh."

"Sometimes I think I see another version of myself. She looks just like me, but she wears camouflage and combat boots, and just seems, I don't know, maybe more militant. I thought I saw her once at a shopping center and another time at an antiwar rally we held at the school. She was with the SDS organizers, but when I went to find her, she'd vanished. It makes me feel really creepy. And then of course there's the girl in the painting."

I got chills listening to her. This girl had seen SDS Daphne! She had seen her more than once. I knew I should probably tell her everything then, but something primal made me keep my experiences secret. Instead I sang, "*Look for the girl with the sun in her eyes, and she's gone.*"

"Ooh, exactly! 'Lucy in the Sky with Diamonds.' Sometimes I'm afraid I'm going to see myself everywhere."

I knew exactly what she meant. There were days at school when any auburn-haired girl could take me by surprise and I'd find myself searching for Daphne in her.

I decided to do some reality testing. "Let me ask you this," I said. "Do you still live at home? Are you staying at the same school?"

"Yes and yes. By that I mean to say, yes, everything is the same, sad as that is. I'm not going to get away anytime soon."

"Do you know a guy named Terry Collins?"

"How do you know about him? I've heard of him. I've never met him. He started an SDS chapter in the next town. I'm against the war and all, but lots of older hippies hang around with him, and there's a lot of pot smoking, and I'm really just not ready for all that. I learned my lesson from going around offering myself to two men and

then coming face to face with a nude picture of myself."
She laughed, seemingly no longer upset about the painting, or overly burdened by the ambiguities surrounding it.

This was still the Daphne who'd come with me to the
gallery. I'd been right, of course. The Daphne whom I'd
met up with at the New York Public Library was a new
girl. "Are you sure you're not a good girl?" I teased.

"Maybe I am, but I hate the war."

"What convinced you of that?"

"Last year I saw a photograph taken by a French
photographer. Henry Huet, I think his name was. It was
of a helicopter lifting up a dead paratrooper. And then I
thought of all the American guys being drafted and of all
the Vietnamese people being killed, kids included, and I
just knew it was wrong."

I remembered talking about the same thing with SDS
Daphne. When I asked her the same question about how
she'd become an antiwar activist she had given me a different answer. She had told me of her letter from a young
soldier named Rick Lopez and of her meeting with Terry.

"Can I ask you another question?"

"Fire away," she said.

"Did you ever have a pen pal?"

"Is this *This Is Your Life*? You seem to know everything about me. How do you find these things out? I was
supposed to have one, a guy named Rick, but he never
answered me back after I wrote to him."

"What did you write about?"

"Nietzsche."

That was exactly what the other Daphne said her first
letter was about. But she had received an answer, though
only one.

"Do you want anything else?"

"I'll take a TaB."

TaB was this awful diet soda that Coca-Cola had introduced a few years back. But who was I to judge what Daphne drank?

After her TaB came we chatted a bit longer. She told me about the books she was reading. I told her I'd read the R.D. Laing book and thanked her for it again. We talked about how much we both loved *Sgt. Pepper* and she ordered me to get *Blonde on Blonde*.

"Whenever I feel like too much of a good girl, I just listen to Bob Dylan, and I know that in my soul I'm a rebel. I can't wait to get home to take off these pearls."

CHAPTER ELEVEN

I STAYED AT THE DISCOUNT HOTEL that night. I caught a movie in Times Square and bought new bathing trunks. I thought about a gift for Caroline. I wasn't sure why she was giving me another chance.

I showed up at her place the next day at ten a.m. on the dot carrying a bottle of chilled champagne that I had just bought from a liquor store in the Village, my new swim trunks, and an unopened copy of *Blonde on Blonde* I purchased on the way over from a street vendor. I handed them all to Caroline. Her bed was already put away, and she had some picnic items set up on a little hinged fold-down shelf next to the baker's rack. She put everything in her huge straw bag, including my trunks. She had laid out bittersweet-orange towels for us both, and was now packing them.

"Where are we going?" I asked.

"It's a secret, but I can tell you I have a light lunch already packed, and the champagne will be perfect." She walked over to one of her shelves and added two plastic cups to the bag.

"You're beautiful," I said. Even her sundress was black, though there was a profusion of white flowers scattered across the fabric. "What do you call those kind of flowers?"

"It's a Jacobean print," she said.

One of the things I appreciated so much about Caroline was the well-thought-out and artful way she did everything. I didn't know if that was Smith, her art background, or just the sensibility she was born with.

"Where are we going?" I asked again.

"I think you can guess where we're going. You've lived around New York your entire life."

"Then I guess we're going to Coney Island. It will be crowded on a weekend in August, and it's not in the best neighborhood these days. But you know that, right?"

"I'm sure it's unbearably crowded, and I don't care about the neighborhood." She was grinning. "Come on, Garrett. Live with the common folk."

"Spoken by my Modigliani odalisque who can't wear ordinary florals."

"You know an odalisque is a concubine, right?"

"Isn't it just an elongated, beautiful woman?"

"Nope. You're thinking of the Ingres painting. But he means concubine. From a harem."

"Okay. You're not an odalisque. But the sound of the word describes you perfectly."

"You chose our Russian Tea Room date. Today is mine. And I say Coney Island."

"Yes ma'am." I offered to get the car, but Caroline said the subway was fine. She even insisted on carrying the straw bag herself.

"You are the consort today," she said.

"No problem."

When we got to Coney Island the first words out of Caroline's mouth were, "It is soooooooo crowded here."

"Well, yeah. Have you ever been here before?"

She just shook her head. The expression on her face would have been comical if she weren't so upset. "I wanted to have a real New York summer experience."

"Well, you are," I said. "It's always this crowded. Tomorrow, Sunday, will probably be even worse."

People were everywhere in various states of undress. Some women wore bikinis so scanty they were almost naked. Some glistened with oiled tans. Others were so white that it seemed to be their first summer day out in the world. Girls wore sunglasses. Guys blinked at the sun, their muscled chests walking before them. Children of a hundred ethnicities speaking a hundred languages, like little voices piping above the crowd, slipped between the legs of their parents and ran after each other. Dogs barked and chased their tails. Bathing suits, towels, sundresses, and shorts made a rainbow of colors. Hippies wore tie-dyed T-shirts with metal peace signs dangling from chains or strings. More militant kids wore surplus combat fatigues, even on this boiling day. I wondered what SDS Daphne did on the Fourth of July. Then I came back to Caroline.

"Well, the first rule in New York is that if you're out at an iconic place, and it's crowded, it's okay. We can have fun. Beach or rides?" I asked.

I had been to Coney Island many times as a kid with my dad. Sometimes we came in the winter when it wasn't crowded at all. He had run away from his family and run away from Harvard, and until the war, he had never really found his place in life. He did a lot of different jobs, but nothing stuck. He was often out of work. He was one of those guys always dreaming big, and the quotidian de-

tails of life were just pit stops between dreams. A day
at Coney Island with him was magical, but my mother
was never with us because she was always toiling to get
our lives to work, whether it was behind a bar or in the
apartment. She admired his education and his manners,
and she'd fallen hard for the rosy world he saw and always believed he could bring about. By the time he'd left
for war she must have been completely on to him, but
she had an Irish girl's pride, and she never complained.
Danny Malone was nothing like him, and for my mother,
that was mostly a good thing.

Caroline wanted to go on the teacup ride, but I nixed
that. "That's kid's stuff," I said. "When we have a daughter,
I'll take you both on that." I can't imagine how those words
came out of my mouth, but we both ignored the comment.
"Let's just do it. Ride the Cyclone," I quickly added.

"Really? Isn't it scary?"

"That's the point."

We put the heavy basket in a locker. It must have taken
an hour on line to get our turn, but we finally climbed
onto the old wooden roller coaster. As we rode, she clung
to me, screaming with terror and delight.

My father had taken me on this ride the last time we
came to Coney Island, before he went into the army. I was
one of those tiny boys who grows in his teens and finally
reaches a respectable height, so for years I had been too
little to ride the Cyclone. I didn't think about the fact that
it was a weekday and that he'd kept me out of school.
I concentrated on not acting scared because I knew my
father needed to see that I was brave. That control was
easy to summon up now. I had fun watching Caroline
lose control while I played the straight man.

"Worth it?" I asked. She nodded, eyes wide.

After the Cyclone the other rides would be anti-climactic, so we retrieved the basket and walked to the beach. She had brought a light sheet to sit on. I found rocks for the corners, and we went into a cabana to change. True to form, Caroline's suit was a one-piece black bandeau that really flattered her. In contrast, I was unattractively pale—white and pasty.

The beach was even more crowded than the amusement park. I could hear snippets of so many different songs on the transistor radios almost everyone carried. I heard the Monkees sing "Last Train to Clarksville," and the Beach Boys sing "Wouldn't It Be Nice." I heard Chuck Berry's "Rock and Roll Music." These were songs from earlier summers that some deejays had thrown into the mix. From every direction I heard Procol Harum singing "A Whiter Shade of Pale," the big hit that summer. I ruefully concluded that their lyric aptly described my legs.

We ran into the water together. The blue-green waves of the Atlantic knocked us down and buoyed us up, and Caroline held tight to my neck, and deeply exhilarated, we kissed and licked salt from each other's mouths. Since we didn't swim far out, the water was clogged with other couples as well, like a huge school of lovers gathered in the shallows.

She asked me to watch her as she floated, and when she stood up again, we decided to push past the others and swim out a bit. We were both strong swimmers. After a while, we turned around and headed back toward shore.

"Wow, I'm hungry," she announced. We sat on our

sheet with Caroline's towels wrapped around us. We drank the champagne out of the plastic cups and ate hard-boiled eggs, crackers, and grapes. Since we were both still hungry we walked along the beach and found the Nathan's hot dog stand. Apparently 1967 marked the 100-year-anniversary of the hot dog, and we each had one with mustard and sauerkraut, and then I had to get some french fries too. We shared a Coke and went back to our spot to doze in the sun.

We held hands as we lay on the sand. Nearby a radio played "Mr. Tambourine Man."

"That was so nice of you to bring me *Blonde on Blonde,*" Caroline said. "Of course, I've heard some of the songs, but I've never listened to the album all the way through. I can't wait. We can listen to it together, the way we listened to *Sgt. Pepper.*"

"Sounds great," I said. "Daphne told me to buy the album." I don't know why I said that, but I could feel her body suddenly stiffen.

"Daphne?" She was angry. "Did she tell you to buy it for me? Does she know about me?"

"No. She just wanted me to hear it."

"So you thought of giving it to me all by yourself?" Her voice was cold and sarcastic. What had happened to our ecstasy in the water?

"But I thought you wanted me to keep working on the Daphne mystery. I saw her yesterday, and because of you I really want to solve this. Remember when you said the way to do that was to get the two Daphnes in a room together? So I tried."

"Maybe I would be more interesting to you if there were three of me, Garrett."

I hated the way my name sounded at that moment. The t's resonated with such harshness. Maybe I needed a nickname. Gar or even Gary. No one had ever called me anything but Garrett, just like my dad.

"Don't you want me to solve this mystery?"

"Either that, or give it up."

"You know I'm not crazy, right? I mean you saw her. You saw Daphne. You saw the portrait. You saw her upset. You know I'm not crazy."

"That's not what makes you crazy. It's what it all means to you that is crazy. You think she's a harbinger of new dimensions of reality or something like that. And anyway, one would think that you'd have enough common sense not to bring her up in relation to a present for me."

I was scared now. I was afraid she'd vanish. I thought of Helena, my young ex-wife, and how wispy she'd felt to me. When I was with Caroline I knew I wasn't alone.

"Why did you decide to keep seeing me?" I asked.

"I don't know. I feel like there's something between us. There are some things about you I really like."

"Like what?"

"I can't give you a list right now."

"I know how you feel about me disappointing you. I really do."

"You do? How do you know?"

"My father had some strange ideas, and I know he made my mother suffer. But I can tell you that when he died he took a special quality with him, took it right out of my life, something I've never been able to get back. Not until this year when I met you . . . and Daphne. It's the feeling of unexpectedness and possibility. I wouldn't want you to lose that from your life, Caroline. Can't we just enjoy the rest of the day?"

She shrugged. She was angry, but not angry enough to waste a day at Coney Island. We finished off the champagne, had another hot dog because the swimming had really given us a big appetite, and watched the sunset. I saw her back to her place.

It was late, so I started to go. I was glad I had taken a room. But Caroline put her hand on my arm and asked me to stay. "I don't want to have sex or anything. But I don't want you to go."

We each took a shower to get rid of all the sand. Her bathroom was so tiny I could stand in the shower and close the bathroom door at the same time. My underwear wasn't too sandy because I'd spent most of the day in my swimming trunks. I put my T-shirt and boxers back on. Caroline put on a flimsy white nightgown. She had washed her long black hair and it streamed wet over her shoulders.

We lay down on top of her white bedspread and kept our clothes on. It was too hot for covers anyway. We tried to lie as still as possible so our sunburns wouldn't hurt. Caroline got up and put on Dylan's record. We took turns getting up to change the album's four sides.

The gibbous moon looked so close that it felt as if I could reach out and touch it like everything in Caroline's bathroom. I asked her to leave the shutters open so I could watch the shadows fashioned by the moonbeams. We didn't talk. Instead we listened to Dylan's tapestry of songs. His "Visions of Johanna" kept us up past the dawn, just as he says in his tune.

After sunrise I put on the rest of my clothes. I leaned

over and kissed Caroline on the top of her head. "Get some sleep," I said. "Don't worry about anything. It will be all right."

CHAPTER TWELVE

A DAY OR SO LATER, Galen's Daphne called from Bronxville. "I'm so sorry, Garrett," she murmured, obviously embarrassed. "Galen decided at the last minute that he didn't want to go to the city after all. I tried calling you, but there was no answer."

"That's okay. Don't worry about it. I was in the city anyway." Jeez. I should have told her why I was in the city. Maybe Jerry could explain to me why I needed to keep these girls secret from each other.

"I'm sorry we couldn't see each other," she went on. "I was really excited." I heard something very forlorn in her voice. Maybe being a muse was taking its toll. She probably didn't have anyone to confide in.

"Are you all right?" I asked. "You sound sad."

"I'm all right. I was just worried you'd be upset with me. Things are fine. I hope we can see each other soon."

"Me too. I'm here if you ever want to talk. Or if you want to get together, Bronxville isn't very far from here. I'd be happy to come see you."

"Yeah, sure. Thanks. See you, Garrett." And she hung up.

I realized she and I were developing a phone-only relationship, and a stilted one at that. I couldn't get past her new reserve. She seemed animated only when she talked about art, either her classes or Galen's portraits of her. It was hard to remember that somewhere in there was a developing sixteen-year-old girl.

Since I'd gone into the study to answer the phone, I walked over to the time line and inspected the picture of her by the swan boats. Daphne was smiling into the camera, yet I saw that there was something shadowed in her eyes, or maybe she was just squinting against the light. Galen must have been taking the picture. I tried to imagine what I'd see if I didn't know her. I'd see a beautiful auburn-haired girl working to appear older by wearing a chignon and sophisticated clothes. Her smile looked as if she was trying to be brave.

I glanced over the rest of the time line, just as I had hundreds of times. There was nothing new to glean.

I had received an invitation from Jane Pinsky that had been buried on my desk. She'd been awarded an honorable mention in her juried show, and now a tiny gallery in Bronxville had agreed to mount a small show for her just before Labor Day when business was slow. It was a formal invitation, but she had scrawled at the bottom, *I'm having people over afterward. Please come!* The show was just a few days off. I figured I'd see Daphne there, so I resolved to go.

For the show, Jane had hung paintings like the one I'd seen: representational paintings in primary colors with block lettering. She painted centaurs, lovers, horses, nude warriors, all facing the viewer with a challenge. She had stenciled the name of every canvas as part of its composition, like *American Warrior* and *Love in the Time of War*. Taken together, I thought the show was effective, although it was obviously the work of a very young artist. I would have brought Caroline, but I'd decided not to mention it to her since anything having to do with Daphne could potentially start a fight.

Jane wore a long, flowing skirt and another bandanna, boots, and dangling earrings. She was a picture herself, a portrait of a hippie. She approached me warmly, clasping my hands and giggling. "Isn't this boss? You just missed Galen and Daphne. It was so great of him to come."

So, I had missed her, but Jane's pleasure made my visit to the gallery worthwhile anyway. I made the best of the little cheese cubes and white wine. Jane gave me directions to her student house.

Only in Bronxville were the student houses so pristine and well-appointed, much more elegant and luxurious than my own little house in New Paltz. Five students shared this one, each with a bedroom. The large and gracious living room had a fireplace, but today the air-conditioning was more important. My house in New Paltz got really hot, and I didn't have any air-conditioning. Most houses didn't.

The environment was gracious, but the party was not. Jane was still a kid, and she had the usual college snacks out: pretzels, chips, dip, and brownies. There were a few jugs of really cheap wine and plastic cups. I saw the album cover of the music she was playing on a fancy stereo system, Jefferson Airplane's *Surrealistic Pillow*. I hadn't listened to the album, but the strong American sounds matched the Americana theme of her canvases. I drank my wine in the corner, watching the kids. When the album was almost over, and as I was getting ready to leave, Daphne came in by herself, while I heard Grace Slick sing "White Rabbit" for the first time, telling the story of Alice, ending with the resounding chorus, "*Feed your head*"—a druggie manifesto from the Summer of Love.

Daphne approached me, still elegant, still subdued. "Garrett," she almost whispered. We shook hands. Her beautiful eyes shimmered like jade, cool in the summer light. This *was* surreal. But she was as real standing before me as the girl in the bookstore exploring Schrödinger. As the song finished I thought of the day we'd met and the two little girls sitting on the floor of the bookshop listening to *Alice in Wonderland*.

Jane sat cross-legged on the floor. Then four or five other people followed suit, and Daphne sat on the floor too. I'd never been a flexible guy, and my legs complained as I crossed them as the kids were doing. I guessed that a joint was coming. I had never smoked marijuana before. My generation just drank, but I thought, *Sure, why not?* I'd give it a try.

I hadn't considered that this Daphne smoked pot. I thought of her ensconced in Galen's world with his habits, but she was in college now, after all. She took the joint first, and I watched her hold her breath as she pantomimed what I was supposed to do. I gathered that keeping the smoke in my lungs was the most important part. I didn't feel anything the first time the joint came around, but by the second hit I began noticing its effects. Someone had walked over to the stereo to play the previous few songs again. The final notes of the last song on the Airplane album lingered and elongated. I started to giggle at the absurdity of everyone sitting on the floor like we were in kindergarten, but in a corner of my mind I was worrying about how I appeared to others by sitting there giggling. I had never smoked cigarettes, and my lungs felt like they would burst at the harshness of the smoke held in my chest.

I stood up, drifting over to the brownies. Daphne followed. I took three small brownies; she took one, and drew me out into the backyard. They were soooooooo chocolaty. The house had a fancy rich-person garden. Obviously, it hadn't always been a rental. I sat down on a curving stone bench that was next to a small pond that might have once held koi. She sat down next to me.

"So, Garrett. Your first time stoned?"

I just nodded. "How about you?"

"What do you think college kids do in Bronxville? Actually, I got stoned once when I still lived on Long Island."

"You did? When I met you you'd already smoked pot?"

"Sure. Why are you so surprised? We smoked during school, in a ravine near the railroad tracks that ran by. Anyone could. There was someone there almost every period."

"Wow. Even when you stood in the bookstore in your rain slicker you were a druggie?" I joked. "I would never have guessed."

She was laughing uproariously, and I started to also . . . *and something is happening here, but you don't know what it is, do you, Mr. Jones?*

We laughed like that for a while until a wave of sadness washed over me.

"I'm worried about you. Are you okay?" I knew I was enunciating slowly, with odd emphasis, but the drug was emboldening me to say things I might not have said otherwise.

Daphne had only taken one drag on the joint, so she was not as high. She said, "I couldn't be home anymore. And just see where I am. In a beautiful garden with a friend, stoned on some good grass, celebrating a painter friend. Not bad. Do I have to think about anything more than that?"

"No. You don't have to think. Where's Mr. Green?"

"He's at home. This obviously isn't his scene. He'll pick me up when I call him."

"I'll drive you home."

"You're super stoned."

"We'll wait a little while then."

An hour and three brownies later we were in my car, top down. She told me about the paper she'd written at the end of her last semester and about the art history courses she'd be taking in the fall. "I wrote a paper on odalisques in French art, centering on the Ingres painting."

Of course I thought of Caroline and the day I'd called her an odalisque. Isn't that always the way it is in life? The things we notice and the things we say circle back to us until we have to ask if these repetitions are mere coincidence or evidence of some design.

I was completely sober by the time I met up with Caroline in New York. When I walked into our date at a bar near her place, she was nursing a gin and tonic and softly drumming on the table. Her beauty impressed me as always, enhanced by the black sundress enlivened by a profusion of the tiniest white polka dots. She was wearing a chignon like Daphne's. Her face had a weariness I hadn't seen before. She glanced up as I neared, but she seemed too tired to smile.

"Garrett," was all she said. Then, after a pause: "What are we doing?"

"What do you mean?"

"Oh, please don't play dumb. I don't think I can get through this if you do."

"Okay. I won't." I didn't want her to hurt, but I honestly didn't know what I could do about it.

"We seem to have an insoluble problem."

"I think I need a drink before I can begin to deal with problems with no solutions." When the waiter came I just ordered what she was having.

She began again without missing a beat, as soon as my drink was served: "I don't know how much longer we can continue like this."

She said this every time we met. Sometimes she got angry when I didn't seem to react strongly enough to her observation, but I honestly didn't know what to say, and I was becoming inured to her ambivalence.

"Look," I answered, "everything is all right. Really. I am not in a loony bin, I am still earning a living, I have no complaints against me at school, I just have a very unusual hobby—tracking Daphne." I should have known better than to make a joke.

She groaned, though her mood changed. "Tell me everything you've come up with since we talked about this." I guess for Caroline it was like putting her tongue where her tooth hurt. She couldn't stop herself from doing it. She had to know every detail of the Daphne saga.

"I spoke to the guidance counselors from the high schools two of the girls attend. At one high school she was brilliant in a debate, that's SDS Daphne, and at the other high school my first Daphne sang a solo in a choral concert on the same night. One guidance counselor, Mrs. Winter, told me Daphne's a soprano, and the other, Mr. Tyler, said Daphne won the debate for them."

"Wow. Really?" It seemed as if she'd forgotten to be upset for a moment. "That's wild. It really is. Is that all?"

I should have said it was, and I wanted to say that it was, but I must have had the same compulsion she had, to make things hurt. "And I saw her—Galen's Daphne— today, just before I came to the city. It wasn't planned. She just walked into a party at Jane's. I met Jane when she was feeding Daphne and Galen's cat. I'd tried to visit Daphne that night, but she and Galen were away." I wasn't being completely honest because the main reason I'd gone to Jane's show was to see Daphne.

"So, you saw her. How was it?"

"It was fun. We listened to Grace Slick, you know who that is? Jefferson Airplane? Singing 'White Rabbit.'" Caroline's tawny eyes remained mild and curious, so I pressed my luck: "Tell me again why my interest in Daphne is so bad. I really don't see it. I don't see why you have to be so upset or why our relationship has to change so much and be put in endless limbo."

"Because your life isn't moving forward; because it's all you really think about. Because you have strange ideas about it. Because she's a young girl. Excuse me, *girls*. Because Jerry thinks it's a bit off. Because you're not thinking about your work or a promotion or about our future. Just . . . because."

"*You* won't let me think about our future. But think about all the things I am thinking about that I wasn't before. Like the war. Like music. Like the nature of reality, for god's sake."

"And those things are going to move your life forward how?" She was almost pleading now, pleading with
me to understand. Her dark hair tumbled about her face
as she fought for our future.

The worst thing about our disagreements was the role
Caroline got cast in. In trying to save me from an obsession, she was volunteering for the role of bitchy girlfriend. I wished I could have spared her that.

Although my job was just a thin membrane that separated me from the vagaries of being a guy like my father,
someone who just could not grasp onto life, I would not
give Daphne up. Until I saw her holding up the Schrödinger
book I had concentrated on making my mother happy
by not being like my father. The Schrödinger girl had reminded me that it was important to live for myself.

"How do you know I'm not doing important detec-
tive work like Sherlock Holmes?" I asked.

"Because you don't have a deerstalker hat," she answered.

"I just want to know the truth."

"Sherlock, the final evidence is never in. That's just
the way things work."

I should have left things like that, and let her have the
final word, but I needed her on my side so badly, and she
was letting me plead my case. "When Leeuwenhoek first
peered at a drop of pond water through his homemade
microscope, no one had ever seen those microscopic creatures before. Was he crazy?"

I watched Caroline's face become more composed
as she realized how important these questions were to
me. She answered in a considered tone, "I don't know
if he was crazy or not, and I don't know if seeing his

animalcules made him crazy. I know some people have
gone crazy even if what they've seen is real. The problem
is that it's not the seventeenth century. People don't just
study things on their own, and you're not a physicist.
You're not even willing to write up your observations for
other scientists to talk about. You won't tell the whole
story, even to Jerry. I don't think Leeuwenhoek kept secrets. Why don't you take this to a physicist, or a reporter,
and go public in some way?"

"I feel protective of Daphne. It's *my* mystery to solve."

The smoky bar was filling up. The late-August night
was so humid that customers were coming in just for the
air-conditioning. I saw people eyeing our table, so I mo-
tioned to the waiter to order us another drink, but before
I could, Caroline said she wanted to call it a night.

"We'll see each other properly next week," she promised. "For dinner."

CHAPTER THIRTEEN

BUT WE DIDN'T HAVE DINNER TOGETHER for a while. Caroline's boss sent her to troubleshoot at his San Francisco gallery. She was out west when the fall 1967 semester began. Three weeks into the semester, I was teaching Introduction to Psychology in a large hall when I heard a commotion outside the room. Someone was banging on the window very enthusiastically, presumably to get the attention of a friend in the room. I tried to carry on with my lecture, but it was no use. All the kids were distracted and staring out the classroom window to the hallway to identify the disrupter. More than a little peeved, my attention found the large picture window, and my entire body jumped. I glimpsed SDS Daphne in a black dance leotard, jeans, and the side braid she had worn the first time we'd met.

This Daphne irked me, though I didn't know why. I asked the class to excuse me and went to the door. "What are you doing here?" I blurted out when I was just one foot out of the classroom.

"We came to confer with student leaders here at New Paltz about the October 21 demonstration. You're coming, right?"

I ignored her question. "You were making a racket."

"Aren't you happy to see me?"

As soon as she asked this question I realized that I was actually ecstatic to see her. I invited her in to hear the end of my lecture, and then we'd catch up.

"I can't. I have to get back to Terry. He's in a meeting right now. I just wanted to say hi."

I couldn't let her disappear. "How about later?"

"Nope. No can do."

"Don't I get to meet this Terry?"

"Are you kidding? That would be an awful idea. I don't think you two would hit it off at all. And you might lecture him about me. That would be so embarrassing."

I was thinking more of taking him aside and giving him a piece of my mind. "You're underage."

"That's exactly why I don't want you two to meet—because you think crap like that."

Changing the subject, I asked, "So all the noise was for this brief hello?"

"I think I could spare another half hour or so."

I considered the situation; I watched myself walk into the lecture hall and cancel the rest of the class.

We walked back to my office. I sat behind my desk, and she sat, as she had so many times in my imagination, in the chair reserved for students. She eyed the artwork on the walls. I'd hung the van Goghs I'd taken down from my study walls, and I had some photographs of Jane Pinsky's work. Daphne studied the snapshots as if she'd never seen them before, which of course she hadn't. Only Galen's Daphne had.

"Those are cool," she said. "Who did them?"

"A young painter who goes to Sarah Lawrence and studies with Galen Green. Ever hear of him?"

"Yeah. You mentioned him the day we spent in Times Square. Why are you so interested in him? I don't know his work."

"Ever meet him?"

"Well, sure. I always hang out with famous artists. I had lunch with Picasso just yesterday." She gave me a fishy look.

"Because I saw a portrait that looked just like you. By Galen Green, as a matter of fact."

"Really? Describe it."

Sitting together in my little office, I didn't want to tell her the painting was a nude. I had made us tea using two immersion heaters, coils of metal that warmed water in a mug. The mugs had been a gift from Jerry, and they read *Id* and *Superego*. I had broken the *Ego* mug awhile ago. Figures—the ego is meant to be the synthesis. The water never really got hot enough for great tea, but Daphne was polite enough to not complain. She did use three packets of sugar, though.

"So what does the painting look like?" she repeated.

"It's abstract, but you can see a girl with auburn hair."

"Abstract, eh? Bourgeois art. Come the revolution we are going to outlaw all that decadent art."

I was relieved to see her impish smile that said she was joking. "What about your parents?" I ventured. "How do they feel about you living with Terry?"

"Oh, why do we have to talk about parents? That's a boring subject."

No luck there. I remembered that Galen's Daphne had told me that her parents had been okay with her going to live with Galen. Maybe they were okay with Terry too? But who were these parents? Simulacra, like the Schrödinger girls? Was everything repeated in alternate universes, like each drop of pond water teeming with life under Leeuwenhoek's microscope?

"I have to go now," she said.

"Do you want a ride?"

"I think I can make it across campus on my own. I remember exactly which dorm Terry is in, Bliss Hall. I have a good sense of direction. Make sure you go to the demonstration. That's really what I came to tell you."

Look for the girl with the sun in her eyes, and she's gone. Daphne was always disappearing.

I decided to follow her. Since I'd parked my car right outside the building, I could easily get to the dorm before she did. Luckily, I was able to find a parking spot that had sight lines to the door of the building where trees would block an easy view of me. After just a few minutes I saw my plucky SDS Daphne walk into the dorm. I wanted to catch a glimpse of her SDS leader. I had seen Galen, and now I wanted to see Terry too.

While I waited I listened to the radio, WOR FM, whose signal just reached New Paltz. It was a beautiful late-September day, and I put my top down and enjoyed listening to "Strawberry Fields." I decided that I liked it better than "Penny Lane," though it had officially been designated the B side. Perhaps Caroline was right. Maybe I was becoming unbalanced. Now I was stalking teenage girls. Thank god I didn't have any binoculars or a camera with a telephoto lens. I could lose my job if anyone caught me spying.

Just then Daphne walked out. I turned off the radio and peered at the guy behind her. He was of average height, slightly stocky, with a dark beard and hair too curly to grow long. He wore a flannel shirt and was neater and more personable-looking than I'd expected. I saw him put his arm around my girl in a companionable way. She leaned into him. He said something to her, and she laughed. With Terry, Daphne, this political, strident girl, gave signs of being *happy*. After my brief glimpse of the two of them together, they got into a car and drove away.

As Ur-Daphne had predicted, when I finally started to really study the politics of the war, I began to oppose the conflict. Jerry, who'd been a dove for a while, had teased me, saying, "What's this? Garrett Adams abandoning his famous scientific objectivity?" But objectivity wasn't meant to be a license for blind neutrality in the face of self-serving colonialism. For a girl who might not be real, the Schrödinger girl was surely changing my life. Soon, I began to see flyers for the October mobilization posted around campus. There were buses heading to Washington from all over the country. Two buses were leaving from New Paltz, and I arranged a ticket to travel with the doves from my department. However, just days before we were scheduled to leave, Ur-Daphne called and asked me to go with her. She had bought tickets for us on a bus that would leave from the parking lot of her high school. She thought we'd be good company for each other. Of course I accepted Ur-Daphne's request. The minute SDS Daphne showed up talking about the demonstration, I'd fixated on the idea that my first Daphne might be going too. I needed to see them together, so I would *know what was really real*, as Bob Dylan said.

Caroline called two nights before the march. She was

finally back from San Francisco but needed to work. "I wish I were going," she said, "but you're going, right?"

"Yup. Bought the ticket and everything."

"With your department?"

"Uh-huh," I answered. This was my first out-and-out lie. I wasn't sure why she wanted to know, but I wasn't about to tell her that I had changed my plans to march with Daphne. It wasn't great hiding the truth, but what harm would it do to let her think I was riding down from New Paltz with my school? I had donated my New Paltz bus ticket to a student who couldn't afford to buy one.

The night before the march I tried to get to sleep early, yet all I could do was toss and turn. Every time I would drift off I'd startle awake. Finally I slept for an hour, but woke up around eleven thirty. I must have felt guilty about misleading Caroline. I decided to call Jerry seeking absolution. Of course I wouldn't tell him about the betrayal outright, but I'd hint around enough so he could reassure me that all relationships have secrets. As the phone kept ringing I wondered whom I was kidding. Friday and Saturday nights had always been Jerry's party nights, and he probably wouldn't be home. I held the phone to my sweaty ear, sitting on the bed of the cheap motel that was close to Daphne's school. We were leaving too early the next day to have driven down from home. The cord didn't reach very far, so I sat upright near the night table of the lumpy bed. The black receiver registered ring after ring. Jerry's private number didn't connect to the answering service he used for his patients, even though both lines rang in the same rooms at his apartment. I lazily let the phone continue to make its hollow sound, too stubborn to give up. After the eleventh ring I heard his confused "Hello?" Maybe it was too late to call, but there was no going back.

"Jerome?" I said, using his full, discarded name for comic effect.

"Who's this?" he asked suspiciously, his voice thick with what I assumed was sleep.

"It's me." Who else called him Jerome?

"Garrett?" he said as though experiencing a great revelation. "Whaddaya want?" he demanded with hostility. This wasn't the Jerry I knew. Maybe he was with a girl. Or maybe he'd had one too many. I'd seen him do that before, but it was only eleven thirty, early for Jerry on a bar night.

"Is this a bad time? Do you have somebody there? Did you just get in?"

He seemed to have collected himself. "No, it's fine. I'm alone. I've been alone here all night."

"On Saturday night? That doesn't sound like you." I wondered idly if something was wrong, but I was too preoccupied with my own problems to give Jerry much thought. "I'm going to the march tomorrow."

"Mazel tov," he said. "Garrett Adams is developing a political conscience. I love it." But then he seemed to sink back into his earlier confusion. "What march?"

"You know. The big march in Washington to protest the war."

"Oh yeah, yeah. Now I remember." There was a time when Jerry would have been trying to drag me along to one of his political events. "What can I do for you, kid?" he pleasantly inquired, now sounding like his old self.

"I just wanted to ask if it's normal for a couple to keep things from each other. You know, for the good of the other, things that would only hurt. White lie kind of things."

"Everyone has secrets, kid." And he hung up the phone.

I wasn't sure that was very reassuring. *Secrets* sounded ominous. But when I got back into bed, even the scratchy sheets didn't keep me awake this time, and I fell into a dreamless sleep free of worries about Jerry or Caroline or the deceit I was visiting on her.

The bus from Long Island left at four a.m. When I arrived early at the parking lot of Daphne's high school, I saw a two-toned beige and brown Oldsmobile dropping her off, though the car drove away before I could get a glimpse of her parents. She rushed toward me and said, "Hi, Uncle Garrett!"

That sounded really weird, but she didn't want to have to explain our unusual friendship. Every secret and deception should have set me wondering if there was something wrong with my preoccupation with the Schrödinger girls, but at that moment I was happy to go along with her little fiction.

The coach bus was comfortable, with large blue seats that reclined, and tinted windows. Daphne brought sandwiches, American cheese and lettuce on kaiser rolls, and I brought a thermos of coffee and hot cups in my backpack. I had prepared answers, should she ask me about the Galen Green portrait again, but she didn't. She was no longer entranced with physics or psychology and had begun to read French and Spanish literature. Her two greatest finds were Rimbaud and Borges. I had never read either.

"Borges wrote this story," she told me, "'The Garden of Forking Paths.' He created a character who is a spy. He's Chinese and he works for the Germans because he wants to show them that Asian people can outsmart Europeans. It's sad, really, because he despises Germans. He finds an English professor who is studying the work of an ancestor, a Chinese ancestor, who has built a labyrinth, except it turns out that the labyrinth is really a novel in which all possible outcomes of events occur simultaneously, and each event leads to further possibilities that have their own forking possibilities."

I was electrified. Daphne had no idea that she was describing the very reality I had discovered about her life—that all events and explanations have their own forking possibilities and complex conditions. My being on this bus represented the intercession of two Daphnes: SDS Daphne had focused on changing my position, and Ur-Daphne had asked me along. I still hoped to catch a glimpse of both girls together. I was certain SDS Daphne would attend.

"What did you make of the Borges story?" I asked her.

"It's cool. Maybe a little scary."

"Scary? Do you ever feel you're in a world like that?"

"Sometimes. Like when I catch glimpses of myself, it's as if the world is a mirror. Only it's not me I'm seeing, it's someone else."

"Do you think we live with these forking paths?"

"Maybe."

I sat for a moment thinking before I explained the connection between Borges's story and the Schrödinger equation. We'd never discussed the specific science before, this central mathematical description of the quantum reality in which we actually live.

"Do you think Borges studied physics?" she asked.

"I can't be sure, but I think he must have." I was finally having the discussion neither Caroline nor Jerry would have with me, and I was just getting started. "So what do *you* think is happening when you see this doppelgänger?"

I looked intently at her flushed cheeks as she held her breath, but instead of answering my question she avoided my gaze and began talking about the logistics of the march.

The Mobilization Committee to End the War in Vietnam had planned a grand scheme for this first national antiwar demonstration. An unsanctioned march of three miles to the Pentagon would follow a day of speeches at the Lincoln Memorial. Roughly 100,000 people gathered at the memorial and listened to Dr. Benjamin Spock, Abbie Hoffman, who wore an Uncle Sam top hat, Norman Mailer, and Robert Lowell. I wondered how I was going to find SDS Daphne in so large a crowd. The weather was fine, and there were guitars and music everywhere. Demonstrators held up signs, chanted, and sang. Placards read, *LBJ, Pull Out Now, Like Your Father Should Have Done.* The crowd chanted, *"Hey, hey, LBJ, how many kids have you killed today?"* We sang, *"It's one, two, three, what are we fighting for? Don't ask me, I don't give a damn. Next stop is Vietnam,"* and Phil Ochs's "I Ain't Marching Anymore."

Daphne occasionally walked over to teachers and kids she knew from school, but mostly she stayed by my side, so I didn't have a chance to go off on my own to sur-

vey the crowd. Our bus was due to leave at ten p.m. Some
of the demonstrators wandered off to go to the Smithso-
nian or to visit the National Mall, or just to find a nice
restaurant, but Daphne wanted to stay and hear all the
speakers. I was determined to march for political reasons,
of course, but I was also hoping to catch a glimpse of SDS
Daphne. Apparently, I had been so restless and craned
my neck so often for better views of the mass of people
before us that my young companion finally asked just
whom I was searching for, but I answered that I wasn't
missing anyone, just recording history.

"If you want to march, it'll be okay," I assured her.
"Let's go to the Pentagon. It's what we're here for, right?"

She narrowed her eyes and half raised one eyebrow.
"But what if things get hairy?"

"That's why I'm here," I replied, hoping she was mol-
lified. I didn't particularly like the pressure I was putting
on her, but I couldn't escape my compulsion to find the
other Daphne, whom I was certain was close by. Using
electric bullhorns, the organizing committee asked for
volunteers to march, warning us that there might be rioting and arrests. I listened carefully for her voice through
the bullhorn. I sneaked a peek at this Daphne. I could see
that the organizers' plea was having an effect because she
had set her jaw in resolve.

"I feel like we should go," she said.

Although I wanted to have the chance of finding SDS
Daphne, I had begun to change my mind; I couldn't in
good conscience totally abandon my chaperone duties. I
decided that we shouldn't march, SDS Daphne or no.
"You heard that it could be dangerous, right?"

"And I heard they need volunteers. Abbie Hoffman

said it's where the real statements would be made. I've decided. I'm not going back to the bus. Kids my age are in danger in Vietnam. They're not going to shoot us or bomb us or napalm us, are they? I just won't walk on the Pentagon lawn."

I thought about this further. I might be able to make some progress on solving my mystery, and I couldn't stop Daphne anyway. "All right, but we have to be sensible," I replied. "Absolutely no walking on the lawn."

The crowd had thinned out, and only about 35,000 gathered for the more risky action. As we marched we sang "We Shall Overcome." People linked hands. People shared water from canteens. Hippies carried bouquets of flowers.

When we reached the Pentagon, the air was still bright and sunset was almost an hour away. I saw troops with bayoneted rifles lined up along the perimeter of the lawn. They were so achingly young. Their close shaves revealed that the tops of pimples had been sliced off. Under their caps their heads had been so recently buzz cut that you could see the irregularities of their skulls. As they stood with their rifles pointed out, it was their turn to chant. At set intervals they warned: "Stay off the Pentagon lawn." Above all, these army guys seemed scared. They were facing their own countryfolk with standard weapons of war. Their eyes darted, taking in the children, teenagers, and elderly among the throng. They stayed rooted to their spots, but they were not so densely arranged that it would be impossible to breech their position.

Daphne threaded her way to the front of the crowd, and I followed. Still no sign of SDS Daphne. Near the military guys the tension was visceral. They stared out at the crowd through narrowed eyes that said that if Command told them that their fellow Americans were enemies, then they were enemies, no questions asked. But their pleading eyes also begged the throng not to tread on the grass and force them to use their weapons against us.

Police hovered near the perimeter, itching to arrest any trespassers. As soon as a protester got a toe close to the grass, a hovering soldier with a rifle would stare her down. A young hippie girl sauntered up to a soldier and pushed a daisy into the rifle of his gun. He flinched, and she taunted him, "You're not afraid of a flower, are you?" Then other hippie women followed suit, scampering onto the lawn and then scampering away. Soon all the rifle barrels sported flowers. Guitarists strummed "Where Have All the Flowers Gone?" and the hippies chanted, *"Flower power!"* The soldiers stood immobile, sweat forming on their brows and trickling down their cheeks.

Daphne was riveted by the scene, but I was still frantically searching for SDS Daphne. She had to be here. If I could put all my own doubts to rest and see them both at the same time then I'd know once and for all that they were both real, and Galen's Daphne too.

I stood close enough to my Schrödinger girl to pull her back should she think of walking on the lawn. I didn't know how far she'd go. For a moment her body stood as still as the Bernini statue of Apollo and Daphne, and I worried that she was emotionally overwhelmed. I wanted to put an arm around her, yet I knew by instinct that she would shake the arm off. She wanted me nearby, but she wanted to face her establishment enemy alone. I still scanned the crowd, seeking that auburn side braid that SDS Daphne always wore. I thought I caught a glimpse of it, but before I could be sure, the Daphne standing next to me rushed up on the grassy mound.

A toddler, a blond mop-top wearing only overalls, had become separated from his parents and waddled onto the Pentagon lawn on his naked chubby feet. The poor soldier nearest the child automatically responded and pointed the rifle at the boy. Just then, other waiting protesters rushed the grass in groups. Daphne ran to save the child. She scooped him up while the police, seeing a volatile situation developing, released canisters of tear gas noxious enough to cause the child to vomit on a choking Daphne. She hugged him tightly and scurried off the lawn. The child began wailing with a cry that alerted his parents. They hurried over and took him from her. I wondered why they'd brought him into such a dangerous situation.

I rushed to Daphne's side and asked a stranger for some water. Someone thrust several napkins into my hands and I handed them to Daphne to wipe the vomit off her gray ribbed top. When she had almost soaked the shirt through with water, she turned and threw up herself. I begged another cup of water from someone nearby. When my young friend recovered from being sick, she was still coughing and struggling to breathe. I was able to get her to drink the water, and she kept it down.

"I didn't think they'd do it, Garrett. I never believed they'd really hurt us. But when I saw that toddler in danger and the determination in that soldier's eyes, I had to save him. They wouldn't have shot him or bayoneted him, would they? I can't believe the soldier would have. He was only a baby. But who would point a gun at a baby? Who does that?"

I could only murmur, "There, there." I was too shaken myself. I had just witnessed the most disturbing sight I'd ever seen—an American soldier pointing a bayoneted rifle at an American baby. I wouldn't recover for a while, but now I had to take charge.

"We're going back to the bus. No discussion. Come on."

I would have to give up my quest to find my other Schrödinger girl. This Daphne was just too sick. Since she was still coughing, I approached protesters until I could find someone who would drive us to the bus, so Daphne wouldn't have to cover the three miles on foot.

When we arrived at the tour bus people were dozing, playing cards, and listening to music very quietly. A pixie-haired, wiry, middle-aged brunette, the school librarian according to Daphne, jumped up upon seeing her and cried, "My goodness, you look like a wreck!"

"I was teargassed."

"Really? How awful. Is there anything I can do?"

Daphne shook her head. She didn't want to speak about the incident involving the child. Maybe she was afraid she'd break down in tears. One of the girls gave her a hug that she accepted after warning, "Be careful of the vomit."

We made our way to our places. My backpack and her bag were waiting for us. Daphne was so small she was almost hidden by the tall seats. I think she was grateful for the privacy. I peeked at the other passengers. They were eating their packed sandwiches and cookies. Some kids were making out in the back, and several riders had their lights on to read. I tapped Daphne on the shoulder and pointed to the panoramic windows. We could see the last rays of sunset. Tendrils of pink streaked through the blue and then faded into the surrounding gray.

"Have some coffee," I told her. "You need it. It's still a little warm." I was glad that thinking of her, I'd added cream and sugar. I suspected she would be unable to eat until the effects of the tear gas wore off. She sipped the coffee without saying anything. She still appeared to be ill. Someone on the bus was playing "Light My Fire" on a DC FM radio station. Daphne had turned me on to rock, but I suspected I was just too old for the radically sensual sound of Jim Morrison and the Doors.

"Do you think that baby is all right?" she asked.

"I'm sure he is. I don't think tear gas does permanent damage, and you got him out of there pretty fast. That was really heroic, by the way."

"No. Anyone would have done it."

"No one else did. You did. I didn't. The other adults standing around didn't. You did."

"Garrett?"

"Yeah, sweetie?" That just kind of came out.

"I didn't feel like a teenager. I felt like an adult. Like a maternal adult."

"Well, you were. How are you feeling?"

"Better."

And then she fell asleep, her head on my shoulder. Today she had learned to feel maternal, and now I found myself thinking, *This is what being a father must feel like*. I felt good having someone trust me, and I was glad I'd been there to shepherd Daphne back to the bus, yet I felt a keen disappointment that I hadn't seen SDS Daphne at all.

While everyone slept I stayed up, thinking. It's a lonely but oddly exhilarating feeling to be the only one besides the driver awake among a group of sleeping humans. Perception becomes somewhat distorted, and it feels as if the world exists just for you. My thoughts kept returning to the brief moment when I thought I'd caught a glimpse of an auburn side braid. Was that her, or was it just someone else with a side braid? I didn't know. Things happened so fast after that—the baby, the vomit, Daphne's vomit—I didn't have another chance to look for her. I wondered if she'd sought me out. Probably not. She had surely been too busy with the logistics of the march. I felt thwarted. Was I never going to be able to solve this Schrödinger mystery?

My mind kept flashing back to the young soldier who'd pointed his rifle at the child. Was there another universe in which the soldier actually used that bayonet? I hoped not. Borges must have known something of what I was going through. I wished I could have asked him what he thought. It was impossible to know how many Schrödinger girls were there, maybe even ones I didn't know about. Perhaps Galen and his Daphne had come. But I hadn't seen another Daphne.

Somewhere in southern New Jersey, I fell asleep. The bus movement made me dream of the ocean and harpoons like bayonets and whaling ships and schools of auburn-haired girls swimming like mermaids through teeming seas. I awoke as the bus pulled into the parking lot at the high school, just as Daphne was also stirring. She busied herself with packing up her bag and then she kissed me on the cheek for the first time. She got off the bus just ahead of me but turned back and said, "Goodbye, Uncle Garrett," and then walked toward the waiting Oldsmobile I could just see through the windshield of the bus.

CHAPTER FOURTEEN

I DROVE TO NEW YORK through the darkness. We had left the high school parking lot at four a.m. Saturday morning and returned exactly twenty-four hours later. I passed by the bridge exits that would have taken me to New Paltz because I wanted to see Caroline. I made great time driving on the early-Monday-morning roads. I parked my car near her street and dozed for a couple of hours until sunrise. Even with all her prickly ambivalence, I missed Caroline, and wanted to talk to her about the demonstration, but I planned to stick with my little deception.

When the day grew bright I consulted my watch, which read 8:00, late enough to risk one of Caroline's moods. I had no classes until late afternoon. A sleepy but mellow Caroline answered the phone. She immediately asked, "How did the march go?"

"I'll tell you in person, if you're okay with seeing me. I'm near your apartment now. I could take you to breakfast." As I said this, I realized I was hungry. I tried to suppress the thought that I'd lied to her and betrayed her by going to the march with Daphne without telling her, but that knowledge kept surfacing in my mind. I had almost blurted it out when Caroline answered.

"Give me a half hour," she said.

We ate bagels, the standard breakfast in New York. We weren't at a fancy place, just a nearby bagel joint where the coffee wasn't too awful. We sat at a small Formica table with rickety old wooden chairs. Caroline, the Indiana girl, ordered an everything bagel covered with lox. I had always liked my bagels pristine: plain with just cream cheese. I added a large orange juice to my order.

Caroline hadn't dressed for work yet. She must have just jumped into the shower and pulled on jeans and a sweatshirt. They suited her. Her wet hair streamed over her shoulders in the way I loved.

"So, spill," she said.

I told her everything as it had happened, keeping the story of the toddler and the soldier until last, editing out all mention of Daphne. She blanched.

"Oh my god. You're kidding. No. That couldn't happen. And tear gas? Really?" I saw that she wanted to cry. "Someone is taking away my country. That isn't America. In America soldiers don't kill our babies, or even threaten to."

"I know," I said gently. "It's quite a shock, isn't it? But I've had hours to think about it, and what I keep thinking is what does it matter whether it's an American baby or a Vietnamese baby? How can *any* soldiers point rifles at toddlers? Of course, it's more shocking to see an American threaten another American, but I am also haunted by images of Vietnamese children threatened, napalmed, shot. Seeing the threat of violence up close makes me realize that it has its own taste. And I tasted violence at the moment that baby was threatened and when the tear gas was introduced into the crowd." Now that I had taken a stand on the war, all these suppressed images flooded me.

"Awhile back you asked me why I keep seeing you, Garrett. Saying things like that is one of the reasons. It doesn't matter what nationality a child is. What happened to the baby?"

"My reactions seemed slowed by shock, but fortunately someone else rushed onto the grass and rescued the kid. By that time he had already breathed enough tear gas to vomit on the Good Samaritan."

Then making the intuitive leap that women do, she said, "It was Daphne, wasn't it? The Good Samaritan."

I tried to avoid the moment. "What?" I started to say. But I quickly caved in. She'd caught me. It had been futile to try to keep it from her. So much for secrets. "Yes. How did you know?"

"Her image just flashed in my mind. Why didn't you tell me?"

"I didn't want to upset you. I wanted to talk to you so much this morning. I needed to. I didn't want Daphne to come between us. Maybe we could just let it be, just this one time."

"It's not upsetting at all finding out you lied to me," she said, in a voice hard with sarcasm. "I should let go of the reality that you were hiding something important?" Her nose became long and aquiline when she was angry or hurt.

"This is what I was trying to avoid."

"Sure. I get that. But lying?"

"I can't explain it. I have to find out about her, about them. I just have to. It doesn't have anything to do with you, but you keep thinking that it does, so I guess I try to hide my involvement."

"How am I supposed to feel about that, in your little universe?"

"I don't know. I can see I had poor judgment. I want you to be my girlfriend—"

"Whom you don't trust."

I decided to cut to the chase: "You have to decide, Caroline. Not me. You have to decide if I'm crazy."

She sat considering this, and went back to eating her bagel without saying anything. There was no wait service, so I went to the counter and got us both coffees. I set Caroline's in front of her and drank my own with feigned concentration, making a point of showing her that I was giving her space. I waited for endless minutes before she addressed me. Whenever the conversation turned to the idea of my being crazy, I thought of Jerry. He had kept his true assessment of my mental state to himself, but now I was worried about him. *Is everyone crazy?* I wondered.

"The jury's still out about whether or not you're crazy. Don't lie again. Ever. You get one pass today. Come back to my place."

She was inviting me to make love. I had dozed enough to take the edge off my exhaustion. Caroline was entirely in charge of our sex life, which varied with her moods. I had decided that if I were going to stay in the game I could never turn down one of her invitations.

I took a shower to wash off the last twenty-four hours. Her tiny bathroom and shower stall left only enough room for one, and she kept trying to talk to me over the noise of the water from the big room, but I had no idea what she was saying. More relaxed and refreshed, I went to her bed where she was completely naked, her nipples already erect from the lingering morning chill and anticipation. As I neared she laughed, "You're still too wet. Dry off!" She took the towel I had wrapped around my waist and began toweling my back and shoulders. That was too much, and I realized I was quite aroused.

Daphne was not between us that morning. As we embraced and caressed each other, I felt both the sadness of the war and the exhilaration of being alive. I remembered that the first time we had made love, Caroline had cried. This time I wanted to exult in the magnificence of being close to her. I was not guarding some worthless grass with a rifle and a bayonet, but I was still guarding secrets.

Caroline had to be at the gallery by eleven, so she left me dozing in her bed. I fell into a dreamless sleep. I awoke hours later and left to make my class. Walking to my car I read the headlines as I passed newspaper stands. The confrontation between the protesters, the police, and the army had gone on all night. The police made arrests. I was glad we'd gotten out of there.

I drove home with images of Caroline and Daphne: Caroline's body welcoming me into her bed and Daphne covered in baby sick, and Galen's Daphne looking wan by the koi pond. And then there was my SDS Daphne, suddenly happy when Terry put his arm around her. Caroline held out love to me like a full cup, but Daphne represented all the tantalizing mysteries of the universe. Why was everything so complicated? Although she denied it, I got the feeling that Caroline was hiding something from me too.

CHAPTER FIFTEEN

I BECAME FIXATED ON WHAT CAROLINE could be hiding from me. That she was finally dumping me? That she had gotten a new job in Hong Kong? That she had met someone else? That she was suffering from a serious disease? Every time I asked her if there was something she needed to tell me, she always said no, but was very cagey about it. She had arranged a leave of absence from the gallery because her parents were considering selling their farm and had a lot of work to do sorting possessions, painting dingy walls, and getting the place shipshape. Whenever I got her on the phone, she was very noncommittal, so I flew out to Indiana the day after a lonely Thanksgiving meal in the only restaurant open in New Paltz.

Caroline met me at the airport. I couldn't imagine my sleek Modigliani beauty on a farm without her sophisticated black dresses, but here she was, a local in jeans and a flannel shirt. She had always insisted that she was an Indiana country girl at heart, but I didn't find this incarnation of Caroline as convincing her New York self. Her family lived near Fort Wayne, and we drove around like tourists to Amish settlements and consignment stores, but seemed to have less to say to each other than when we were in New York. She was restless and unfocused. She came back to my hotel and we had mechanical sex in the nondescript room. Then she drove us downtown for a very good cheeseburger. Conversation still stalled.

Finally, Caroline asked, "What are you doing here exactly, Garrett?"

"I came to see you."

"Of course. But why? I mean you're not here to tell me you're giving up on this Daphne business, and I don't think you're here to propose, so why the drama?"

"I don't want to lose you. I missed you. New York is empty without you."

"Well, that's corny," she said.

"You don't believe me?"

"No. I actually do. But love, it's okay if I say love, isn't it? Love is sacrifice. And besides, I told you. Your Schrödinger obsession is really starting to scare me. I need you to be sane. I think that's a basic requirement."

"You go back and forth so much. You say you're backing away but you ask me into your bed. I'm not sure what that means. And I want to meet your parents. When do I get to do that?"

"You don't. It would only get their hopes up. They think I'm an old maid and that New York has ruined me." Then she laughed a little ruefully. "You can't imagine the locals they are lining up for me to date. These gruesome blind dates—kids of their friends. The ones who didn't leave Fort Wayne."

"You're not actually thinking about staying, are you?"

"Sometimes. I feel like life is slipping away."

"I'm not supposed to leave till Monday morning. Should I change my ticket?"

"We'll go to the zoo tomorrow. You can leave on Sunday."

Fort Wayne has one of the best children's zoos in the country. It had begun as some kind of preserve in the fifties, and they had just opened the shiny new zoo in 1965. We walked around eating popcorn and looking at animals. Amos, a pygmy chimpanzee, was the zoo's most famous resident and unofficial mascot. Caroline let me hold her hand when we spent some time with him, though I'd always felt uncomfortable around chimps. They reminded me too much of myself.

Even the day at the zoo failed to lift her spirits. She couldn't tell me what was going on except what she'd already said, that her life wasn't really making too much sense. She wanted to hear me say that I would never think about Daphne again. Maybe she even wanted me to say that I'd brought a ring. We just stood and stared at Amos playing with a stuffed lizard.

Back in New Paltz, my professional world began to fall apart. Dr. Dyer, our department chair, called me into his office for a little chat. He was a portly, excitable man around fifty.

"Dr. Adams," he said with forced formality when his secretary ushered me into his office. He gestured for me to take the seat across from him. "We're not too happy with your output lately," he said.

I nodded. My mouth felt dry. Funny—I had put all of this out of my head.

"Working on anything? What happened to the work you were doing with those listless rats you bred?"

"It didn't pan out," I said. "Nothing interesting."

"Any articles in the pipeline?"

"Not at the present."

"I'm not going to lie to you, Garrett. We were pleased, very pleased, with data you were getting before you were granted tenure. You were going gangbusters. But your output seems to have slowed down, a post-tenure slump. I've seen it happen before. You're going to have to have more to show the committee if you're ever going to get a promotion or be happy here."

"Should I consider this an official warning?" I asked. "Is there a report in my personnel file?"

"No. Nothing like that. Just a heads-up between friends."

Without Caroline and with this new anxiety, neither Christmas nor New Year's were very festive. Jerry and I caught a movie and had Chinese food—the Jewish Christmas. He asked me to go barhopping with him on New Year's Eve, but I stayed home and watched those dumb movies they show to losers who have no parties to go to. I nursed one shot of Baileys for the entire night. I just wasn't in the mood to party. I was screwing up everywhere—with Caroline, who was still in Indiana, and at work. I guessed I shouldn't have thrown that briefcase in the dumpster when I left the bar with the Yankees losing. In the end they hadn't come in last, but it was almost as bad, second-to-last. And to make matters worse, there was no sign of Daphne.

1968 promised to be a bad year, I thought, as I sat watching *After the Thin Man* in black and white, finishing the last drops of my Baileys. It had been either that or Guy Lombardo.

It turned out I was right. At the end of January, just after midnight on January 30, the Viet Cong hit American forces hard in the south. The attack was completely unexpected because the Vietnamese had always observed a cease-fire for the holiday of Tet. The element of surprise was on their side. The battle continued into the next day, when they attacked Saigon. This was catastrophic for American forces. I thought we should get out right then.

Then a call from Jerry came to interrupt my isolation and gloom. He proposed we meet at Hunter Mountain to ski. Back in our Cornell days, we had learned to ski on a dare from a group of guys who thought it would be fun to humiliate the city boys. Jerry took to it more easily than I did. He excelled at so many things. But I was persistent, and I learned. After that, we skied as often as we could.

It had been a long time since I'd done any diamond trails, but we'd skied together at least once a season since we graduated. We used to go back to Greek Peak near Cornell, but now we just met at Hunter. Jerry had to drive almost three hours to get there, whereas I could be there in an hour. They'd built a new base lodge about five years before, and I read that they'd installed a new lift and that the snowmaking apparatus was now one of the best in the world.

Jerry had to get up before daybreak, but I could linger over morning coffee. The day he chose was perfect—one of those days that recalls a child's drawing, with a cloudless sapphire sky, a big yellow sun, and conical hunter-green trees covered with snow.

Our ritual—which had been Jerry's idea—was to have coffee together before starting our day of skiing.

Jerry had pointed out that we might have news to share, and an outing provided a chance to catch up.

I was surprised to see Jerry already at a table because I hadn't noticed his car in the parking lot. He seemed a little worn, and his eyes had a wistfulness I wasn't used to. A tall, rangy waiter with wheat-colored hair came to take our order. We always drank Irish coffees. Jerry had once convinced me that a little alcohol was a perfect way to warm us up before we hit the slopes, and this had become part of our skiing ritual. I started to order when Jerry said, "Just plain coffee for me, Garrett."

I ordered two coffees for us and waited for him to speak. After all, my issues had dominated our last two meet-ups. This morning was his turn. I tried to be patient, yet I was itching to get out on the slopes; I hadn't done anything completely physical or exhilarating since the day months ago when I'd swam in the ocean with Caroline.

The Adirondack-style lodge was built with exposed beams and wood paneling and decorated with forest-green upholstery. The vaulted ceiling was vaguely Alpine, and the roaring fire was homey. While we waited for our coffee, Jerry plunged in: "I know you weren't comfortable the last two times we saw each other, Garrett, but that day in my office I was just trying to help."

Trying to help. I was surprised by the constriction in my throat, and my own anger, and I said, "I felt like you were condescending to me. The great white healer and his messed-up friend." I could plunge in too.

Jerry sighed. "Of course it would feel like that to you. But I wasn't thinking that at all."

We'd been waiting for this fight for years.

"Admit it," I said. "You think being a psychoanalyst is way better than being a professor."

"No, *you* think that, Garrett. Not me. You were always measuring yourself against me. Who says we have to compete at all?" His tired face was hangdog and sallow. The coffees came. We sipped them in a kind of silent truce.

He tried again: "I don't want to compete with you. I want us to be friends, equals."

"I suppose I am competitive. As students we were on a par with each other, but now you have this apartment and all this money. I *am* jealous." I surprised myself by being so honest. I couldn't see any reason to continue this covert war.

"I am no one to be jealous of."

We finished our coffee, and he resumed: "And then at the bar, I know you had things to talk about—"

"Time to hit the slopes," I cut him off. "Let's save all this for another time."

"I wanted to talk to you about that. I don't think I feel quite up to skiing right now."

"You don't want to go skiing? You could have called me last night. You didn't have to put both of us through this trip."

"*Bubbeleh*. I guess I could have, but I wanted to see you. I *needed* to see you."

"Why?"

"Because I need a friend."

This was getting weird. Jerry always had this hardiness about him, a kind of blustery humor that muscled through everything and charmed everyone. It was the thing about him I envied the most. Next to him, I'd always been the tall, skinny, bespectacled sidekick. Seeing him deflated should have felt like a victory. Instead, I felt uneasy.

"What's wrong?"

I put aside the anger, and suddenly we were two eighteen-year-old kids again, before life became a pissing contest, and before we measured ourselves in dollars and publications and renown. He shifted a little in his seat, his face showing just the faintest beginning of jowls.

"I'm in the beginning stages of cirrhosis of the liver. There's been some scarring that can't be reversed, but I can live with that." He winked at me there to lighten the news.

"Cirrhosis? You're only thirty-seven."

"We're almost thirty-eight, kid. Think about it," he said. "Really consider the idea."

Suddenly the ritual of having Irish coffee before skiing suggested something very different. It wasn't the whiskey that was the addition; it was the coffee. Jerry couldn't very well have suggested we go for beers at eight o'clock in the morning. I remembered the time in his office when I wondered why we weren't in the living room. Maybe it was because of the decanter of Scotch. He could walk over and take a nip without the fuss of bottles. I remembered now that he'd poured himself one first, and then offered me one with just a raising of his eyebrow and the tilt of his head. I remembered how much he resisted my request to go into the living room. Maybe he just wanted to stay where the booze was. I hadn't really considered the fact that he left his liquor out in front of patients. I had rarely seen him out of control, but the last time in the bar he was really drunk, and not just the letting-off-steam kind of tipsy.

I said, "Liquor has been part of every one of our meet-ups for a long time. Ten years maybe."

"It's been longer than that."

"You never seemed drunk, not until last time."

"I'm a functional alcoholic, which only means that I hold my liquor very well, and that I can drink large quantities of it. Or at least, I could."

"How long has it been since we were together without you having a drink?"

"I doubt that you've ever seen me without alcohol, until today. Not since the first few weeks at Cornell anyway, before we really knew each other."

My clenched jaw relaxed and I felt sorry for my friend, and a little abashed at my own blindness. I had suspected nothing, even when he was so out of it. "So, you're done with all drinking for good?" I asked.

"I have to be. It's been four days." He said this in an odd voice that showed both agony and pride. "It's going to be really tough. Ski lodge without Irish coffee? Unthinkable. But here we are."

"What happens now?"

"I'm in a program."

"AA?"

"No. That's not for me. That higher-power stuff."

"But you're Jewish."

"Jews are atheists. You know that. Part of our covenant. When you get circumcised you become an atheist."

"I thought you trotted God out for special occasions, like Rosh Hashanah."

He laughed heartily at that. I was relieved to see it.

"But you're in a different program now?" I asked.

"Yes. It was the only way to get off the sauce. I'm at a rehab center near here."

"They let you out? I guess they don't know about your love of Irish coffee."

"Of course they do. Ski lodge equals Irish coffee for an alcoholic. They know that. I got dropped off here for a two-hour furlough. Someone will pick me up."

I had imagined the morning all wrong. He hadn't gotten up in Manhattan at the crack of dawn and driven up here. He was with aides and other residents.

"I'm terrified of running into one of my patients," he confided.

"Then why don't you go somewhere else?"

"Only the best for my patients. And I shouldn't have the best?"

"What are you telling them?"

"Just that I needed to be away for a month. I arranged for other analysts to cover for me, especially for emergencies. It would be awful for both my sobriety and my clinical practice to lie to them. It would be awful for my clinical practice to tell them the whole truth."

"Do you really believe in psychoanalysis, Jerry?"

"Not as a cure for alcoholism, I don't."

"That's not what I meant."

"Maybe that's a conversation for another day."

"You don't even have skis with you, do you?"

He just sat there resignedly for a good thirty seconds. Then he said, "I thought you'd understand."

His eyes glistened with new tears, and his mouth sagged with a vulnerability I wasn't used to seeing in Jerry. I felt myself relenting. "Yeah, I get it," I said, letting him off the hook.

Then the old Jerry surfaced, and he said, "It should be you. You're the Mick. I'm the Yid. Jews aren't alcoholics." Then his humor faded. "Except when we are, I guess. I envy you, kid."

"Envy me? Why?"

"First, you're not an alcoholic. I wouldn't wish this on anyone. Second, you're in a stable relationship with a fabulous woman."

"I wouldn't really say it was stable. Soon you may have nothing to envy."

"What do you mean?"

"We haven't seen much of each other lately. She's been in Indiana. She can't handle the Schrödinger mystery."

"That girl?" he asked.

"Those girls," I corrected. "I met another one, and I talked to two separate guidance counselors about two different girls."

"That's also a conversation for a different day, but don't let Caroline get away. Soon we'll be forty. You have to connect with someone, Garrett, and I have to stop running around and having all these dalliances. I can't even take a girl out for cocktails now. But I do want to find someone and have a child."

We had both married young, divorced, and spent years on our own. Jerry and Annie had stayed married for five years, at least four years longer than Helena and I had managed.

"Why did you and Annie get divorced anyway? You never said."

"We drank together. One of us might be dead if we'd stayed together." He stood up then. "I'm going to wait outside for my ride, but as long as you're here, why don't you take a few runs for both of us?"

I agreed that I would.

I followed our usual ritual. I drove my car close to the lift I liked. Although they'd added a new triple lift, I went back to the one we habitually used. I wore my ordinary boots because the parking lot was slippery. I carried my ski boots, gloves, scarf, hat, sunglasses, and sunscreen in a large camping backpack. I carried my skis too, of course. I bought a ticket for just a half day. I stashed my walking boots in a locker, and geared up. I chose an intermediate run. I hadn't skied in a while so the first run required my total concentration. It was just the mountain, the snow, the sun, and me. The next run was pure exhilaration: speed, freedom, and joy. I stopped then. I hadn't come with the mind-set for a day alone on the slopes.

When I was back home, although I rarely drank hard liquor on my own, I poured myself a Scotch. I had misunderstood so much for fifteen years, Jerry's brio and confidence were fueled by alcohol. What would he be like now, without it? He seemed almost like another person, so vulnerable and raw. I had a newborn sympathy for him and all the hiding he had done. Because I had defined so much of my adult life through competition with him, I wondered what I'd be like from now on.

New information was forcing me to reinterpret all that I thought I'd known about Jerry. His illness had humbled him, but even with these changes, he remained one person, not splintered into three like Daphne. He couldn't help me now. I was on my own, missing both Daphne and Caroline without Jerry for a sounding board, so I took stock.

Caroline and Jerry both thought I was crazy, and I got an uncomfortable chill down my back that maybe they were right. I had failed at getting any two Daphnes in the same place. Was I crazy or was it a quantum anomaly? I had so little to go on and no way to create an experiment in the way I'd been taught to do. I would have to decide. It was like Schrödinger's two cats, but I had no mechanism to open the capsule and discover the truth, just my own intuition. I had to believe that the world I was seeing was real. If I couldn't trust my own perceptions and conclusions, my entire life would unravel. By uncovering hidden connections, I fantasized, I could understand some deep code about the world—though maybe I would never really understand anything.

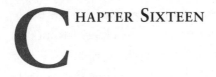

C HAPTER SIXTEEN

THE ABSENCE OF THE SCHRÖDINGER GIRLS put me in a state of chronic agita, but I had set rules for myself—that I would not call Ur-Daphne or SDS Daphne, the two high school girls.

So, I called Sarah Lawrence and got the art department secretary. "I'm looking for Professor Green," I started to explain.

I was about to recite the lie I'd prepared, that I was writing a feature article on Galen Green's Daphne paintings, when the obviously overworked staffer sighed in exasperation and cut me off. "He's in the low countries for two large-scale international exhibitions."

"Low countries?"

"In Brussels and Antwerp."

"Thanks," I managed to get out before she hung up. So, they were off in Europe again. I was jealous and annoyed. Why wasn't Daphne around when I wanted to see her?

At least I could happily anticipate Caroline returning to New York. After months in Indiana, she had called and asked me to pick her up at JFK on Valentine's Day. She didn't want to talk at her apartment, she said, because we inevitably ended up in bed.

This was a make-or-break visit. Since I didn't know her agenda, I couldn't prepare any talking points, whereas she must have been mulling over what she wanted to say for weeks. To prepare, I took down the Daphne time line after I'd studied it again, still hunting for clues. I folded it in half and stowed it in my center desk drawer as I cast a random glance at the calendar. I had drawn a circle around Valentine's Day. I planned on rehanging it after her visit.

I could acknowledge the day, or just ignore it. My instinct would have been to ignore it completely, but I was going to be on my best behavior with Caroline. I made the half-hour drive to Woodstock, where I found a gift, a little print in the Japanese style of a full amber moon, a shimmering disc rising over a slate-blue lake foregrounded by rushes and wild violet irises. The moon hovered close to the lake, full of expectation.

As I drove to the airport one of the FM stations was playing *Magical Mystery Tour*, the entire album. I would never have listened to the Beatles if I hadn't met Daphne. *Where were the girls?* The day was almost ten degrees colder than average for the middle of February, in the low twenties when I left, but it was clear now. The snow shone pristine white on the fields I passed. The album finished as I approached the airport. The final cut, "All You Need Is Love," made me even more anxious with its Valentine's Day sentiment, and I worried about the day's outcome.

I saw Caroline immediately, bending over the luggage carousel. She struck me as adorable in a very retro black-and-white houndstooth coat, the epitome of the

swinging-sixties look that was now out of style in favor
the San Francisco hippie look. I rushed over to her and
tried to embrace her, but she sidestepped my hug and
handed me the suitcase. Something was up, but at least
the listlessness of Thanksgiving was gone. This woman had
a subterranean purpose, though I had yet to discover it.

I gave her the print during dinner. She had no gift for
me, but that didn't bother me. In fact, I would have probably been uncomfortable accepting a gift in the midst of
all this ambiguity.

"I don't know how I found my way to art history," she
said, gazing admiringly at the print in her hands. "Going
home this time made me realize that there was absolutely
no art at all in my parents' house. Ever. This time at home
I really missed the consolation of paintings. I forgot how
bleak winter in a farm community in Indiana can be. Yes,
there's Fort Wayne, but the farm was just so lonely. I'm
relieved that my parents decided not to sell after all, or I
would have had to spend more time packing them up."

"You seem tired."

She nodded.

"Are you going to tell me what the hell we're about
to discuss?"

"Not today. Tomorrow. I'm too tired from traveling."

More suspense.

"I've been on tenterhooks for months."

"Relax. It's not as bad as all that. I promise. What
have you been up to?"

I told her about Jerry.

"Oh no. How's he doing?"

"I assume he's doing very well because they're letting
me pick him up for the day next Saturday, although they

extended his stay. He tried for an overnight, but his psychiatrist said he isn't ready."

"It's strange to imagine Jerry with his own psychiatrist. I hope I'll get to see him again . . . We agreed that if I dated you it would be inappropriate for me to be his patient."

"How did you afford all those sessions—five days a week at those rates?"

"I didn't go for psychoanalysis. Just therapy once a week."

"I thought Jerry only did psychoanalysis."

"Apparently there are a lot of things about Jerry you don't know."

I paused. "He said he wanted to settle down."

"Right now he needs to concentrate on his recovery. I saw a lot of alcoholism growing up in the sticks. It's a demon disease."

I was relieved when Caroline said that she wanted to go to bed, but then she said that she wanted to use the guest room. Okay. So, there was to be more frustration. I showed her to her room.

I left for class before she was up.

When I got home, she met me with high spirits. "At least someone's happy," I said. She seemed to have made some decisions because all the unfocused, lost demeanor she'd had when I saw her in Indiana had vanished.

"I slept pretty well, but that room doesn't really get warm, Garrett. Let's go find a second quilt for that bedroom." I couldn't believe it. She wanted to go shopping? Did she have a strategy in mind? She had the air of a general, yet her objective mystified me. We faced each other like large wary cats, she a panther, sleek and black, with her liquid dark hair, and me a lion with a scruffy mane and a pair of spectacles. I wished I'd known the rules of engagement.

"Is this elaborate foreplay? Right now my stomach's in knots."

She shook her head playfully. "Nope. I just want to buy a quilt." Her exuberance was not contagious. She was singing "Good Day Sunshine," just like the first morning we'd spent together, but I still felt anxious. The weather, however, had turned a bit warmer, the sky a radiant blue.

In Woodstock, we entered a store that displayed quilts and other handmade items on consignment. I enjoyed watching Caroline haggle with the salesclerk. She bargained the price down, and we purchased the quilt, a simple patchwork design in soft, faded colors. *So, being domestic feels like this,* I thought. Helena and I had lived in student housing, worried about tests and writing papers and the coming baby, and never made it as far as buying household items, or going to a nearby town just on a lark.

Back at home Caroline raced upstairs and put the quilt on the bed. The second bedroom became inviting. She confused me. Did she plan on spending many nights in my guest room?

She turned to me and announced, "Now we'll talk."

We seated ourselves in the parlor of my nineteenth-century house. Wide pine planks made up the floorboards with wide joists that allowed tiny objects to fall through to the basement. The mellow amber wood was so soft that a woman's high heels had dented the surface throughout. I had lived here for over five years, and it was my first real

home—the first place I'd ever furnished. I'd splurged on a
leather couch, and sometime later I purchased two arm-
chairs covered in soft brown velvet. I'd found the coffee
table at the side of the road. The discarded glass-topped
wrought-iron piece had been meant for the garden, but
functioned perfectly in my living room, even with all its
flaking paint. I had tried to repaint it, but the paint just
kept chipping off, and I decided that I liked it that way.
The legs were decorated with vines that I now glanced at
for the hundredth time as Caroline sat on the couch. This
was the first time I noticed they were laurel leaves. Of
course, I thought of Daphne.

I sat in a velvet chair facing Caroline. She took a deep
breath and said, "Garrett, the thing is . . . I want to have
a baby."

Her statement was so surprising that I blurted out,
"No way."

She went on. "I'm thirty-three. When I was engaged,
I daydreamed about the two perfect children we'd have,
and the home we'd make for them. We even had a dog in
these fantasies. When the engagement ended I focused on
establishing a place for myself in the art world."

"You've done a great job."

But she held up her hand to signal that she wasn't
finished. "I never met anyone else special, so I gave up
thinking about that future. My thirtieth birthday came,
and I figured that was it. You know, we live in a world in
which almost anyone who's going to marry is married by
then. But the night we made love, and I cried, all those
dreams came rushing back."

I tried to respond, but she still wasn't finished.

"When we saw each other again, a few weeks later

at your house, I felt the same connection. And then I saw the time line."

"I don't know why I didn't take it down."

"It scared me. I had imagined you to be the perfect father and saw this house, and pictured the white picket fence, and the dog and all of that, and then it just seemed like you were crazy, and my whole fantasy fell apart. I've been going back and forth about you ever since."

So, Caroline wasn't exactly who she seemed. I'd been right. She'd been run by a hidden agenda, and now so many of her reactions made sense. I had been auditioning for a part I knew nothing about. She'd been keeping this baby hunger from me. No wonder any sign of my instability sent her into a tailspin.

"I don't know what to say."

"I'm old enough to know that nothing is really perfect. But they start you out on these dreams when you're little. When they give you a doll. Then they read you *Cinderella*, and you dream of Prince Charming."

"I guess I'm not Prince Charming."

"Well . . . I've been struggling to let go of Prince Charming. He's only in a story. Anyway, I don't need a Prince Charming. People compromise."

"So I'd be a compromise?"

She said nothing to that.

"I had no idea you were thinking about children."

"Men are dumb."

"You *are* asking me to have a child with you, right?"

She nodded. "But I still want you to give up your Schrödinger girls."

Happy Valentine's Day to me. "I give them up, or what?" The ultimatum just hung in the air.

"There's something else. I don't want to have sex with birth control. Baby-making sex, or no sex."

"That's why you slept in the guest bedroom."

She stared at me, trying to glean a crumb of my reaction, but I had so many conflicting feelings I wanted to hide that I worked at keeping my visage neutral. *She's the crazy one if she expects me to give up the Schrödinger girls.*

"Why are you telling me this now?"

"My trip, I guess. Seeing people just getting on with their lives. And I can finally admit that I miss you when we're apart."

"That's good to hear. I have something to say too, but I need some tea."

My teapot was a squat, gunmetal-colored, Japanese-style vessel. A few years back I'd gone through an Alan Watts Zen phase, like everyone else at the time, and the teapot was its only legacy. I heated the water in a teakettle, but I removed it from the flame before it could whistle. I poured an ounce of hot water in the pot, rolling it around to heat the metal evenly. I poured the water out and spooned in the loose leaves of Irish breakfast tea and filled it with the boiling water. My mom had loved the ritual of teatime, and she had given me a cream-and-sugar set that I put on a tray with the teapot and two creamy china handleless cups that seemed Japanese. The tray was a charming amalgam of Japan and Ireland.

I watched Caroline's beautiful, long-fingered hands pour cream in the cups and spoon in the sugar. She held the pot at the perfect angle to avoid getting the loose leaves in the cups. Without handles, the cups were a little hot to hold, but the heat brought comfort too. An old house in upstate New York is drafty on February 15.

I began, "Most men just don't think that much about having kids." Not once had I ever considered Caroline and me having children, not even when Jerry talked about wanting kids. The thought of her wanting them hadn't entered my mind. She never cooed at babies on the street or dragged me to the window of a baby store or mentioned her friends' babies. "You remember me telling you about Helena? About how we got married as kids and got divorced soon after?"

"Of course."

"We got married because she was pregnant. And the baby, who was a girl, was stillborn. The umbilical cord choked her. Helena named her Amy. We fell apart after that, and then I stopped thinking about them—Helena and Amy."

I could see a shadow of anguish in her eyes. "Why didn't you tell me?"

"I don't know." I sounded shallow and evasive. "I just didn't know what to say. Jerry says it's because I never dealt with the pain of their loss. I only saw . . . Amy . . . once . . . so briefly. And I was ashamed to feel so little."

"And you couldn't tell me?"

"I never tell anyone. Jerry knows. He was at the wedding."

She was nodding to show me she understood. We finished our tea and repeated the tea ritual to have something to do. That's the beauty of having a metal teapot—it holds the heat without a cozy.

I broke the silence: "I resolved to never have children. Things can go wrong. Why open the door to pain?"

"But when we were at Coney Island and I wanted to

ride the teacup ride, you said you'd take our daughter and me on the ride. Don't you remember?"

I did. I had no idea why I'd said that except as a ploy to go ride the Cyclone. Talking about a hypothetical daughter had led Caroline to hope. Now she stared deep into my eyes. I felt uncomfortable. I thought of my glasses, my eyes hidden behind the lenses.

I said nothing, so Caroline continued: "You were young. You can change your mind."

"I would make a horrible father. Behaviorists do. The children of John B. Watson didn't fare well. One tried to commit suicide multiple times, and one succeeded. The other two had severe, lifelong stomach problems. There were rumors about B.F. Skinner doing experiments on his own two daughters, and he invented a crib that some derided as the 'Skinner box.' Though I don't believe the stuff about Skinner."

All the skeletons were marching out of the closet.

Caroline went on, "We don't have to raise her that way." And then she asked, "Does any of this have anything to do with your father?"

"Maybe, but you know I don't like to think about the past." I didn't want to acknowledge that psychoanalytic thought was beginning to influence me.

"Maybe John Watson was just a prick," she said.

"Maybe he was."

We were at an impasse.

"Let's table this for now. It's a lot to absorb," I said.

"No." She was adamant. "We should go on. What else are you keeping back? Tell me. More skeletons?" As she spoke, she stood up and began pacing. She wasn't as in charge of herself as she seemed.

"I'm worried that I'm stalled in my career. Behavior-ism isn't the 'it' thing anymore, and I don't know if I'll be able to publish or get promotions. Maybe I won't even be able to support a child."

"Is that all? That's called the human condition. You can expand." She still stood over me, but she had stopped pacing.

"I don't know if I can."

She spared me further reassurances.

"About the time line," I began. Even though I had taken it down, it was still very much on my mind. I wasn't giving up on my exploration of the mystery of Daphne. Not for Caroline, and not for a child. I missed those girls, and I was still convinced they held the clue to something important. "I just can't agree to give all that up. Not now."

Making quotation marks in the air, she ironically asked, "Do you have a 'time line' for when you might be willing to?"

"I don't."

"Being in Indiana, seeing my parents' dysfunctional lives, makes me want us to do better. My father drinks. My mother thinks she talks to ghosts and makes ridicu-lous hats she tries to pawn off on people. They haven't spent an entire evening together in twenty years. They go their separate ways. I want more than that. But they raised me anyway. And I want that too."

"Aren't you interested in the Schrödinger girls at all?"

"How old is Daphne?" she asked.

"About to turn seventeen."

"And how old would Amy be?"

I paused. "The same," I finally said.

"Do you need help putting these tea things away?"
she asked.

"No, it's nothing."

"Then I'm going upstairs for a nap."

I could hear her climbing the stairs to the guest bedroom while I remained downstairs tidying up. I imagined
her folding back the quilt we had just bought. She never
articulated the *or else* part of her ultimatum. I could have
described our relationship in two different ways. Either
we were two people deeply in love trying to make our way
toward each other, or we were adversaries, each fighting
for self-fulfillment while trying to cede as little freedom
as possible. Caroline was fighting for a child and a mate
who conformed to her picture of normalcy. I was fighting
for the right to see my Schrödinger girls and continue my
relationship with Caroline at the same time. Both were
true—we were loving friends, and we were adversaries.

We resolved nothing that day, but we agreed to keep
talking to each other. She seemed to have crossed a bridge
to more acceptance and was less angry.

Then, soon after this conversation with Caroline, I
heard from Daphne again.

CHAPTER SEVENTEEN

Daphne Note
Date: February 23, 1968
Days since last Daphne meeting: 124
Time line entry: Daphne at Stony Brook

A WEEK LATER, I HAD JUST gotten off the phone after checking on Jerry when it rang again. The voice on the other end of the line was young, female, and tentative.

"Dr. Adams?" she said. "This is Juliana Schloss. A friend of Daphne's? She's not in a good way, and we just didn't know who else to call. She had your card."

Which Daphne is this? I could feel the roller coaster of exhilaration and confusion that started in me whenever I had a chance to see one of the Daphnes. "Where are you calling from?"

"Stony Brook University."

"On Long Island, right?"

"Yeah. We're in my suite in the dorm. Daphne is sitting in a corner, high on drugs, and we can't get her to eat, shower, go out, or go to bed. This is the second day, and we're all very worried."

"Can I speak to her?"

"I'll go see if she'll come to the phone." After a pause

of several minutes she came back and reported, "No. She won't get up, and the cord doesn't reach that far. Could you come?"

Of course I'd go, but I considered for a moment. I had no classes the next day, Friday, so that was fine. "Should I come tonight or can it wait until morning?" I had never been there, and I didn't know how long it would take, but I figured somewhere around three hours.

"Tonight," she said immediately in a hoarse voice. "We have been taking turns watching her, but no one has been getting much sleep, and she hasn't slept for two days."

As I packed a few things in an overnight bag, obsessive thoughts circled repeatedly: *How did she get to Stony Brook? What's wrong?* My fingers compulsively drummed on the steering wheel. It was a long drive in the semi-black. I also gave some thought to which Daphne I'd encounter. Not Galen's Daphne for sure. My money was on SDS Daphne. Her rebelliousness might get her into this scrape.

Finding the dorm wasn't easy. The roads were dark and lined with barren trees. I drove around a little more, feeling increasingly anxious about the girl I'd find. In the darkness of the car, I couldn't make out the directions I'd written down. I reached into the glove box and retrieved a flashlight, and I was finally able to find the dorm. A cacophony of songs assailed me. Each room seemed to be playing a different album with stereos cranked up to maximum volume. I wondered how the kids could stand it. The sweet, earthy scent of marijuana was unmistakable. Juliana's suite was on the first floor at the end of the hall.

After my vigorous knock, she came to the door, an athletic, curly haired girl with the same wispy voice I'd first attributed to nerves. "I'm so glad you're here," she said. "I just didn't know what to do." She must have been nineteen or twenty.

"No, of course you didn't."

"She's this way."

I strode though the large common room and found Daphne rocking in the corner of Juliana's bedroom. There were three beds in the room: a set of bunk beds and a single bed with Daphne on it, facing the wall. She sat with her legs crossed on top of a navy blanket.

"Daphne?"

She turned. When she raised her head I saw butchered hair, hacked off unevenly, sticking out at all angles under a Yankees cap. Dirt dimmed its usual red hues, and her dull skin lacked color.

"Garrett." Her voice was flat. She had never said my name like that before. I couldn't be sure which Daphne sat before me.

I said, "All your beautiful hair."

"Yeah. I'm a real Jo March," she remarked sardonically.

"Joe March?"

"You'd have to be a girl who read *Little Women*. What are you doing here?" She spoke in a one-dimensional monotone.

"Juliana called me. She was worried."

"Okay."

I still had no idea how she felt about my visit, but decided to deal with practicalities and so I exited into the common room to consult with Juliana. "Can she sleep here tonight?"

"Yes," she assured me. "We have an extra bed."

"Which one do you want her to take?"

"She can have the one she's on. My roommate and I will take the bunks."

"Is she a student here, Juliana?" I asked, trying to glean enough information to solve this puzzle.

She shook her head.

"I'll go back to her and see if I can get her to sleep. Where is your roommate? And where are the other girls?"

"She's studying with her boyfriend, and the others are around. They'll be back soon, but they knew you were coming, so they wanted the room to be quiet. Everyone is worried."

"Why is she here? And why have you all taken her in?"

"You'll understand when you hear her story."

I walked back into the room, and Daphne was in the exact position in which I'd left her. "What's going on?" I asked. "Are you okay?"

"No. I felt good about two hours ago. Now I feel like shit."

"You're stoned on something, right?" Teaching at a college had brought me into contact with a lot of drugs. Kids came stoned to class all the time, and on occasion someone even came to class tripping on mescaline or LSD. Her affect struck me as different.

"I smoked a big wad of sticky black opium in a hash pipe," she announced with a touch of triumphant relish, her head nodding in rhythm with the drug.

Then Daphne curled up like a snail in its shell, still rocking on the bed. I sifted through everything I knew about opium, but all I could remember were images from the movies of Chinese opium dens and men in long braids and beautiful brocaded robes nodding off in the corners. The dorm room wasn't exotic, and neither was this sad girl in front of me, nodding out and far away. She uncurled herself, stopped rocking, and sat ramrod straight, her emerald eyes smoky with defiance.

"What happened?" I asked.

"They killed him."

"Killed who?"

Her expression was withering. "Come on. You can do better than that. Wait a minute. I'll show you." She reached for a large canvas bag and pulled out a copy of *The Portable Nietzsche*, the thick paperback with a purple cover. I had the same book. Then she held out a picture. I saw a handsome young Latino man in uniform.

"Who is this?" I asked.

"Don't you remember? The one I talked to about Nietzsche. Rick. He couldn't get a deferment because he wasn't a citizen. He only had a green card. He was a musician and knew Zappa from the downtown scene, but everyone there started calling him 'Baby Killer' when he went off to basic training, even though they would have deported his family if he hadn't. It was so unfair." I could hear a catch in her throat.

SDS Daphne had once told me about this young soldier. Ur-Daphne had tried to start a correspondence with an army private, but he had not written back. That meant that this girl was either SDS Daphne or a new Daphne who'd branched off from her. I wanted to find out just whom I was talking to. Then I remembered that SDS Daphne had only gotten one letter from Rick.

"Your pen pal, right?" I asked first. Then I tried to be nonchalant. "So, remind me. We saw each other last when?"

She nodded. "My pen pal. Rick told his friends to send me these mementos, the book with his signature, the picture, and the Yankees cap. He loved the Yankees, even though lately they suck."

I thought about the day I'd met Ur-Daphne, when I was so upset about the Yankees. This past season they hadn't done much better.

That poor kid was over in Vietnam rooting for the Yankees . . . "How did he die?" I asked.

"What does it matter? He's dead. He was twenty-three. Now I'll never get to meet him."

"What about Terry?"

"You mean the SDS guy? What about him?"

She hadn't answered my question about the last time we'd seen each other. Getting off the bed she said, "I got a long letter from Rick the day after I met you."

I felt relieved just to see her get off the bed. *This is progress,* I thought. She sidled over to the stereo and pointedly chose a record from the sprawl of albums on top of the bookshelves. The album cover featured a decal banana. The song she played was about heroin, the music raucously recreating the action of the drug. I could hear the lead singing, "*When I'm rushing on my run, and I feel just like Jesus' son, and I guess that I just don't know . . .*" I got chills listening to him.

Daphne returned to her cross-legged position. I went over to the stereo and gingerly lifted the needle off the album. I saw that the name of the group was the Velvet Underground, the singer, Lou Reed. Just hearing this snippet told me the group was talented but very close to the edge, and I shivered again. This new Daphne was close to the edge too.

"Planning on heroin next?" I asked. Then I decisively said, "No more Velvet Underground, and no more drugs."

"What does it matter?"

"I'm not going to have a philosophical discussion. You're not shooting heroin."

"I want to," she said. "And I know where to get it."

"That's really stupid. That's a way to become an addict. What would you do then?"

"Not everyone gets addicted. That's an ignorant old wives' tale."

"No, it isn't. Not absolutely everyone gets addicted, but most people do."

"How do you know?"

"I studied it. I'm very sorry about Rick, but do you think he'd want you to stick a needle in your arm? He wouldn't." Taking in her overall pallor I added, "You should have something to eat."

"Nah. Not after the opium."

"Could you sleep?"

"Maybe."

She took off her jeans and crawled under the covers, her head on the pillow, in a fetal position. She was asleep before I left the room.

Juliana stood waiting for me just outside, in the common area of the suite.

"Mission accomplished," I said.

"She's sleeping?"

"She is. Can you tell me what happened?"

Juliana launched into the story. Daphne had gone to a rock concert with a high school friend five days ago. Juliana hadn't gotten it straight if they'd been at the Felt Forum at Madison Square Garden that had just opened its doors right at Penn Station, or at Café à Go Go, or the Fillmore East, or somewhere else. She also wasn't sure what band they saw. Daphne hadn't been too forthcoming. Juliana knew that Daphne sat next to a young kid who happened to have a lot of drugs. He gave her handfuls of uncut grass, which she ate. Then he gave her seven Nembutal, which she swallowed, one by one, with no thought of the dosage. They must have been the very lowest dose available, or Daphne would be dead.

"Do you think she was trying to commit suicide?" I asked Juliana.

"I have no idea. I don't really know her."

"Go on," I said.

The friend Daphne was with wanted to go home, but Daphne didn't. Daphne was just straight enough to get to Penn Station with her friend, but in a stunning show of poor judgment she decided to stay in the city, even though her friend was leaving. According to Daphne, they parted ways when she was still standing and mostly all right. Soon after the girl got on the train, Daphne was overcome by such sleepiness that she just lay down in the middle of 34th Street in front of the Statler Hilton Hotel. She only remained alive because of the sparse traffic at that late hour, to hear her tell it.

A young guy, a Good Samaritan on speed, took pity on her and picked her up off the street. Mr. Speed Freak had an open invitation at Stony Brook to visit friends. He chose that night, and took this wasted girl on the train with him going east. He crashed with friends and Daphne slept on an empty bed in the room. The Nembutal was so powerful that she awoke in the boys' suite twenty-four hours later.

"The awful thing," Juliana told me, "is that when she came to, Mr. Speed Freak was having sex with her without a condom. According to Daphne, she just shrugged. I told her that this was a form of rape and wanted her to report him to the police, but she just said she just didn't care who she fucked and besides, he had rescued her, so he deserved a reward."

I couldn't bear to hear any more of this. I should have been there and protected her, although I knew these were irrational thoughts. I understood Juliana's charity. "You were hurt like that once?"

"Yeah." She clenched her jaw to hold back tears, and her whispery voice grew almost inaudible so I had to strain to hear her. "When I was fifteen. By my mother's brother. I can't call him my uncle. No one believed me, especially not my mother. It almost killed me. When one of the guys from the suite in the boys' dorm thought Daphne should be with women to take care of her, he brought her here. He knew my history.

"Mr. Speed Freak sold drugs and had sex with half the women on the floor, and abandoned each one just as fast. He was using everyone. Finally, the boys came over to eject him from campus. They put him on a train and warned him never to come back. But Daphne is still in really bad shape. She's grieving for the guy in Vietnam, feeling sexually exploited, fucked up on drugs, and she has nowhere to go. She's been camping out on people's couches, living with friends, or sometimes on the street for a while now. I get the feeling that she dropped out of high school. Something in Rick's letter. You have to do something." Juliana urgently grasped my hand.

"I will. I'll figure out something."

I went to the bathroom and leaned my forehead against its cool tiles. I thought I might throw up. I couldn't process the desperation Daphne must have felt to swallow seven pills that could have ended her life. I felt angry that she would throw away her future because Rick had lost his. I tiptoed into the room and was gratified to discover that Daphne was still asleep. I would have been glad to sleep on the floor of the common room, but boys and men were prohibited from sleeping in the women's dorms.

After I checked into a motel I walked across the street and sat in an all-night donut joint. I wasn't ready to go to sleep so I ordered a coffee, which I nursed for about forty-five minutes till it turned stone cold.

I thought of my little Junior League Ur-Daphne sitting in our coffee shop wearing the pearls we'd ridiculed. I had been put off by that Daphne's primness. How I'd laughed when I discovered that I had not lost her to a more conservative vision of herself. Now that reaction seemed foolish and indulgent. That Daphne did not know the sadness of this hollow-cheeked girl. My first Daphne was still connected to the nourishing roots of childhood, whether she wore pearls or a hippie bead necklace. This young woman in the Yankees cap had been severed from childhood completely. Both girls seemed made of the same stuff, but life events had shaped them so differently. An open question in psychology was whether personality and character keep evolving. Now I was certain they did.

Their dissimilarities went beyond the simple observation that circumstances conditioned each Schrödinger girl to react in a different way; this was something more. Just as in Borges, these were forking paths. At the pulsing point of divergence, one girl became four different girls, and even the inner kernel of self became reshaped by the path she traveled. The Schrödinger girls both were and weren't the same person. The metaphysical implications were dizzying, raising questions about the nature of the self that psychology might never answer. Behaviorism didn't ask any of these questions, and the rest of my training as a psychologist hadn't prepared me to answer them either.

That Saturday morning I had more pressing concerns. I was up early, after only a few hours of sleep. Dawn was an uneventful display. The darkness gradually lifted to reveal a charcoal-gray sky that lightened into a pearly, almost nacreous silver. Then it was day. There was no room service, but I'd brought back a couple of donuts from the night before; I'd get coffee later. It was too early to return to the college. I had already decided to consult Jerry about how to help this girl, yet it was also too early to call him. I had brought something to read, but instead I stared out the window in mindless absorption. In the early-morning light this stretch of commercial road was dull. I was about five miles south of campus, and the large stores, gas stations, motels, and car dealerships were uninspiring.

At eight a.m. I called Jerry. Any calls to him had to be screened through a switchboard. *Poor Jerry. He can't even screen his own calls.*

"Garrett?"

"Yeah, it's me. How are you doing, friend?"

"As well as can be expected. I might become a holy roller now that I'm no longer a sinner."

"So you're not still an atheist?"

"Kiddo, what's going on so bright and early? We're still on for tomorrow?"

"I'm not sure. I encountered a new Daphne, and she is seriously abusing drugs and is suicidal. She definitely needs professional help. I don't know where to take her or what to do."

"Does she have parents you could involve?" If he thought I was delusional, he didn't show it.

Although I had resolved never to involve her parents, Jerry's question made sense that morning. "I'm not sure. Trust me, that wasn't a question I could ask last night."

"Where are you?"

"I'm at Stony Brook, way out in the boonies on Long Island."

"If I could arrange it, could you drive her to this re-hab center?"

"She's not eighteen yet. I don't know if I could get parental permission. Does that make a difference? And I don't know who'd pay for it."

"Let me work on things here. Can I speak to her?"

"Not right now. I'm at a motel. I couldn't very well stay in an all-girls' dorm."

"No, of course not. Call me back when you're with her."

I waited an hour and half before driving north along a street with only trees and traffic lights. The five miles were just a blur of barren branches. I could see that the school was being built in a particularly undistinguished style. Puddles and mud filled in all the space between buildings, but the dorm was easy to find by daylight. I parked in the large student parking lot.

Juliana must have been expecting me, or seen me through the window, because she was right by the door when I knocked. "Yes, Daphne is up," she said before I could ask.

"Will I be disturbing anyone if I walk straight into the room?"

"No, not at all. Most of the suite is at the train station to go home for the weekend. Daphne and I are alone."

Daphne seemed to have recovered from the night before. The pink had returned to her face, though she still appeared tired and pale. "I was a brat to you last night," she said, avoiding looking at me.

"You were fine, just unhappy. I am so sorry about Rick."

She took off her baseball cap. I could see that she'd gotten up early enough for a shower. Her hair still hung in uneven bunches, but at least it was clean now. Her copper-penny auburn strands shone in the eastern morning light.

"I need to ask you some questions," I said.

"Okay."

"The first is about your parents."

"I'm an emancipated minor."

"That makes things easier. Would you consider going into rehab?"

"I guess so. Everything hurts and I don't know where to go."

"Let's get some air. Get some breakfast. Ask Juliana if she'd like to come."

Both girls climbed into the backseat of the car. It was a cold, hard, bright morning. Light fell in spiky darts, and crisp air shone blue against an even bluer sky. We drove until I saw a beach, *West Meadow*, the sign said, deserted in the winter. The blue-green waves crashed and receded. We walked along the sand, holding our collars against the wind. After ten minutes we were too cold to keep walking so we went somewhere close by for hot chocolate and buns. After eating, I took the girls back to the dorm. This time I called Jerry from the common room phone.

He had gotten his lawyer working on things. God bless Jerry. Since Daphne was an emancipated minor there was no problem making arrangements for her without her parents' consent. He had somehow finagled a scholarship, if that's what you'd call it, from an affiliated facility nearby. Apparently, a lot of people from New York City went into rehab there, just north of the city.

Jerry said, "I thought it better that we not be in the same facility anyway. Too many potential entanglements."

"But didn't you say yours is the best?"

"Me and my big mouth. Don't worry. It will be just fine, and she'll have somewhere safe to be and a chance to work through this . . . Now I have to talk to her."

Daphne got on the phone. I heard her confirm all the details I had given Jerry. Then I heard her emphatically declare, "Yeah, I'll go into rehab. I'll try to get better."

She had come so far in just one day from the alienated, emotionless girl I was with yesterday. Or maybe that had just been the opium. She sounded more like the old Daphne. She would spend one more night with Juliana, and then I'd drive her to the facility upstate.

CHAPTER EIGHTEEN

WHEN WE ARRIVED AT THE REHAB CENTER, just before Daphne got out of the car she gave me a Russian painted box. It was only two inches round, black with colorful Russian birds and flowers painted on it. I tried to open it, but the top was screwed on tightly.

"Thank you. I'll keep this," I told her. It would be part of my collection that included the snapshot, the postcards, the books, and the albums—all the objects that Daphne had brought into my life.

The girl stood in front of the large glass doors, small and forlorn. She had known me for almost a year, but I had known this fourth Daphne for only two days. This Schrödinger mystery gave life an odd quality. Each new girl knew me better than I knew her. She had met me in April 1967, her memory of that day was intact, but when a new avatar entered my life I would be meeting her for the first time. I had to be careful to hide the discrepancy from her and act as if we were old friends, which in a weird way we were.

She disappeared into the building, and I drove a little way to see Jerry. Despite the twenty-degree weather, he was waiting outside, jumping up and down to warm up. "Finally an adventure," he said.

I chose Rhinebeck because I'd taken Caroline there, and Jerry was fine with anyplace. The colonial setting of the old inn had a charm that I thought would be a welcome change from the sterile environment of rehab. Without beer, wine, cocktails, shots, and Irish coffees, we would have to find new rituals.

"The thing is," he began, "I don't know how to be without the hooch. It was like the yellow-brick road, giving me direction."

"Can't you just be the person you were, but sober?"

"The person who designed my life was a drunk."

"Do you still believe in psychoanalysis?"

"Maybe I don't believe in penis envy or the castration complex. Maybe I don't think people need to lie on a couch five days a week free-associating. But I do believe in having a trained and responsible friend to hold your hand when you're exploring the most painful aspects of your life."

"I don't revere behaviorism the way I used to either. I don't know what I believe, but I can't agree with the denial of the idea of a self."

"Man, professionally we're a mess, aren't we?" But his voice was playful, and the corners of his mouth turned up ever so slightly. "I like being in therapy. It helps you see what makes you tick. It's been years."

"Maybe I could use that," I said.

"It wouldn't hurt."

"Do you believe me? About the four girls?"

"Um, no. It's too far-fetched, but I did talk to a very unhappy girl."

This was a blow. Simultaneous realities represented by the different avatars were evident to me, but not to anyone else. If only I could uncover irrefutable proof. Yet I still hadn't seen two of them together.

"But Jerry? What else is there to think? What is your explanation?" He ignored my question, and then my mind wandered. Eventually I clued back into to what he was saying about himself.

". . . family came from the Old Country they were seeking a savior. A big, gaudy, American-style success. My father worked his heart out as a catering waiter, but we were always really poor. The Lower East Side was no picnic. Gangs. Getting beaten up all the time for being Jewish, often by you Irish boys. So who was to be the savior? Who was the darling *tateleh*? Me, of course. My mother told anyone who would listen that I was going to become a doctor. It was an act of rebellion to become a psychologist and not a doctor. But to make her happy I had to bring in big bucks."

"We weren't exactly rolling in it either, Jerry."

"But being from his wealthy family, your dad had already been to Oz and seen behind the curtain. Your parents didn't expect you to rescue everyone. My family did. Grandparents, even aunts and uncles."

"And the drinking?"

"Ambivalence. Fear. Even at eighteen I knew I would never be able to save them all. And then there was the Holocaust and the survivor guilt. We all had it."

"Ah." I understood everything he was saying. I had reacted to my past in the opposite way: I'd built a snail shell of research psychology around me and crawled into it, behind my glasses.

"Even sports. I needed to be the big man. Always competing."

"Do you miss drinking?"

"Only every minute."

As we drove back I put on one of the new FM stations. I saw Jerry stiffen and become restless. Dylan sang, *"There are no truths outside the gates of Eden . . ."*

"You really listen to this music? I can't get into it. And Bob Dylan's voice is so grating."

"Whoa," I said. "Hmm. Dr. Freud, what do we make of this hostility?"

Jerry laughed. Then we heard "It's All Over Now, Baby Blue," also from *Bringing It All Back Home*. *"You must leave now, take what you need, you think will last, but whatever you wish to keep, you better grab it fast."* The lyrics, the tune, and Dylan's voice found their way straight to my core.

"Give Bob Dylan a chance. He'll turn you inside out."

I silently thanked Daphne, who had led me out of the straight jacket of the fifties and into the openness of the sixties. I had traded a black-and-white still for a Technicolor movie, and I wanted to share this transformation with Jerry, who had helped me rescue Daphne. I wanted him to hear how the Beatles and Bob Dylan and so many other bands talked about their inner worlds the way I did.

I got out of the car at Jerry's rehab center and practiced my newfound openness by giving him a big bear hug. His startled expression was comical, but then he returned the embrace. I waved as he glanced back before entering the one-story, tidy, modernist construction that was made more open by walls of safety glass, decorated with a neat lawn and well-kept topiaries. A tidy garden is a tidy mind? I reflected on the odd coincidence of both

Jerry and Daphne being in rehab at the same time, and felt gratitude that whatever my problems were, I wasn't there with them.

CHAPTER NINETEEN

ALTHOUGH CAROLINE'S ULTIMATUM defined the space between us, now that I had met this fourth, vulnerable Daphne, I was even more committed to my Schrödinger girls. I fiercely hoped that Caroline's demand would prove negotiable.

We had a date set for St. Patrick's Day. I didn't usually celebrate this holiday out at bars. I had a kind of self-righteous *I'm a real Irishman* chip on my shoulder, but I made an exception. We arranged to meet in Kips Bay at Molly's, a great old Irish pub owned by a real Irishman. A version of the tavern had been at that location since the 1890s. The bar sported sawdust on the floor and was as close to being in Dublin as you could get in New York. I'd spent a lot of my life in an Irish pub doing my homework at a table while my mother tended bar. It would be a big night for her pub too. Even in Florida people wanted to be Irish on March 17.

When I got to the bar it was so crowded I could barely squeeze in. It wasn't going to be the same without Jerry. St. Patrick's Day had always been a day he performed. He affected a great Irish brogue and recited speeches from *Ulysses*. He was a much more literary guy than I, who had never made it through Joyce's novel. I couldn't recite any Yeats either.

Gazing out into the dense crowd I saw a sea of green shirts, green ties, green dresses, green hat ornaments, and green carnations. Even hippies were in green tie-dye and green bandannas. The place wasn't that big and so many people shoehorned in that I had no idea if Caroline was there yet. As I tried to get through, a few single women, longing for an Irishman for the night, decided I'd do and accosted me in exaggerated Irish accents. "Hi, darlin'," one blonde enthusiastically crooned, and another carrot-topped redhead called out, "Paddy, free for the night?"

My mom had always told me I looked Irish, but I didn't really see it. I didn't have the family's bright blue eyes or black Irish raven hair. I had the middling coloring of my Boston father. "It's the face," Mom said, and maybe so. The holiday didn't have much to do with the working lives of my family of cops, teachers, and nurses. My mom had begun tending bar to put herself through nursing school, though she decided she liked the conviviality of a bar more than the atmosphere of sickness at a hospital. Even so, it had been a hard life for us both.

The corned beef and cabbage and penny whistles also had little to do with the life of the old sod where we still had relatives. Ireland was all poverty, verdure, and stories. Still, it was fun to hear all the Irish songs and see so many Irish movies on television for the day. But after St. Paddy's Day I had no desire to see *Darby O'Gill and the Little People* or *The Quiet Man* until the next year.

After elbowing my way through the crowd for a while, I gave up and stood in place like a rock in the middle of a current of swarming people. I wasn't having any fun, and I was nervous about seeing Caroline. She hadn't given me a deadline for my decision about Daphne except to point out that she was only getting older.

Finally, after what felt like eons of waiting, I heard Caroline's contralto voice: "I'm here, Garrett." She was tall enough that when she lifted her arms over her head I could just see her waving hands. I made my way over to her, though to my surprise and chagrin, she wasn't alone. *Who the hell is this guy?* She was arm in arm with an extremely attractive man. Men may claim we don't notice things like that, but it's a lie. He reminded me of an actor whose name I couldn't remember, whom Caroline and I had seen in the movie *Barefoot in the Park*. I wanted to punch him in the nose just for being with my girl and for being so handsome. Neither he nor Caroline wore green. She introduced her friend as Tom, explaining that they had dated when she first came to New York and had run into each other, quite by chance, a few weeks ago.

Caroline had a Cheshire grin on her face, but we guys were awkward.

"I'm an actor," Tom began. Of course he was. The loud buzz in the bar was beginning to make me feel dizzy, and his vibrant blue eyes made me even more self-conscious about my glasses. That settled it. I was getting contacts. "Nothing interesting. Just some commercials. Toothpaste." He grinned in an exaggerated manner, comically showing his teeth.

Yup. He had perfect teeth. He also had a deep baritone voice. If Caroline had a child with this man, the kid would win the genetic lottery. I had a fleeting paranoid thought that she had hired him to show me that I couldn't dither around for long, that she could do better than me.

Tom was saying something about my being a professor, but the noise distracted me.

Tom went to the bar for three pints. "What's he doing here?" I asked her.

If she heard me over the roar of the bar she gave no indication. I had no idea what she'd told Tom to get him to come along. He returned with the pints, but after downing them, we all got tired of the din, so we gave up on St. Patrick's Day and found a quiet little coffee shop.

When we each had our coffee in front of us, I said, "So did you guys hear that Bobby Kennedy announced his candidacy for the presidency yesterday? It's a perfect St. Patrick's Day announcement. Members of my family have a shrine to the Kennedys in their homes. The Kennedys and the pope. I'm not kidding."

"What do you think of McCarthy?" Tom asked.

"Too cerebral," Caroline responded. "I would rather have Kennedy. I'm just so afraid it's going to be that bastard Nixon. RFK is the only one who can beat him."

Tom must have discovered that being a third wheel wasn't all that much fun because he excused himself and walked over to the pay phone. When he returned he announced that he had to leave. Back to a bar, I imagined. I've never been the kind of guy to make a scene, but I wanted to make one then. I itched to tell him to stay away from my girl, yet he was such an affable guy that when we got up to leave we just shook hands like gentlemen. If Caroline wanted Tom instead of me, there was really nothing I could do about it.

When we were finally alone, Caroline and I almost glared at each other. "He's a real looker," I said.

"He's great. Smart. Starting to have some success."

"How far has it gotten?"

"I'm not sure our present contract allows you to ask questions like that," she replied. "How far have you gotten in renouncing this crazy Schrödinger obsession?"

"Not very," I admitted. "In fact, I met a fourth girl."

Caroline's face took on a wary, hardened expression. When she heard Stony Brook Daphne's story she murmured appropriate words of concern, but her eyes were noncommittal. Then, surprisingly, she asked me to go back to her place. We had gotten to a very cynical space with each other, where some sex was better than none, but neither of us was happy about using each other.

"What about your edict about not having sex with condoms?" I asked.

"I'll get a papal dispensation."

"I don't know, Caroline. Bringing Tom was quite a stunt."

"Yeah, I guess it was," she said, laughing. "But all's fair in love, etcetera."

"You're playing hardball."

"I'd like to play with your balls." Then Caroline blushed. *She must be really horny*, I thought, which meant she wasn't yet sleeping with Mr. Blue Eyes.

When we got to her apartment, we wanted each other, but each of us came with baggage that made things complicated. As I kissed Caroline's delicate breasts, thoughts about the babies they might feed crept in. Nothing was as simple as the first times we'd made love, when the world sang with joy. Still, as usual, we were good together.

I loved having her body curled against mine, her head on my shoulder. "Have we seen the end of Tom?" I asked.

"I don't know. Have we heard the last of Daphne?"

Her implication was unmistakable—forget them, or she'd pursue Tom. I understood that it must have been difficult for her to watch me think so much about these mystery girls when she longed to create a real child. Caroline was tireless in her attempts to rescue me from my quixotic allegiance and return me to a reality she recognized.

"You explained to me theories about different realities. What if this is true for all of us, and we are unaware of these realities, in the same way we can't hear a dog whistle or see ultraviolet light, but we know those sounds and sights are real? What if there are as many Garretts as there are Daphnes? What if reality is so complex that there are worlds upon worlds of alternate realities and alternate Carolines, Garretts, Daphnes, and Toms? What if there's a Garrett who is running a rat experiment right now, and one who's a physicist and one who is serving his country in Vietnam, but we have no access to these realities?"

"Exactly," I said. "What if? And what if for some reason a barrier dissolves and we can see four of these alternate realities?"

"Then the outstanding variable would not be Daphne, it would be *you* and your ability to see these realities. What if we are all part of realities we never know? What if you and I are already married with three children in an alternate universe?"

These were stunning thoughts—that Caroline and I were already parents, that Daphne was not the anomaly but the rule, and that the only weird circumstance would be the unexplained break in the membrane keeping these different realities separate.

"But how does that help us? I would still want to spend my time thinking about my ability to perceive these alternate universes. I do wonder what happened that day in April last year in the bookstore that brought this mystery into my life. And the day at the gallery, the third time I saw Daphne, when we first glimpsed a different reality when we viewed the portrait. You were there too, when I first discovered there were two Schrödinger girls. And I started to fall in love with you. That was magic too. You're part of this, Caroline."

"Maybe, but I don't feel like it, though it is a kind of miracle whenever we meet anyone who truly moves us. We don't meet many of these people in one lifetime—the people who lead us forward. Why should this idea, the idea of these simulacra, be so engrossing to you instead of the miracle that we found each other at all?"

"They show some kind of rent in the fabric of many universes, a momentous exception. That has to mean something."

"You are so stubborn. Is it crazy to be so obstinate? You know for a fact about these many universes? And anyway, you can only live in one reality."

"But I could do that and still make visits to these other realities."

"You're not going to give up on this Daphne mystery, are you?" she asked, her voice sinking rhetorically.

"Not right now." I could tell I was being a jerk to her, yet I couldn't do anything else. I wondered why she put up with me at all. We were good in bed, but it couldn't be just that.

"I have no idea why I feel so comfortable with you when you drive me bonkers. So much for my ultimatums."

CHAPTER TWENTY

CAROLINE'S CAMPAIGN WAS GETTING TO ME. I had to consider the possibility that I wouldn't be able to keep both her and the Daphnes in my life. The thought made me feel as if I were drowning—the premonition of grief. I experimented with imagining my life without Caroline, then without the Daphnes. The drowning feeling only got worse. Somewhere I had read the sentence, *The first death is the worst.* That was my father. His posthumous nocturnal visit allowed me to keep breathing, but as soon as he disappeared for good I began sinking into my grief. I had spent days at Yankees games learning baseball statistics to have something to hold onto. This preoccupation served me so well that I got really comfortable with numbers and was a statistics whiz in grad school.

But I'd shut down when Amy was stillborn and Helena just drifted away. The random girl in the rain slicker had been the first person in fifteen years to penetrate my shell, and once she had, I'd been able to allow Caroline to slip in too. I didn't want to go back to the petrified state I'd been in, impervious to history, impervious to art, and impervious to love.

No matter how many people thought I was crazy, I'd hold onto the reality of the Daphnes now. Caroline was my life, but the Daphnes were my signposts, directing me toward real engagement with life.

However, things could not go on like this. Caroline was too concerned about her biological clock, and I keenly felt the pressure she exerted when she spoke about the adventures she had with Tom. I didn't know exactly how things stood between them, but I would have to do something soon.

I began rereading the book that had brought Ur-Daphne and me together, hoping for an answer I might have missed. I could just about follow the math that led up to the Schrödinger equation, but that was as far as I could get. I had an acute wish to be a physicist, although when I went to one of the guys at New Paltz for some insight, he didn't understand quantum physics any more than I did. He was unperturbed, and explained, "To be a race car driver you don't really need to understand exactly what's under the hood of the car." He was happy just manipulating the math he did understand, and teaching it to each new crop of beginning physics students. He left the unanswered questions of the universe to someone else.

Although it was a superstitious idea, I decided to return to the scene of our first encounter, the Bookmasters on Columbus Circle. I stopped by Jerry's beforehand, for the first time since he'd gotten out of rehab.

"Hey, kid." He'd come to the door in a silk robe and slippers, even though it was already past ten in the morning.

"Are patients coming soon?" I asked.

"No. I'm free for about three hours."

"You seem to have a lot of time of your hands these days. Are you having trouble getting back into your practice?"

"No. Why would you say that?" But he turned away as he answered.

"How about a walk? Twenty blocks to Columbus Circle?"

"Not that stupid Bookmasters," he groaned. "Still with that Schrödinger business?"

"Yup."

"How's Caroline?" he asked.

"Fine. Having a flirtation with someone else."

"You're being dumb. Maybe I should make a play for her. I don't have a professional connection to her anymore. She's an incredible woman. That would serve you right."

"Shut up, Jerry. I can't help it if she can't stand my Daphne investigation."

"Of course. I forgot. You have to solve the mysteries of the quantum universe. And while you're at it, find out if there really is free will, and then make sure you're quite sane."

"I don't think analysts are supposed to talk like that."

"I'm not your analyst. Just give me a minute." He went off to change.

I had become a sucker for spring. The crocuses and daffodils were everywhere, and the West Side cherry blossoms were poised to open any day. When we got to the bookstore there were a few high school kids buying Regents exam study guides, and a geezer or two leafing through magazines. We both headed over to psychology. I picked up Ulric Neisser's *Cognitive Psychology*, which had been published in the past year, and Jerry found something too—*Gestalt Therapy: Excitement and Growth in the Human Personality*, a book that had been around since the early fifties. It seemed like a book I should be familiar with. Meeting Daphne had prompted a new interest in personality theory. Before now, Jerry and I had both dismissed any approach not narrowly defined by our loyalties to psychoanalysis and behaviorism, though it seemed our horizons were widening.

"You're interested in Gestalt now?" I asked.

"Yeah, Fritz Perls is shaking up therapeutic practice. I'm too stuck on Freud, as you've always said."

"Hallelujah! *Ding dong, the witch is dead.*"

"Hey, let's not throw the baby out with the bathwater," Jerry said. "Freud is still Big Daddy. What do you have against Freud anyway?" Obviously, he knew what I had against Freud—his discussion of internal drives without empirical evidence.

The book on cognitive psychology was a groundbreaking look at perception and thought beyond the mechanical investigations of behaviorism, so with my quarry in hand, I left Jerry in psychology and walked over to the physics section. Among the volumes, a book with a bright red spine caught my eye. It was a recently published overview of quantum mechanics. I immediately went to the index and found the Schrödinger references. I got goose bumps when I read this: *Schrödinger and Simultaneous Realities.* I raced to the entry.

According to this volume, while lecturing in Ireland, where the scientist repatriated, Schrödinger had announced that although the audience might think him crazy, his equations led to the strong possibility of simultaneous realities. *So here it is in black and white!* Schrödinger had actually predicted the possibility of simultaneous incarnations of Daphne. I wished for magic powers that could summon the four girls to the store right then and there. I closed my eyes, but of course, no Schrödinger girls appeared.

I called Jerry over and showed him the entry. "For god's sake, Garrett!" he bellowed.

I jumped back in surprise and hit my elbow on one of the bookshelves. Why do they call it the funny bone? My elbow really hurt. I let out a small yelp of pain, but he was undeterred.

"I am so sick of this shit. We've been talking about this for months now. You are letting a great woman get away while you are off on a Don Quixote quest for mysterious girls who are going to reveal to you the nature of reality. Give me a break! Are you in love with these girls?" His voice boomed so loud that the clerk asked us to leave. That had never happened to me in a bookstore before.

"Wait for me outside," I said. "Give me your book. I'll buy it."

I was angry as I walked out, and the tinkling bells that alert the clerks to new customers annoyed me. I was rehearsing the complaint I'd make to Jerry when I found him around the corner of the building, but seeing him like this jolted me into the awareness that something really was wrong. He'd never just gone off on larks in the middle of the day. He'd always been too busy. And his clothes. I couldn't remember the last time I'd seen him in sneakers and a sweatshirt.

"Don't you have patients to get back for?"

"I have time," he said dismissively. He crossed the street and ambled over toward Columbus's statue. Columbus Circle was a sleepy place, without any of the bustle of Times Square. Besides the famous landmark, it was just a traffic loop. Pigeons marked their territory and there was a flurry of flapping wings as I followed him to the Columbus monument.

"This is the heart of the heart of the city," he remarked. Then his mood changed, and he impatiently said, "Let's go home."

Being three inches taller, I had no difficulty matching his stride.

When I was abreast of him he said, "I lied. Things aren't okay."

"No kidding. Do you still see patients?"

"Yeah, sometimes."

"What are you doing for money?"

"I saved a lot. I mean, *a lot*."

"What happened to your practice?"

"I hate psychoanalysis without the booze. People's problems are just so boring. And they repeat themselves. Like you've been doing for almost a year now. Move on, kid. And did you notice that even Schrödinger thought he himself might be crazy? And what was the deal with moving to Ireland with his scandalous ménage à trois? Booted out of Germany and Austria, probably. Isn't there a story where he chases around a fourteen-year-old girl? Sounds very Apollo-and-Daphne, doesn't it? And that's the guy you want to emulate?"

I ignored his outburst. "I thought you loved being an analyst."

"I was drunk. The patients were more interesting then. Now I know why Freud did cocaine."

"Wasn't that for research?"

"Don't be such a stickler."

"You can't get interested in your patients while you're sober?"

"That's about the size of it."

"What are you going to do?"

"That's why I'm reading up about Gestalt. It's interactive and might keep me more engaged."

"Don't you need training for that?"

"That's the thing. I'm thinking about going out to California. To Esalen."

"That kooky hippie institute?"

"The very same. I thought you were the one going all sixties. Perls is there. Right now, I can't even bring myself to make appointments," he explained with the slight hostility I'd been hearing in his voice all morning.

"Are you always this irritable now?"

"Pretty much. I miss being drunk."

"Then, yeah. You do have to do something. But does it have to be something as drastic as leaving, giving up the practice it's taken you ten years to build? Give it some time."

I guess he didn't want to hear that because when we reached his stoop he abruptly said, "Gotta go," and took the steps to his brownstone apartment two at a time. He disappeared without giving me a backward glance, and left me standing there on the sidewalk feeling abandoned and angry. I knew I should have been more understanding. Jerry was still trying to find his footing after rehab.

I worked off my annoyance by retracing my steps to Columbus Circle in long, loping strides. This time spring made no impact on my mood. I headed to Caroline's gallery. She was talking to a potential customer when I walked in. As usual, she wore one of her little black dresses.

She was so beautiful I almost laughed out loud. I could feel my eyes widen when I glimpsed another Daphne painting on a nearby wall. I had seen all the paintings from this series with Jane in Galen's studio, but I hadn't been giving the work much thought. Each deserved its own viewing. And now here she was—half nymph, half tree, caught suspended in a moment of transformation. She was *uttering green leaves*, as my SDS Daphne had said at Bryant Park. My sharp intake of breath was just audible and Caroline glanced away from her potential buyer and toward me.

As her customer exited the gallery she ambled over and said, "Trust you to be standing under a Daphne painting. Never mind, I don't want to talk about our problems at work. Why are you here?"

"I wanted to see you. Have any time?"

"Actually, I don't. I'm leaving a little early to have dinner with Tom before he goes on stage. He's in an off-Broadway play. Do you want to come? To the play, not the dinner."

"Maybe. How far have things gone between you two?"

She narrowed her eyes, trying to decide just how much she wanted me to know. "We're seeing each other. It's not that serious. Yet."

"What's the stumbling block?"

"That information is beyond your security clearance."

"I think I'll pass on the play."

"I thought you might."

"Jerry is thinking of leaving New York," I said. "And I had the brilliant idea of taking over his apartment." I had improvised that on the spot. Although I really had no chance of being able to afford it, I thought it would pique her interest. Yet even I could hear that I said this with anger and defiance. Then I pivoted on my heels and abruptly left. I felt estranged from both Jerry and Caroline as I reflected on the fact that intimate relationships were often war zones.

CHAPTER TWENTY-ONE

JERRY HAD LEFT ME ON THE SIDEWALK without ceremony, and now I'd added to my alienation by doing a similar thing to Caroline. What was going on? The ambiguities of the Schrödinger mystery were weighing on me, and both my friends had made it clear that they didn't believe in the validity of my experience. If your best friends won't back you up, who will? It should have been obvious to them that the more they questioned me, the more I would want to prove them wrong.

But it was worse. Jerry, who had been my sidekick since we were eighteen, was seriously considering quitting New York, and Caroline was flirting with replacing me with Tom. I couldn't blame either of them. Kudos to Jerry for trying to build a sober life, and as for Caroline, our little dance had been going on long enough. Although there was desperation to her attempts to satisfy her intense desire for a child, there was nobility too. I'm sure I didn't come across like this to her. But I couldn't help being the person I was, and who I was now would forever more include Daphne.

Why had I said that about Jerry's apartment? I had no idea. Was it merely to entrance Caroline, whom I feared was drifting away, or did I secretly harbor a desire to move back into Manhattan? Jerry had always joked that I envied him his apartment; clearly, I did. In truth, I hoped Jerry would come to his senses, drop all that Esalen business, stay in New York, and return to his practice.

I had taken the train so I could leave my car with the mechanic for a new set of brakes, and on the way home the early-spring Hudson River Valley scenery was whizzing by outside the train window. I had the whole two-hour ride back to study my new physics book. After I'd followed up on all the Schrödinger references I perused the index and found this entry: *The Many-Worlds Interpretation.* Here was a detailed, cogent discussion of the ideas of Hugh Everett III, a man who'd earned a doctorate in physics from Princeton with a thesis that postulated this idea of many worlds. His idea explained what happens to the Schrödinger equation over time—in other words, the progression of a quantum system, that portion of the universe under investigation for its wave-particle duality. Since light operated as both matter and energy, composed of both particles and waves, depending on the conditions of observation, the quantum model created problems that Newton's model hadn't, but it also proved more accurate. Physics now needed to find explanations for the ambiguities quantum mechanics introduced, and so far Niels Bohr's model, called the Copenhagen Interpretation in deference to his Danish nationality, had been the most popular. The problem with the Copenhagen Interpretation was that it privileged the observer and set him apart from the rest of the quantum system, sort of the way Caroline had suggested that I was the linchpin of the Daphne phenomenon.

Everett argued against the Copenhagen Interpretation.

He asserted that physics needed to accept its own math and embrace the obvious implications that arose from its calculations, no matter how surprising the real-world implications. His conclusions had the great advantage of restoring the observer as a part of the quantum system and removing his privileged status. Everett accounted for all anomalies by an idea that was directly suggested by the math: every time a quantum system interacted with the world, a new reality branched off. His simplest example was an intersection. When a car reaches an intersection in one reality the car will go right; in another it will turn left. Voilà! A new reality. This process of branching realities occurred throughout quantum systems, generating new universes, perhaps an infinity of universes. Borges had described this process in his "Garden of Forking Paths," the story Daphne and I talked about on the bus ride to Washington. Once the two universes separated, however, they would never interact again. To put it more simply, there were an infinite set of possibilities for Daphne, for each of us actually, and it was arbitrary which possibility manifested in our universe. In another universe, a different possibility would manifest.

I reviewed these implications in my mind, assuring myself that I understood what I had just read: Daphne was a set of possibilities, and each possibility became manifest in a new universe when the universe branched off, as Borges had said it would. But once this new universe branched off, it could never interact with the previous universe. They split completely.

But the question still remained: why could I interact with all four?

Everett's model insisted that I could never get two

of the girls together. The laws of physics as described by
Schrödinger's equation, and interpreted by Everett's hypothesis, prohibited it. That much I understood, but then
why could one Daphne see another's portrait? Why had
one Daphne glimpsed another at a school teach-in? Why
could I see all four? Which reality was I in?

I reread the Everett section. Everett's conclusions
were clear.

But poor Everett had been ostracized for his elegant
and daring theory and forced to leave physics. People had
found him crazy, just for suggesting his Many-Worlds Interpretation as an abstract model, even without the concrete example of auburn-haired teenagers. A quantum
conference in Copenhagen had pronounced him so, and
so had the great man Niels Bohr himself. I would certainly always be found crazy too. Even so, I resolved to
track down Everett and ask him about Daphne. And I
also resolved to stop using the word *crazy*. Surely there
were other words for bold ideas that frightened people.

I didn't want to waste the time going over to the
Vassar library, so the next morning I holed up in the
less-impressive New Paltz library. I discovered that when
Everett had been forced out of physics he created his own
firm that designed weapons systems for the Pentagon. I
even found a phone number for that firm. I took my notes
home to make phone calls. I got bounced from one office
to another, until finally I was speaking to Everett's very
businesslike secretary. I explained to her that I wanted
nothing more in the world than to meet her boss. I expected her to explain to me why this was impossible.

Instead she said, "He had a cancellation, and I have a
fifteen-minute appointment tomorrow at three."

"Tomorrow?" I wanted to see Everett, but I was imagining a time frame of months, not hours. "I'm in up-state New York. I'd have to get down there, and there's a problem with my car—"

"Excuse me. Dr. Everett never takes appointments like this without some pressing relationship to his business life. I'm giving you this slot because the only thing he might hate more than talking to someone just off the street or talking to someone about physics is having a gap in his schedule. He is very particular about time. He would not want a fifteen-minute break with no one across the desk from him on the day he sees people. However, he will not be receptive to your interest. I hope that's understood. It's tomorrow or never. It's up to you."

"Tomorrow. Thank you so much. I'll be there."

My mechanic had replaced my brake pads and assured me that the car was in good enough shape to make the trip to DC. Twenty-four hours later, after a night's sleep in a favorite little hotel in Georgetown, I found myself sitting across from Hugh Everett.

"I've read your article in *Reviews of Modern Physics* and found other references to your work. While I can't claim to follow everything, I understand enough to know that you are the first proponent of the Many-Worlds Interpretation, MWI."

Everett was a sweating, portly man with very short hair styled in the fashion of ten years earlier who wore the same Coke-bottle glasses I did. He reeked of Scotch, from lunch, I surmised, and it seemed like he'd had more than one. He could obviously hold his liquor, but he seemed irritable, as if he were working to keep his temper under control. I had only been in his office for one minute, yet I had already watched him stub out the end of one cigarette and light the next. His immaculate walnut desk had a glass ashtray overflowing with the day's butts. He had no pictures of family. His office had no artwork or decoration of any kind, not even the expected framed diplomas. The blinds were drawn, obscuring what must have been a spectacular view of the Potomac. In front of him was a yellow legal pad and an array of identical pens lined up like soldiers.

"I don't do that work anymore, " he answered in a clipped voice that prohibited any questioning. Through our two sets of lenses, his eyes bored into mine with determination and some impatience.

" Yes, I realize that, but I've run across a phenomenon that seems to prove your theory. I keep watching one girl split, first into two, then three, then four iterations of herself. Each iteration branches off into a radically different future."

"That's impossible," Everett pronounced.

"No. It happened."

He seemed to ignore my response. "Once a new universe branches off, it has no further interaction with the one before. You would never be able to see all four girls. That's not my theory."

"How do you know?"

"Schrödinger's equation."

"But observation is the basis of science."

"Observation, yes. Under controlled conditions that can be reproduced."

"I am sure that what I am observing is related to your paper. I just know it."

"Perhaps. But it is not an example of the Many-Worlds Interpretation. It just doesn't fit the math we have. Perhaps you should consider a more mundane explanation, like a problem with your mental health." He began writing on his pad and evidently had no more interest in talking to me. There were no handshakes or goodbyes. There were four minutes left to my fifteen-minute consultation, so I just sat there, deflated, watching him work.

I thanked him for his time, and at 3:15 on the dot his efficient secretary returned to usher me out. "Dr. Adams, do you want me to validate your parking pass?" she asked right after she closed the door. I walked to her desk so she could stamp my ticket. "Is something wrong?" she asked. "You've gone a little pale."

"I'm fine, thanks. Which way are the elevators?"

"Through those doors to the left. You can't miss them."

I had already checked out of the hotel, so I got on the road.

That Dr. Everett had discovered a theoretical framework for the idea of multiple Daphnes had given me hope of understanding this eerie experience life had brought me. That he had been thought weird and had been ridiculed had given me someone to identify with, and led me to conclude that there were worse things than being thought odd. Now I *knew* there were. Being told by Niels Bohr your model was crazy, as Everett had been, was one thing; being told that your experience was crazy by Hugh Everett was entirely different. Bohr was a great man defending his own theory; Hugh Everett was a failure in physics, rejecting an example that might validate his theory, however problematic the four Daphnes were. If he thought I was crazy, maybe I was.

Everett had solved his problem by walking away from physics, just as Caroline insisted that I could solve mine by walking away from these Schrödinger girls, only there weren't really Schrödinger girls after all, if Everett was to be believed. But how could I ignore my own experience? One option was to accept the conclusion everyone else was drawing—that I was mentally ill. I didn't feel it. Daphne felt as real as Caroline, and if I had to see her as a fantasy, maybe Caroline was a fantasy too. Maybe I had imagined the entire web of reality I'd experienced, or maybe my observations had distorted what I saw so much that the universe manifested itself completely differently from the way it seemed to me. If I pulled that one thread, the thread of the Schrödinger girls, what would be left? Would everything I knew start to unravel? I imagined myself peering into emptiness. If my perceptions of the Daphnes, who seemed so ordinarily real to me, were faulty, how could I construct any reliable reality? Perhaps reality was a fantasy.

Or maybe my perceptions were as real and accurate as they felt to me, and someday the math would be discovered to prove that I was right. Perhaps I alone lived in a tiny pocket of the universe that defied the laws of physics. One of my professors had insisted that the laws of the universe were really based on probabilities, and that anything was possible, even phenomena that defied the laws of physics. They just have an extremely low probability. I would never question my nocturnal meeting with my father when he told me that I was now the man of the family.

Things were just that strange now. For Everett, the Schrödinger girls presented no problem; the problem arose from the fact that I could interact with all of them in my one universe. I was grandiose enough to wonder if I had found a glitch in the space-time continuum. Of course, I also questioned if everything I had discovered about Daphne could exist only in my own mind. I had to reject that idea when I remembered the snapshot, the guidance counselors, the Green portraits—all the manifestations of multiple Daphnes that existed in the real world, even if I was the only one of billions of people to know the reality of the Schrödinger girl.

CHAPTER Twenty-Two

SO NOW I WAS A MINORITY OF ONE, except for Daphne, but who knew what she'd think? I was in my study, as usual, making notes and culling my journals, now that Everett had rejected my experience. That was decisive. I could no longer turn to science; he had been my best hope. He had unceremoniously dismissed me, and indicated that I was a boring crank. Goodbye. I had expected a better reception. Driving down to DC, I had played fantasy scenarios in my head in which he was excited by Daphne and couldn't wait to hear more and together we studied the math, and even coauthored a paper. Maybe in some other universe we did. In this universe he closed his door.

I had done an admirable job of alienating both Caroline and Jerry with my fixation. I had no friends in New Paltz, only distant colleagues. I thought about calling Jane Pinsky to meet up, so I could pump her for information about Daphne and Galen. Who was I becoming? A creepy, middle-aged guy fixated on a young girl—exactly who everyone thought I was. I typed up all my notes on my Stony Brook encounter with my last Daphne.

The rehab facility didn't allow her visitors for five weeks, which was still a few days off. I was tracking her progress on one of my graphs. She sent me updates in little missives, posted once every few weeks. My time line had blossomed into a huge chart that occupied an entire wall, and I had traced each iteration with a different color marker. Stony Brook Daphne was a bright cobalt blue. Just this past week, the last week in March 1968, she had sent me this update: *Doing well. No drugs. Beginning to work in the garden.* I had recorded her garden work in my time line, which was becoming a dizzyingly detailed design. Galen's Daphne was green, but whenever I checked in, she was off somewhere for a show or a gallery opening. I don't know how she got her homework done. That's why I wanted to talk to Jane. SDS Daphne, marked in red, seemed to have disappeared, so her line just stopped. I hadn't heard a peep from her since that day at New Paltz, right before the mobilization.

And my Ur-Daphne? Her trajectory, marked in purple, stopped the day of the march. She had given me her phone number that day, and I had called her house several times, but one of her parents always answered. I was afraid they'd think me a creep stalking their daughter, so I just hung up. One time, feeling desperate to talk to her, I tried to sound younger, and I left a message with her mother for Daphne to call me, but she never did. I wanted to sit in the parking lot of the high school and wait for her by the buses, yet I was afraid she would resent it.

Even Dylan and the Beatles had stopped releasing albums.

I felt like I was at the event horizon of a black hole. I had just read that term in a magazine article. The event horizon, as I understood it, was the vicinity of a black hole when you get too close to escape its gravitational pull. I was probably using the term wrong, but after seeing Everett I knew that I wasn't going to be a scientist.

Before things had gotten out of hand, although I had never been the most prolific researcher or the most popular teacher, I had provided careful instruction on behavioral psychology that sent my students into the world a little better informed, thinking a little more precisely. I knew that they called me Dr. Stats, for statistics, but every year I had my followers, and my classes attracted just enough students to continue the behavioral track in the department. I began to worry that I would lose my job along with my friends. Everett had as much as told me that my preoccupation was a symptom of a mental disorder. He had turned his back on his own theories and intimated I should too. At least *his* model was rooted in reliable mathematics, whereas my thoughts were rooted only in random encounters with the Schrödinger girls, a phenomenon that only I had experienced.

Soon, events interrupted my self-absorbed brooding. That spring the fabric of history began to unravel for everyone. On April 4, after delivering his famous "I've Been to the Mountaintop" speech, Martin Luther King Jr. was shot in Memphis, Tennessee, standing on the balcony of his hotel. Evidence pointed to James Earl Ray, and a manhunt began.

On hearing of Dr. King's death, Robert F. Kennedy, in Indianapolis about to give a campaign speech, delivered a stirring extemporaneous eulogy pleading with us Americans "to tame the savageness of man and make gentle the life of this world." But the pain brought riots in Baltimore, Boston, Chicago, Detroit, Kansas City, Newark, Washington, DC, and many other places across the country. Forty-six people died.

Tragedy brought the Daphnes back to me. On the back of a postcard of Michelangelo's statue of Apollo in the Bargello Museum, Galen's Daphne had drawn two weeping faces and signed her name. Still living with Terry, SDS Daphne sent a standard postcard, no picture, with just my address. She had written only two words: *those fuckers*. From high school, the always-generous Ur-Daphne had sent me a single of Joan Baez singing "We Shall Overcome," recorded in 1963 in the UK, right after the folk singer presented the song at Dr. King's big speech in DC. I couldn't imagine how she'd gotten ahold of the recording, and I didn't know how I would ever repay all her gifts to me or express my gratitude. I played the record so many times I was afraid of wearing it out. Did anyone sing as purely as Baez? I wished I could have been at the march, but in 1963 I had been too dumb and too self-involved to even think about going. Knowing Daphne had changed that.

From the rehab center, Stony Brook Daphne had written me a letter:

Dear Garrett,

Besides being heartbroken, I am doing well. You and Jerry were amazing to find me this place. I am making friends and don't feel so alone in the world. I have people I can live with after I leave, but for the time being I will be staying here. I have jobs I really like. I get up early and bake the bread for everyone every day. Dr. Miller says that if I

*want to stay, we can call this a real job, and it will
cover room and board. Then in the afternoons,
around three o'clock, in good weather I work in
the garden. In the winter I couldn't do much—
just pick up twigs and branches left by storms, but
now that it's spring, the earth needs to be turned
over.*

*I am working on my GED. It's very easy.
There is an educational consultant who is helping
me with ideas for college. So far the standouts are
Stony Brook (where you found me) because I can
get a Regents scholarship and some additional
scholarship money, which would make attendance free. The other college is Wellesley because
they have a special program for girls like me, and
it might also be free. Emily, the consultant, is really pushing Wellesley, and not just because it's so
much more elite, but also because it's so small, all
women, and she thinks I'll feel safe there. I'm not
so sure I want to feel safe. Maybe I want something big, and something bustling, where I can
feel like someone who'd rather have an adventure
than be safe. I think I might like to go to school
with Juliana. She was so good to me. Everybody
there was. I might want to study botany.*

*Nothing about this makes sense to me.
Love like Dr. King's just makes people feel even
more hatred, as if letting in the love would just
break them apart. I wish I could tell them that it
wouldn't, and that they'd believe me. Otherwise
there are going to be even more of these deaths.
Love doesn't hurt. Only people who have never*

had any think so. Anyway, if I can get through
this, and I will, I'll be all right.

Love,
Daphne

She was right. Nothing did make sense. Not in the
United States. Hatred was always boundless. In the face
of this anger, I wanted to do what I could to heal the rift
with my friends. Jerry worshipped King. I called to ask if
I could see him, but he insisted that he was fine.

"Still moving to Esalen?" I asked.

"Considering it."

"You're not angry, are you?"

"Don't be silly. Just sad."

I took him at his word and trusted him to stay sober.
Caroline was a different story. I wanted to show her
Daphne's letter from rehab and the rest of my proof, the
postcards from the different Daphnes, each stamped by a
post office at a different location, but Caroline was still
angry with me. I suspected that proof would be beside the
point. People can ignore evidence. Everett had the math
to prove his theory, but his ideas didn't make sense to
Bohr. Now Everett wasn't even a physicist. I despaired of
convincing Caroline. When I called her she admitted, "I
just don't get you, Garrett," her voice strained and weary.
"No. I don't really want to see you right now."

I wanted to ask about Tom, but something in her
manner prevented me from pressing her further. I had no
one but myself to blame. "I'm sorry, Caroline. I shouldn't
have taken my jealousy out on you."

"No, you shouldn't have." She hung up

I spent the spring semester going through the motions of teaching my courses. History was exploding around me, but my response was to crawl inside myself. Jerry, Caroline, and, more importantly, Daphne disappeared from my life again. I found more books on Everett, read more about the Daphne myth, and reread the time line so many times I had each dot of ink memorized. I read Everett's paper seventeen times, and I read Borges's "Garden of Forking Paths" even more. Sadly, I had to conclude that there were no more clues. For a while, my life had been blazing with Daphnes. Now it felt dark.

Although the date came and went when Stony Brook Daphne could accept visitors, when I called and checked with the front desk, her doctor kept putting off the visit. A month passed, but I was busy with grades and tried not to mind too much, though I was longing to see her. Finally, after another month, at the end of May I took my chances and drove to the rehab facility without making a date with the young botanist. At the front desk the receptionist referred me to one of the therapy aides because it wasn't official visiting hours. A comfortable middle-aged woman with a graying flip hairdo and a fifties sweater set smiled at me when I introduced myself.

"Oh, we know all about you," she said. "Daphne says that you're a real gentleman and a life saver. Normally we wouldn't allow visitors at this time of day, but Daphne is no longer technically a patient. She's working in the garden out back. Come, I'll show you."

She led me through the building to a back door that opened onto a respectably large plot. I had to squint to see Daphne against the bright sunlight. She had her hair tied up in a green bandanna, and she wore cutoffs and a sleeveless top marked by sweat. She was weeding and working hard. Roses and peonies were blooming in side beds, but she was tending a big vegetable garden recently planted with tomatoes, corn, watermelons, string beans, and zucchini, their seed-packet markers mounted on sticks. Right now, the plantings were just tiny, tender seedlings with their heads barely out of the soil. She heard my footsteps and turned around.

"Garrett!"

I thought of how wanly she had said my name just months ago. Some of her old enthusiasm had returned. Someone had recut her hair, and it was even shorter under the bandanna, but it wasn't hacked off anymore. The short hair gave her a gamine quality, but she was earnest too. She didn't seem the same girl who had sat in an opium stupor ready to withdraw from life. As I watched her, I saw that her work in the soil had a methodical quality. I noticed that she had lost some of the spontaneity that I always associated with my Schrödinger girls.

"You're working hard," I said.

"I am. We will eat this food. I like watching seeds become food and seeing the food on the table. It's mysterious, don't you think?"

I said that I did.

"Will you excuse me for a minute while I finish weeding? I just have a few more rows to go."

"Of course." I liked watching her work.

When she finished, she walked over to a hose and washed the dirt from her hands. "Okay, I'm done," she said.

"Can we go somewhere to talk?"

"I like to be outside. There's a bench over there." She

pointed to a section of the yard just out of sight. Her nails were ragged and there was dirt under them.

I followed her, and we sat down on a long wooden bench. We each sat at an edge, so two people could have fit between us.

"How's it going?" I asked. I wanted to ask her about drugs, about Rick, about how empty and suicidal she'd been, but it was best to let her take the lead.

"Things are good, if I'm careful," she answered.

I waited for her to go on but she didn't. "Careful?" I finally asked, hoping she'd explain.

"If I'm not careful I can get despondent. If I think about Rick or what happened at Stony Brook with Mr. Speed Freak, or the war, or just being on my own, I can get sad. And here we learn that getting sad like that can make us think about drugs. It's a full-time job, not being sad. I can't even be snarky without going all negative. And that's dangerous for me."

I felt my own pang of sadness. When I met Stony Brook Daphne, although she was nihilistic, she was also gritty and real and compelling. But now she needed to work hard to just to stay optimistic and grounded. I guess it was an improvement because she was no longer self-destructive.

"Do you think about calling your parents?"

"What parents? They don't know me."

"Do you mean that your parents feel like the parents of someone else?"

"Yeah, something like that."

"What if reality is more complicated than you think, Daphne? Would you want to know?"

"Right now, I wouldn't. I'm having enough trouble dealing with the reality I have. Gardening helps. I like

growing food and learning about plants. I passed my
GED with an almost perfect score, and I am going to
Wellesley. Fewer drugs than at Stony Brook, and I got a
full scholarship."

"Wow! Great news! It's a fantastic school. You're going in September?"

"If Dr. Celantano thinks I'm ready. He's my main doctor. He says barring any major relapses, like using drugs
or something, I'll be ready."

"That's a year early for you, right? The rest of your
class has another year of school?"

"Yeah, but I'm glad to miss all that—the prom, graduation, all that kid stuff."

"I get it."

I didn't really know how to keep the conversation going with this pragmatic young woman. I knew which topics to avoid—anything sad—but I had no idea of how to
connect with her. Our friendship had begun with her sadness over the death of Rick Lopez. I didn't know how to
find any other common ground, yet I had missed Daphne
so much, I wanted to try. I was about to ask her about
what music she was listening to when she interrupted my
thoughts.

"It's getting close to dinner," she said. "I really
shouldn't miss it."

"No, I suppose not." I was sorely disappointed, though
it was probably better for me to leave anyway. I shouldn't
talk to this fragile teenager about my metaphysical specu-
lations, or her difficulties, or Martin Luther King's death,
or even her beautiful letter, which might have turned her
thoughts to sad things. There wasn't much left to talk
about.

"Thanks for coming, Garrett. Remember the little box I gave you?"

"Of course."

"Did you open it?"

"No. The cap was on too tight."

"I gave you the last of my stash, so I could really stop using drugs. I don't know if they would have searched the little box, but I was afraid to have it with me."

"Why didn't you just throw it out?"

"I just couldn't bear to."

"What's in it?"

"LSD. You should throw it out."

"I will," I assured her.

"I'm sorry I gave the acid to you. It was before I got sober."

"I understand."

"I shouldn't have tried to drag you into my druggie world. I've changed a lot since then even though it was only three months ago. Keep the box, though. It's beautiful."

I suddenly thought of Caroline's idea that I bring at least two Daphnes together. I guess it was in response to the notion of this Daphne going away to Wellesley and another Daphne already in Bronxville. They would all be scattering. The idea was impossible, according to Everett, although my Ur-Daphne had caught a glimpse of SDS Daphne and been spooked by her. I recalled that when she had tried to talk to her double, she'd failed to catch up with her. I remembered the exasperated tilt of her head when she recounted the feeling that her simulacrum had fled. "She was just out of reach," Ur-Daphne had said, just as Hugh Everett had insisted.

And once again I began to suppose for a moment that everyone was right. But if I was crazy, how had I constructed such an elaborated fantasy world? This was my own personal science-fantasy novel, if the Schrödinger girls weren't real. Did that mean that the aide at the rehab center wasn't real either? Or that Galen's portraits were fantasies? No. Occam's razor, the idea that the simplest explanation was truest, intimated that they were real. Why their presence challenged everything we knew about reality was a question I couldn't answer, but I was profoundly grateful to my Schrödinger girls. Just seeing Stony Brook Daphne made me feel alive again. Even this Daphne, so focused on being sober, exhilarated me. Her love of plants, for example, was inspiring, and her auburn hair glinting in the sunlight looked so joyous. How long could I inhabit my own little pocket of reality? Maybe all the girls would disappear.

Since I couldn't see two of the girls together, I decided to try to do the next best thing and see two of my Schrödinger girls on the same day. I drove to a phone booth and called Galen's Daphne in Bronxville. It was only five o'clock so it would still be early enough when I got there to have dinner with her. The phone rang three, then four times, and I was about to hang up when Daphne answered.

"Hello, Daphne here," she said in a breathless voice.

"It's Garrett."

"Oh, hi. Let me catch my breath. I had to run for the phone because I was outside in the garden. What a glorious day it is!"

"That's a coincidence. I was just outside in a garden too. Sure. Catch your breath while I ask if you're free to-

night for dinner around seven. I could be there in Bronxville in an hour and a half."

"Maybe. Let me ask Galen what he thinks. Can I call
you back in just a minute or so?"

I gave her the number of the pay phone and waited in
the booth. True to her word, the phone rang within five
minutes.

"Hi," she said brightly, and before I could respond,
her answer came tumbling out: "Galen says that would
be fine. He has something he wants to catch up on and is
happy to make himself a salad. So I'm all yours. Oh, and
guess what! I've gotten my driver's license and can drive
myself to town. I'm willing to risk being out after dark
with my junior license."

I congratulated her on the milestone. She named a
favorite restaurant and we arranged to meet. This was
a familiar scenario, meeting Daphne in a restaurant to
chat, but now she would come as an adult. I wondered if
I would feel any different.

On Saturday night Bronxville was filled with Cadillacs
and Lincolns, lawyers and stockbrokers taking their
wives out to dinner. Just as I arrived, a Karmann Ghia
pulled out and I snagged the only available space. I wondered which car Daphne had driven. Probably Galen's
old Jag.

I walked along the main street, which possessed
a kitschy charm with all its fake Tudor facades, until I
found the place. Since I had overestimated the distance,
I was there early, but thoughtful Daphne had made a
reservation in Galen's name. She had chosen a pleasant
restaurant that attempted a Tuscan atmosphere with

arches, earth tones, and centerpieces of lemons. When she walked in I must have been perusing the menu because she laughed a throaty laugh, and I raised my head from reading to see her sitting across from me.

"You must have seated yourself by stealth. Maybe you should be a spy."

"Well, you shouldn't. If I were a spy, you might be dead. You had no idea that I was here." She laughed again. The bodice of her sundress was an ice-blue paisley print that set off her auburn chignon. She was still wearing her hair that way.

She seemed different, though. She was wearing makeup that accentuated her eyes, and very pink lipstick, and her psychedelic print gave her a sixties flair despite the chignon. As I glanced around the upscale eatery, there seemed to be hippies everywhere. Tie-dye outfits, guys with hair way past their ears and wide ties, bell-bottoms, and puka-shell necklaces, and girls in peasant blouses and gypsy skirts with long, streaming hair and bandannas keeping it out of their faces. My mind drifted to Caroline's sleek black locks. *Now none of that. You're here with Daphne.* She wore beads on her sundress, but her tight, low bun set her apart from the other Sarah Lawrence girls.

My head was now spinning with my impressions of Galen's Daphne and Stony Brook Daphne. Their features were so exactly the same, and yet they were so totally different. I know identical twins can be uncanny, but I had satisfied myself early on that this girl wasn't one of a set of twins, or triplets. Now that there were four, I felt even more certain that a multiple birth was not the explanation. It's easy to canvass hospitals to find out about

quadruplets; they are a rare occurrence. Just seeing one
with short hair and one with long hair was unnerving.
They sounded different, yet they sounded the same. Their
energy felt different, yet it felt the same.

"So, you're finally in town," I said. "You and Galen
get around."

"Yeah, we do. But I wish I had been here when Dr. King
died. Too sad. And of course, being abroad just wasn't
the same. What's happening to our country, Garrett?"

"*And something is happening here, but you don't
know what it is, do you, Miss Jones?*"

"I'm serious," she said, in the elegant manner she had
adopted. She seemed somehow taller than the others.
She sat up straight, with an elongated neck. Maybe she'd
learned this while posing for Galen's paintings.

"I couldn't tell you," I said. "I was hoping you knew."
I was acting nonchalant, but just being in a restaurant
with Galen's Daphne inspired me. Two Daphnes in one
day! My head was spinning. She was chattering on about
her career plans. They were obviously influenced by Galen, but that's just the way her universe had branched off,
I supposed.

I began to think of Ovid's rendering of the Daphne/
laurel myth. Of all the Schrödinger girls, she seemed the
only one who had been trapped by Apollo—in this case,
Galen. The others had gotten away. My Ur-Daphne was
still free. Stony Brook Daphne had been saddened by
Rick Lopez's death, but she was making her own way in
the world. I could only assume that SDS Daphne was also
still free and not Terry's puppet. But here was Daphne,
Galen's Daphne, following his pursuits and being painted
by him over and over again. He had shown her fixed and

turning into a tree in many of his canvases. I wondered if she would ever be really free or ever become her own woman.

I began listening more carefully when she said, "I'm going to go to graduate school in art history when I'm done at Sarah Lawrence. Yale or Columbia. Striking distance from Bronxville. That way I can curate Galen's work and do my own academic research. My new love is Turner. He discovered a kind of very early impressionism."

I remembered two Turners from my trips to the Met with my mother—one of whalers and one of Venice. From what Daphne said, I suspected that neither was in the style of which Daphne was enamored. This conversation was more familiar to me than the conversation I'd just had with the other Daphne. At the rehab center we hadn't talked about books, music, or painting at all.

We both ordered pasta and then espressos. Daphne continued discussing painting, especially her interest in Turner. But I wanted to get away from Turner and talk about the Daphne portraits and the myth. "I would have thought you'd be interested in portraits."

"Why?"

"The Daphne portraits. I just saw another one at the Forester Gallery. You were turning into a tree."

"That's not me. That's a character I modeled for," she asserted, bristling slightly. She was too quick to protest.

"But she is Daphne and so are you."

"Mere coincidence."

"Galen's interest in Ovid has nothing to do with you?" She blushed. "Well, maybe a little."

"When did you start sleeping together? The first night after the Russian Tea Room?"

Her green eyes flashed with anger. Her back stiffened. She shifted in her chair. Her discomfort suggested that she might suddenly bolt from the restaurant. "And that's your business, why?"

"We're friends, and I care about you a great deal. I'm sorry if I sound somewhat . . . parental."

Her back visibly softened and her lips twitched into the tiniest of grins. "Oh, all right. Actually, we haven't. Slept together, I mean. Galen is being ridiculous. He wants us to get married on my eighteenth birthday. I'm going to take my junior year abroad in Florence, of course, and Galen is coming with me. We'll be married there next spring, and he wants me to be, you know . . ."

"A virgin?"

"Yeah, that's it."

"He's protecting you? He's the river god, not Apollo?"

"How should I know?" she asked petulantly, suddenly a child, her lovely chin jutting out. I noticed she was playing with her leftover pasta. "And anyway, I don't live in a myth."

Had that been what I was doing? Casting her in a myth? A Schrödinger myth? Was it possible to unmask an unadorned reality of Daphne? Whenever I tried, Ovid or Schrödinger intruded. Still, Schrödinger was science, wasn't it?

She was glaring at me defiantly, her eyes cold green gems. "I have to go," she said, starting to gather up her purse.

But I didn't want her to leave on that note. "Stay. Please. Dessert?" I asked.

"I don't think so. I'm expected for drinks and I don't want to be out too long after dark. I might be able to just make it. We have some art critics coming over, and Galen wants me to be there. Jane is coming too. And before you ask, no, I don't drink."

"Cappuccino then?"

She nodded a grudging assent. Maybe she didn't want to leave angry either.

"How's Jane?"

But we were silent then until the waiter brought the coffee. "I'm so excited to be going to Florence," she announced. Then she said, "You have some foam above your lip."

I wiped it off, making a show of being the buffoon so the awkwardness would pass. "I'll walk you to your car." I indicated to the waiter that I'd be back.

The sunset had organized itself into wide bands of strictly demarcated color—salmon, gold, and fuchsia—which rose over a soft slate blue. I had never seen a sky quite like it.

"It's a sky from Turner," Daphne said. "Constable did all the clouds, but Turner saw all this," and she gestured to show off the sky. We walked apart for a block, until we arrived at the Jaguar and she abruptly hugged me. "I'll miss you," she conceded.

"Me too," I said, before watching her drive off.

I returned to my table and ordered another cappuccino. I took out a small notebook and began to write.

May 23, 1968
I have been taken with the differences in circum-
stances and personalities between the Daphne it-
erations. However, what I failed to observe until
today were the differences in destiny. It is impos-

sible not to notice the striking difference between Stony Brook Daphne, who has struggle and freedom ahead of her, and Galen's Daphne, who has a life of comfort and confinement mapped out already. Destiny is so mysterious. Even with the opportunity to follow four separate existences of the same person, I can't locate the mechanism that creates these separate destinies. They seem random and to occur by chance. The other possibility is some kind of deterministic universe/s in which these paths are prefabricated. This second possibility, while plausible, does not seem probable.

Daphne's admission about her life with Galen changed my assessment of their relationship. Reality was always doing that, wasn't it? Splintering off in a prismatic way when we learned something new or saw something from a new angle. I didn't need Hugh Everett III to explain that to me. The Schrödinger girls presented me with too many mysteries to contemplate. Beyond the deepest problem of their existences, they raised questions about personality and destiny I just couldn't answer at all.

CHAPTER TWENTY-THREE

SEEING TWO SCHRÖDINGER GIRLS in the same day elated me. They were absolutely real. Every time I listened to someone else and doubted their existences, I was plunged once again into self-doubt. If they weren't real, I was crazy. If I was crazy, I had no basis for my life at all. But if they were real, my perceptions were real, and my life was built on solid ground. The only problem now was my estrangement from Caroline.

Since I'd visited Caroline in the gallery and been so rude, we'd barely spoken. I had dialed half her number and then hung up so many times that it had almost become a regular part of my day. Occasionally I called the gallery, let it ring until she answered, and then hung up. Sometimes I waited for her to answer just for the pleasure of hearing her contralto voice. Once I even identified myself, but she dismissed me. I didn't blame her. Sometimes I was on the verge of renouncing Daphne just to have Caroline back in my life, in my arms, in my bed, but I knew I wouldn't be able to make it stick.

Things seemed to be transforming all over the world. In early May, Paris had erupted in student uprisings. And also in Paris in May, formal talks began to end the Vietnam War, though I didn't believe anything would come of them. Before Daphne, I would have taken sides against the Parisian students and trusted the government to do the right thing, but that naïveté was gone now. *Time* magazine had called my generation the Silent Generation, too young for the big war. Now some of us were making noise, but King, just a year older than I was, had died for speaking up.

I tried not to go numb again. Slivers of hope flashed in the campaigns of Bobby Kennedy and Eugene McCarthy, who both promised to end the horrid war. I was just so tired of seeing children burned by napalm and soldiers with guns to their heads every night on the evening news. Without Daphne, perhaps I'd still be oblivious to these realities. I had followed that yellow rain slicker out of my postwar apathy.

On June 5 everything went to shit again. Now it was Bobby Kennedy who was dead, shot in the kitchen of an LA hotel where his supporters in the adjacent ballroom were celebrating his California Democratic primary win. Just hours before his death I had been so hopeful; he seemed unstoppable, and soon he would have been in New York campaigning, bringing his brand of optimism back home, where another primary win would pretty much have clinched the nomination for him. Instead, his body was brought east by train in a funeral cortege that recalled the journey of Lincoln's coffin. All along the route people flocked to the tracks to wave at the train, citizens hoping to end the war, black people who were stirred by his words, people already so bruised by King's assassination. What was America doing? Who were we killing? I needed to talk to Jerry. I needed to lay my head in Caroline's lap. I needed to see Daphne.

I pored over all the artifacts in my study and stared at the Daphne time line for aimless hours. I would have driven to the city or hopped on the train to talk to my pal, but I knew Jerry would tell me in no uncertain terms to move on. He was struggling with his own demons and had no patience with mine. We had been comrades together in buttoned-down silence. Now addiction, obsession, and history had intruded on our friendship, and we were left on our own to struggle out of the shells we had constructed during the Eisenhower fifties. We had turned to Watson and Freud for safety, after the brutalities of World War II that had cost me a father and Jerry all the family he had left in Europe, and we had buried our deepest feelings. Now the sixties were making our strategies obsolete, and Daphne had become my only guide.

What was she telling me? Here everything was, the time line that had grown into a complex chart, with branches like a tree, and the snapshot, the books, the records, and the little Russian box Stony Brook Daphne had given me.

On Saturday, June 8, the day of RFK's funeral at St. Patrick's Cathedral in New York, I thought of going to stand with the thousands who'd be on the street paying tribute, but the idea of being there without Caroline saddened me too much. I stared at the beautiful little Russian box and worked at opening the top. I applied elbow grease and patience, and finally it revealed its secret—two perfect scraps of paper, liquid LSD dropped by eyedropper onto pieces of a pale-blue blotter nestled against the brick-red interior of the enameled receptacle. I caught my breath.

Here was my Rubicon. My drug experience was lim-

ited to the joint I'd smoked with Jane and Daphne on
the day of Jane's art show. Getting stoned had brought
me mostly silliness and a great appreciation for brownies.
Although the experience had been pleasant, I had felt no
urge to seek it out. I knew that acid would be different.
Popular wisdom said that acid devastated lives, like Jerry's alcohol or Daphne's opium, Nembutal, and whatever
else she had gotten her hands on. She had done acid too,
and had told me to discard it, but the nihilism I felt just
then drew me to the idea of tripping.

Before I made a final decision, my body, one step
ahead of me, was already ingesting one of the tiny pieces of
blotter paper. I suspected that it wasn't necessary to actually eat the paper, but since there wasn't anyone there to
advise me, I swallowed the little scrap of paper. Nothing
happened. Of course nothing would happen immediately.

I selected and arranged a stack of records, *Magical
Mystery Tour* the most prominent with pride of place
on the top of the pile. *"There's a fog upon LA, and my
friends have lost their way, we'll be over soon they said,
now they've lost themselves instead,"* sang the Beatles
as the June light streamed into my living room. I had a
glass of water, my records, and a small snack on my living
room coffee table. After I put on the record, I sat with my
feet up waiting for the acid to kick in.

"Please don't be long, please don't you be very long,"
I heard as I began to feel thirsty in an odd way and the
edges of objects began to appear wavy with halos of refracted color around their edges. A prominent purple ring
formed at the boundary of the water in the glass, so I
raised it and tilted it so the ring went sideways, and then
it was level, and then I made it go sideways again. I set

off the toy I always I had on the table, weighted metal balls suspended from a wooden beam, so the spheres hit each other and clicked in a percussion symphony while they made ominous shadows on the walls. I could see rays streaming in from the windows as the visual world crowded out sadness about the funeral and all the other miseries I'd been carrying. I was suspended in a world of purple and green; the ceiling had begun to turn paisley.

I heard a noise that startled me. Perhaps it was an animal, but suddenly I was on high alert, because it sure sounded like someone was walking up the path onto the stoop, and then there was a small rap at the door. I heard the knocking, but I was rooted to the chair in apprehension. I didn't want to telegraph that I was tripping, and I thought if I just sat there on the couch they'd go away. But then the rapping returned. I held my breath and watched the door open a crack. *I am being invaded.* And then the crack widened. Sunlight streamed into the room in chunks of yellow, and a large, tall shape occupied the doorframe.

Something was definitely off in this acid universe, because I thought I saw Caroline's Tom peering in.

"Tom?"

"Yeah. Hi, Garrett."

"*Hi, Garrett?* Didn't you just open the door without being asked in? What's going on?"

"You didn't answer, and I saw the car," he explained with contrition. He stayed in the doorway. "May I come in?" he asked in a strained voice. He was doing a mediocre job of acting like someone uncomfortable. I was amazed the guy got any acting parts at all. I wasn't sure what part I should be acting right now myself.

"Um, sure, yeah, come in," I heard myself say.

"Caroline sent me. She said she has some things in the spare bedroom. I had to be up here anyway to negotiate a part. Summer stock. I have a rental car just outside."

Poor guy. He was really embarrassed. Caroline shouldn't have made him do this.

"Oh, okay. Why didn't she call me and let me know? This is weird."

"I have no idea, buddy. Yeah, she should have. Kind of shitty for both of us. You know women."

"Do I?"

"It's the room upstairs? Do you mind if I go get her stuff?"

"Is she taking the quilt?"

"What quilt? I don't think so."

"Is she mad at me?" I asked. I sounded five years old, and he stopped and studied me, furrowing his brow a bit.

"Is something wrong? I don't know you well, but you don't seem like the guy I met on St. Patrick's Day."

"I dropped acid," I announced. I could feel a wide smile of pride on my face, so big that my cheeks actually hurt.

"Shit. Jeez, man, you did?"

I energetically nodded my head up and down, making my newly long hair bounce around my face.

"Well, I can't leave you alone like this."

"Oh sure you can. I was going to be alone before you came."

"Yeah, I understand that, but I don't think it's a good idea." His voice betrayed weariness and just a hint of resentment. He was clearly trying to do the right thing.

"Have you ever done acid?" I asked.

"Mescaline. Not acid. Same difference, I guess. Just maybe milder. Have you gotten off yet?"

"Your face is purple. You are really handsome, you know."

"I'll take that as a yes."

"I have a second piece of blotter paper for you if you want," I offered generously.

"I'll pass."

I was staring at the folds of a blanket I'd left over the arm of one of the brown velvet chairs. The space inside the folds was bright magenta. I'd never noticed how prominent creases are. The ceiling continued roiling with kaleidoscope designs. *Magical Mystery Tour* kept playing. I'd already replayed it several times. *"I am the eggman. They are the eggmen. I am the walrus. Goo goo g'joob."* The words made perfect sense.

"I'm thirsty," I said, "but I don't remember how to drink."

"Just pick up the glass. You'll remember."

The glass was filled with clear liquid that shone bright fuchsia at its surface. As I drank I thought about what Salinger said in his story "Teddy" about pouring God into God when someone drinks. He was right.

A series of *oh wow*s came out of my mouth, like tiny bubbles.

"How are you feeling?" Tom asked. His voice sounded as if it was echoing through a long tunnel.

"Fine. Except my face hurts."

"That's just because you're smiling so much and so broadly. Let's go for a ride."

We drove around until he found a public garden. The day was so beautiful I thought of Bobby Kennedy and how right it was that he would be eulogized by his brother Ted. It was like the water—God into God. He was being poured back into God, and suddenly for just that moment his death felt okay. I wished he were there with me so I could tell him. When I told Tom this he said, "He already knows."

The flowers, poppies shining orange, peonies bursting open, roses singing, had Day-Glo halos. I was seeing like a butterfly or like one of the bees diving deep for nectar. I buried my nose in the flowers too. When a cloud passed over the garden I became somber, my mood volatile and impacted by that tiny happenstance. "I'm scared," I said. But then the cloud passed, and the day was sunny and bright.

I had no idea how long we were there, but Tom took us for ice cream, though I didn't think I was hungry. I was getting deeper into the trip.

Outside the ice cream shop new flowers bloomed pink white red purple, mixing together, swirling, the colors bleeding onto their containers. The ice cream cold, yummy vanilla chocolate sweet more melting cone crunchy more! More flowers fragrant, buzz, buzz bees, circling, drinking, whispering, *Garrett,* and white, white puffy clouds blue azure glass sky turning magenta purple paisley green.

"Tom!" I called out insistently.

"What is it?"

"I forgot to be sad. It's Bobby Kennedy's funeral. I forgot to be sad."

"It's okay. You'll be sad later."

We went back to the house and listened to music: *Revolver. "Turn off your mind relax and float downstream, it is not dying, it is not dying. Lay down all thought, surrender to the void, it is shining, it is shining . . ."* Suddenly I knew exactly what Lennon meant. Reality was shining, glowing, changing shape, but perfect as it was.

CHAPTER TWENTY-FOUR

I WAS HIGH FOR ABOUT EIGHT HOURS. Tom and I listened to my whole Beatles collection and then Dylan and finally the Airplane singing the same song I had listened to with Daphne and Jane when we had all smoked a joint, "White Rabbit," but by that time I was starting to come down. We both drank a can of Ballantine as we watched something mindless on television. Tom made sandwiches with whatever he could find in the refrigerator, but I didn't want to eat anything.

When I was finally cogent I asked if he had missed his appointment. "I guess you don't remember me calling them. Yeah, I did miss it, but they rescheduled for tomorrow after I explained that I was with a friend high on acid. Nothing to worry about there. I can stay here tonight, right?"

"Sure. Of course. I really don't know how to thank you." I hoped my voice didn't show how embarrassed I felt. He must have read my mind because he said, "It's so embarrassing now, to get Caroline's things. Should I call her and say I can't?"

I thought about it as I walked him upstairs to show him the room. "Wait here a minute," I said, "I'll be right back." He sat down on the bed covered by the handmade quilt Caroline had carefully chosen. I went out to the garage and returned with a small cardboard carton. "I'll help you pack up."

Things were less mortifying for both of us that way. I wanted to ask him about their relationship, but I refrained from making things even more difficult between us. We gathered up makeup, toiletries, some underwear, a nightgown, two or three casual shirts, and a few paperbacks, and packed them in the box. We walked downstairs, and he took the box out to the car while I started on another beer. While I was in the bathroom he must have hurriedly called Caroline to tell her what was going on because he said a quick "Bye now" when he saw me come back into the room, and he hung up. My heart actually skipped a beat at the thought that I might really have lost her for good.

We watched the late-night news with clips of RFK's funeral. When I put my hand up to my cheek I could feel that it was damp with tears. Tom's eyes were misting over too. "Damn shame," he said.

The next morning I made pancakes, and we ate them in companionable silence. We shook hands when he left, and I thanked him again. "I'm sorry I upset your plans," I managed to articulate. "You went above and beyond."

"It's all good, man," he said.

"And you're sure you don't want the other scrap of blotter?"

"No. I'm fine."

I walked out onto the driveway and watched him drive away. Everything in the world was the same as it had been before; the flowers no longer burst out with Day-Glo insistence, and bees were no longer special em-

issaries from a secret realm. I no longer felt as if the sunshine was pouring God into me. I lived in a secular world
again. And yet, although I didn't feel all those things any
longer, I could superimpose my memories of those feelings onto this quotidian day. For the first time in my life
I could glimpse the spiritual possibilities lurking in the
most mundane things. I thought about dropping the other
dose of acid but decided to give myself a break. The last
thing I wanted was to bury myself in drugs and end up
in rehab. The sadness of so many losses was something
I was going to have to learn to carry on my own. I had
been avoiding sadness for a long time now, since my father died, really, and then after Amy's death.

I waited for a week to trip again. My second trip was
darker. I had a patch of absolute terror when I thought
that everything would be all right if I was home in my
own bed, until I realized that I *was* home in my own bed.
But I also had moments of sheer elation. I watched the
trees on the Oriental rug in my living room blossom and
drop their petals, then bud, bloom, and go through the
same cycle a hundred times before my eyes.

I hadn't felt that I could go to my wall and study
the Daphne time line in front of Tom, but on my second trip there was no one watching to see me spend
hours studying its strands of information. Poring over
my graphs, I saw the Schrödinger girls, each in her own
perfect, iridescent-transparent bubble, separate in her
own world. The bubbles floated and crossed, like the
bubbles from a kid's bubble wand. They drifted to the
ceiling and came back to the desk. I saw so clearly that
together they were Daphne, and separately they were

each a Schrödinger girl. Reality splintered and joined and splintered and joined like the blossoms of the tree on the rug that bloomed and died in an infinite cycle. I saw Daphne at my desk, sitting in a chair, drinking tea. I saw her portrait hanging on the wall. I saw her photograph coming to life in front of the swan boats in Boston. I saw the cobalt, green, red, and purple lines merge and separate, each into its own trajectory, a parabola, a hyperbola, a straight line, a circle, reality unreeling before me like a four-projector movie. Each Daphne was whole. Each Daphne was a part of a whole. There was no contradiction.

I pulled out the *Traffic* album so I could hear Steve Winwood sing. *"If for just one moment you could step outside your mind, and float across the ceiling, I don't think the folks would mind."* Winwood was right. *We are not like all the rest,* Daphne and I. And I didn't want to be. We had found each other at Bookmasters and bonded over Schrödinger's cats, and now I knew that reality is a phantasmagoria of which we glimpse only the smallest fraction. Tiny microscopic organisms and large cosmic events exist completely outside of our awareness. Colors hide in folds of fabric; designs decorate the inside of our eyelids. Girls appear and disappear, facsimiles of themselves. So much is real that we know nothing of.

When I was straight again I had to struggle to remember these insights; they had burst, just as any bubble would. I went to the library and got out a book that would help me understand the brain on acid. Timothy Leary, a Harvard researcher, had published *The Psychedelic Experience* in 1964. I'd never been interested before and had avoided any challenge posed to Watson and Skinner, but *something was happening*, and Skinner and Watson couldn't lead me where Leary could. He explained that the drug did not create the experience; it was merely the key to expanded consciousness and permission to opt out of the game of prescribed social roles. Aldous Huxley's 1954 memoir of a mescaline trip, *The Doors of Perception,* explained what the mind experienced in terms of intensity of experience. He was taking me inside the music of Dylan and inside the Beatles. Now there were so many other troubadours and guides in my record stack, like Donovan. *"For standin' in your heart is where I want to be and long to be. Ah, but I may as well try and catch the wind."*

That's what I wanted to do—catch the wind, weave a net for Daphne. I spent the summer of 1968 tripping once a week; I kept a routine. I spent the other six days reading psychedelic literature, writing about experiences, and daydreaming about the Schrödinger girls and the new universe they'd brought me to.

The urge to go talk to Daphne was overwhelming. I had a standing appointment with her. I'd go into my study and steep myself in my notes and artifacts, drop acid, and hope she'd make an appearance in my consciousness. Sometimes she did. Mostly she didn't, but I was living for the times that she did. I was traveling farther and farther away from Jerry and Caroline, and even from the Schrödinger girls as I knew them in life. They were becoming an idea I couldn't live without.

In the middle of August, when I was completely straight, I got a call. On an airless day of over ninety degrees I heard Jerry say, "It's so beautiful out!" and I knew something was up. "Well, kid, I did it. I'm in California. I'm in Big Sur in the wilderness. There's a hillside just covered with wind chimes, a thousand of them maybe. We wait for wind."

"You've moved? What's the deal?"

"I turned my patients over to another analyst if they wanted to continue. I kept my apartment—sorry, kiddo, but you couldn't afford it anyway—but leased him the consulting space. I am a staff therapist here. I'm working with Perls. They're paying my expenses for now. It's wild. It's grand. I feel free."

"How long have you been gone?"

"Two weeks."

"You didn't let me know?"

"I wasn't in the mood for goodbyes. Besides, you're doing all that acid shit. It's not exactly good for my sobriety."

"I get it."

"Be careful, Garrett. I'm afraid you're going to get caught down the rabbit-hole and be unable to get back up. Getting sober isn't easy. And there's always the question of your job. Leary and Richard Alpert lost theirs. We wouldn't want to see that happen to you. Why are you taking all these trips?"

I might have made a mistake telling Jerry what I was doing. Although our ideas about psychology were coming together—we were both becoming "New Age" psychologists, I guess you'd call it—our personal lives were drifting apart. I couldn't stand his moralizing about drugs. I hadn't done that to him, had I? Or maybe I had. Maybe I had been a self-righteous prude. Then I said, "Daphne."

"Daphne? What do you mean?"

"She's why I'm taking all these trips."

"How's that working out for you?"

"Not great."

He just let my answer hang there.

"I left you a present," Jerry said. "Well actually, two presents. I left you my decanter that I always kept on my desk. I won't be needing that. You can pick it up from Jim Carruthers at my apartment." He gave me a phone number for Jim. "And I left you a pair of Yankees tickets for a twilight doubleheader. That's the one thing I am sad about. That we didn't see a game together before I left."

"You're not changing teams, are you?"

"I just might," he said with a twinkle in his voice. "I've been missing the Giants. I had to save myself. I was dying in New York."

I knew exactly what he meant. Now Jerry was gone, Caroline was estranged, and for a while I'd been seeing Daphne only in my acid dreams.

I called Stony Brook Daphne at Tall Oaks, the rehab center.

"Yeah, I'll go to see the Yankees with you. I've never been." I heard a catch in her voice. "After all, I have the hat," she added. I knew she was thinking of Rick.

On the day of the game, when I got to the building in the early afternoon and went to the desk, I was greeted with a note Daphne had left me:

I know you'll understand. I went to Massachusetts a few weeks early to set up my room for Welles-ley. I didn't want to say goodbye. I'm sorry about the baseball, though. I was afraid I'd cry the entire time. Have a good life. I'm going to really try.
—Daphne

Her note felt final, a final farewell. I hadn't known Stony Brook Daphne for as long as the others, but I was already mourning her loss. I retrieved the tickets and the decanter at Jerry's place. I asked Jim if he wanted to see the game, but unlike Jerry in his last months in New York, he had patients to see.

I drove to Yankee Stadium and stood outside waiting for someone wanting a ticket. Like the day I'd met Daphne at the bookstore, I decided to surrender to chance and resolved to give the second entry pass to the first person without one. There were still plenty of empty seats, but all of them were in the nosebleed section. A burly guy with a five o'clock shadow was shouting, "Anyone with an extra seat for sale? I'll pay twice the face price to avoid the upper reaches of the bleachers!" Jerry had paid a small fortune for seats right behind home plate. A deal's a deal, so I had to go with him, still hoping that the encounter might prove magical, like my first meeting with Daphne.

"I've got an extra ticket," I said. But as I handed it to him, he blanched when he saw the ticket price.

"I can't pay twice that. Too rich for my blood," he said, his shoulders hunched in disappointment. I almost passed him by, considered waiting for the next taker. He really didn't present himself as the ideal companion, though I was resolved to keep my bargain with myself.

"No. I meant that I'd *give* you the ticket."

He regarded me, narrowing his eyes suspiciously. "Why would you do that? You could get really good money for that ticket."

"Money means nothing to me."

He didn't laugh but gingerly accepted the ticket. I

could see that he thought he'd be sitting next to a weirdo, but he seemed like the kind of guy who could take care of himself. I could also see that he had weighed his options and decided that he couldn't possibly get into trouble at the crowded stadium.

He showed some grace in buying me a watery beer and a couple of hot dogs, but we didn't converse much, and we cramped each other's style when we got excited at some of the plays. I imagined Stony Brook Daphne sitting here, in her hacked-off hair, wearing Rick Lopez's cap, rooting for his team and talking to me about plants. Or Caroline. We'd never been to a game together. Or Jerry. Saying goodbye to Jerry at a game would have been a bittersweet event.

This time I didn't feel the hand of destiny. My random stranger was just a guy I'd never think about again. Our time together seemed to go on forever; the two games went well into the night. The Yanks won the first with a two-to-one score, but the second game went nineteen innings, past one a.m., and ended in a tie, the first I'd ever seen in all the baseball games I'd attended. I never even learned the name of the guy I'd sat next to for almost eight hours, and the Yankees' tie against the Tigers did not end the day well.

I'd met Daphne just over a year before, but I could barely recognize myself as the guy I'd been then. I'd been complacent and cut off, disdainful of the culture of my students, with little interest in the events taking place around me, and buoyed up only by my unwavering commitment to the principles of behaviorism, secure in the system I was passing on to my students, insular and numb. Now not one of those things was true. I was raw and lonely and open to doubt and experience. Walking back to my car at the stadium I debated which way I was better off. I hadn't been in emotional pain then, yet I had been just so small; I was even oblivious to my best friend's sad predicament. I had to conclude that the hurt I felt now was salutary and the cost of being truly alive.

Late in the evening on August 28, I was watching the news and seeing that riots had broken out at the Democratic National Convention in Chicago. Chicago was a mess. The Democrats were split between McCarthy and Humphrey, the maverick peace candidate and the party regular. McCarthy was running on a peace platform; Humphrey was not. Party insiders had selected Humphrey, and that didn't sit well with young people who were demonstrating. The confrontations between the police and the protesters turned violent. I'd had enough and decided to turn off the news when the phone rang. The voice on the other end gave me butterflies in my stomach, and I turned vigilant with concern.

"Garrett," the familiar voice faltered, and seemed to need to push past her vocal constriction.

"Daphne?"

"Yes, it's me. I'm in Chicago."

Shit. Chicago wasn't safe at the moment. I made a quick deduction. This was SDS Daphne, of course. I imagined she had gone to the Democratic National Convention with Terry, part of some political group.

"Are you with Terry?"

"I was."

Where was the sassy girl who had gotten herself kicked out of an army recruiting center? And how did she get my home number? And why was she calling?

"What's going on?"

"Riots. Tear gas. Beatings."

"Yes, I'm watching all that on TV. Are you safe? What can I do?"

"Can you come to Chicago?" She was sounding stronger. I could feel my muscles relax and my protective instincts dial down a notch.

"Start from the beginning."

"Terry and I came here to be with the Yippies. You know, Abbie Hoffman, Tom Hayden, Jerry Rubin, and the rest. They wanted to disrupt the convention because the Democrats weren't going to nominate a peace candidate. I know it all registers as frivolous from the outside, but we're all just trying to save the lives of Vietnamese people and American soldiers."

"I know that, Daphne. You really don't have to convince me."

"Anyway, with RFK dead, it's pretty clear that Humphrey is just being anointed by the party!" Her old anger flared.

"Why are you calling?"

"Terry's in jail. He's going to be indicted for resisting arrest, criminal trespass, and incitement to riot. I tried to raise bail money, but he was able to get me a message that he didn't want to be bailed out. He wants to stay in jail and go on trial like the big shots. I'm sick of politics being taken into the street and I'm supposed to just hang around while he plays hero."

"But why do you need me?" I didn't mind flying out, but school was starting, and I didn't see what I could do. The rioting would be ending before I arrived.

"I watched it, Garrett. I saw a kid take down the flag,

and I watched the police beat him bloody for it. I can't explain how shocked I feel. It was like watching a newsreel from Nazi Germany. Then the crowd went wild, and the cops began throwing tear gas."

"Did you get sick?"

"No, Terry and I seemed to be all right, but I moved away from the cops and the melee. Terry ran toward it and joined in the brawl. I think he totally forgot I was there. Then he got arrested. I can't stop thinking about the guy the cops beat to a bloody pulp."

This was like the peace march, but even worse. I had just watched a newscaster say that even Humphrey was affected in his hotel room near the convention center.

"But you're okay, right? You're not hurt and not sick?" I asked again.

"I guess." She clearly just needed moral support.

"By the time I get there, all the fireworks are going to be over. Do you have a plane ticket?"

"No. Terry wanted to leave things open-ended, in case he wanted us to do organizing work in Chicago."

"What about school?" I asked.

"I guess he doesn't think high school is very important."

Little shit, I thought, though he wasn't little and probably wasn't a shit, just a self-righteous ideologue.

"Here's what we're going to do. You're going to go somewhere and have something to eat. At least get some coffee. Do you have money?"

"Yeah, I have enough money for that."

"You need to be totally off the street. Find someplace where they say you can take a phone call. Then call me with the number. I am going to see about getting you on a plane. Do you have a credit card?"

"Get real. I'm a seventeen-year-old girl. Even my mother doesn't have a credit card in her own name."

"Right. I'll buy the ticket. You'll just have to get to the airport. Do you have enough money for a cab?"

"Yeah, I think so."

"Okay. Call me when you have a number where I can reach you."

When she called, I had to give her the bad news that it was impossible to buy a ticket at that time of night. Offices reopened at nine the next morning.

"Do you want me to arrange a hotel room?" I asked.

"You know, I can just stay here. This is an all-night coffee shop. The people are really nice. I'll just keep buying coffee and donuts until morning. I don't want to go anywhere, and I can't imagine sleeping. Besides, I don't want to be alone in a hotel room. I have a book in my purse—Vonnegut's *Cat's Cradle*. It's really good." Her voice sounded almost clipped. She had a no-nonsense quality that I didn't recognize.

I called her once during the night to make sure she was okay. At nine fifteen a.m. I called with an update: "A ticket for the noon flight is being held at the reservations desk in your name." I gave her the gate number. "Be there an hour early."

"I will."

"Then I'll pick you up at LaGuardia."

"See you then."

It was late afternoon in New York when her plane landed. I waited at the gate. I hated the harsh fluorescent lights of the airport and its high-pitched hum. Almost as soon as the board marked her plane as landed I saw her flame-colored hair done up in a French braid down her back and not her customary side braid. It made her seem older and more put-together, just as her white oxford shirt and fashionable jeans did.

"Garrett." She gave me a perfunctory hug. "You've grown a beard. It looks good on you."

"Luggage?" I asked.

"Everything is in my backpack. It doesn't make much sense, does it, when we didn't know how long we were going to stay. Terry told me to just pack the basics—a few tops, something to sleep in, a toothbrush, other toiletries, and a couple of books."

We sat down in an airport restaurant and I ordered a coffee.

"None for me, thanks. I've had enough coffee for a month." But she let me buy her a sandwich and a Coke, not that horrible TaB that Ur-Daphne drank.

"I can take you back to New Paltz with me, if you need a place to stay."

"That's so nice of you, but everything is under control. I'm going to stay with a girlfriend. Her mother is really cool. She knows about Terry, but doesn't care. Not a prude. She's happy to have me. Their household is just the two of them, her and my friend Liz. She even said I could stay with them until I finish high school, but I don't know about that. I *do* want to stay at my new school. I'm their star debater, and I think we could come first in the state. But thanks for the offer."

"You've been busy getting everything sorted out. Should I drive you or do you want to take the train?"

"Either is fine, though it would be fun to catch up in the car."

"Car it is."

She looped her arm through mine in a very grown-up gesture and we walked to short-term parking. I had the oddest feeling that I had just met a fifth Daphne. I heard the change right while we were on the phone. SDS Daphne must have decided to stay in Chicago with Terry. Of course, I was just speculating, but this dispassionate girl seemed like she'd be running the world someday. I wondered how many other Schrödinger girls I would never meet.

CHAPTER TWENTY-FIVE

IN SEPTEMBER THE FALL SEMESTER began the way it always did. The two seminars, one on Pavlov and the other on Watson and Skinner, were in smallish classrooms, whereas Introduction to Psychology, Section 3, emphasis on behaviorism, was in the small lecture hall because my classes were never very full, although they were always respectably attended. I was a fair teacher, but I used to be a rather dry lecturer.

Thirty-seven students were enrolled; the class was capped at fifty, which was the capacity of the room. The bookstore had put up a sign that the textbook was mandatory for the first day of class, and I usually got about 80 percent in compliance.

I began my first-day lecture the same way I always did, with a brief history of psychology, until we got to Pavlov, and then I directed the students to open their texts to notice images of the apparatus he used for his experiments with dogs. Somewhere in the middle of my explanation, as they were taking in the illustrations, I stared up at the ceiling, and it suddenly began its green-purple paisley dance. Some would call this experience a flashback, but I prefer to think that in a boring situation my neurology provided some diversion. I now found the world stripped of acid too prosaic, and I felt the class stifling.

"Close your books," I commanded. About thirty books slammed shut at the same time, making an impressive percussive sound. "I'm taking a casual poll. Raise your hand if you would mind switching your section to Intro to Psych, Section 4, consciousness expansion."

"Dr. Adams," someone called out, "that course doesn't exist."

"I know that," I assured him, "but I am proposing to bring it into existence right now instead of the course you signed up for. You guys are in charge. If you want to leave things as they are, we can. But if you want something a little more cutting edge, we can do that too. The textbooks will still be good. So, raise your hands if you disapprove of the change." I gazed out at the lecture hall. I saw beards, shell necklaces, bell-bottoms, bandannas, long hair, tie-dyed shirts, camouflage jackets, long skirts, and leotards. Of course, there were some khakis, polo shirts, and Peter Pan collars as well, but I thought my proposal stood a good chance of carrying the day. Indeed, not one hand was raised.

"So, we're doing this?" I asked. I received a resounding yes in response.

That was on a Monday. By Wednesday all fifty seats were filled; thirteen new people had registered for the class. I told them about a hypothetical experiment that involved Schrödinger's equation, which I put on the board. I could actually explain all its symbols. I also asked if anyone had heard of Hugh Everett, and although no one had, many had seen the *Twilight Zone* episode that talked about alternate realities. "So, we are going to talk about a very hypothetical situation, one that would be utterly impossible in the world, even the world Everett describes, a situation that defies the laws of physics but teaches us a lot about personality. We are going to talk about one girl separating into different iterations, with different personalities. One personality is lighthearted and inquisitive. One is elegant and aesthetic. Another is political, angry, and direct, and yet another is wounded and earthy. How do these personalities come about? How would they react in different situations? Can one personality ever morph into another? These are some of the questions we are going to be investigating through role-play, group work, and speculation. We are going to discuss the roots of personality and the implications of the differing personalities and their relationships to differing destinies. Let's name this hypothetical girl Diana, after the many phases of the moon."

We called this the Diana Project. The class was split into groups and each group was going to be responsible for exploring a different personality and the life events that might precipitate it. I had never used such an innovative teaching approach before.

I outlined the rest of the class for them too: "We are going to talk about perception and the nature of perception, especially the experience of transcendence. We cover abnormal and social psychology in the second half of the course next semester."

By Friday I had a new course outline with Schrödinger, Jung, Leary, Alpert, Maslow, Fromm, and Laing, along with the more historical sections of the text. I put articles on reserve in the library for them to read because not all this new material was in their textbooks. I brought fifty copies of one article I had mimeographed, but they weren't nearly enough. It was still the add/drop period, and my class had doubled to seventy-five. We needed a new classroom.

I had designated Fridays as my day to trip over the summer, and some wicked impulse led me to drop a tiny dose of mescaline before my Friday lecture. I brought the psychology department record player with me, managing its bulky mass across the parking lot. I also carried *Magical Mystery Tour* to play to my class. *The Magical Mystery Tour is coming to take you away, coming to take you away.*

I knew I was skating on thin ice. Any hint that I was doing drugs or advocating drugs would probably have resulted in my immediate dismissal, but I made an ingenious argument. The rationale stated on my syllabus was this: *Course Objectives: 1) To understand the history of psychology. 2) To explore the New Age psychedelic experience without the aid of drugs, to understand consciousness expansion, and to explore human potential.*

I'd carefully disavowed the use of drugs right on this first handout. I hoped that would be enough to protect me from reprimands from the department chair, or worse. After we listened to one side of the album I explained the ways in which the music expanded consciousness. The small mescaline dose helped my insight, though I was so nervous that I vowed never to trip in class again. What had I been thinking?

Back at the psychology department office I returned the record player to its cubby. When I checked my mailbox there was an urgent message from the chair to stop by his office as soon as I got the note. Things were sleepy on Fridays so he would be available.

Alex Dyer's office was at the other end of the hall from mine, and I could hear my shoes squeak on the highly polished linoleum as I traversed the distance between them. Mescaline usually created a very mellow space, but I was feeling paranoid. I felt transparent and afraid I had blown my entire career out of boredom and out of delight in Daphne and in drugs. The institutional sickly green walls had never appeared less aesthetic, even with the traces of tripping paisley that adorned them. I had proverbial butterflies in my stomach again, but my facile brain saw the butterflies actually flying before me, their beautiful orange-gold and black wings the markings of a flight of monarchs.

My mouth felt dry as I entered the room, and time stretched out like taffy as Dr. Dyer, disheveled as ever, slowly turned toward me after I arrived to find him staring out the window. Forever seemed to pass before I could gauge the expression on his face. Had he found out about the mescaline? Was I fired?

"Garrett!" he exclaimed. "Come in. Come in." He seemed to be smiling, yet I didn't know if I could trust my own perceptions. "I heard about your lectures," he began, "and I looked over the syllabus you dropped off with the secretary this morning. We have had to cut off enrollment . . ." *That sounds ominous. Maybe the class is being pulled. Maybe I'm going to be relieved of my duties.* ". . . because the enrollment has reached a hundred, and that's the absolute legal limit for classes in this building. Congratulations, Garrett. Well done. From thirty-seven to one hundred? That's the stuff! And the best thing is most of these kids aren't transferring in from other psych sections; they're coming from religion, anthropology, and sociology classes. If we can get them in our intro course maybe we can grow our department and even add a line. But I'm getting ahead of myself."

My palpitations stopped immediately although I didn't trust myself to appear normal. "You don't mind my not doing my behavioral section?"

"You have your advanced seminar for that."

"You know I don't have training in this area. I'm sort of making it up as I go."

"No, but you're a trained psychologist, and no one really has any training here. You could get some," he suggested.

"A colleague is at Esalen. A good friend, actually. Perhaps I could take a course there."

"Sure. Good idea."

"How about using the word *psychedelic*? You're okay with that?"

"As long as you don't discuss actual drugs in class or make them a part of the curriculum in any way, I think it's ingenious. We don't have to lose the explorers to drugs. I support your syllabus."

"You know that consciousness experiments often come from drugs, right? Indians and peyote, for example."

"Of course. And medieval mysticism often came from ergot poisoning, but we're not going to throw out St. Francis and St. Teresa because of it."

He surprised me. He had always seemed like a stodgy social psychologist, but lately I'd been learning that he'd been a Marxist when he was young and still carried some of his fervor. And now he was surprisingly open-minded and even insightful. Maybe I didn't give other people enough credit.

"One more thing," he added. "I like your hypothetical Diana. I heard the kids were really excited about it." He must have read my mind because he said, "I haven't been giving you enough credit as a teacher. The Diana Project. It really has a good ring to it. I suggest you start keeping notes. It sounds like something you can publish as a unique pedagogical approach."

I could never, ever let on that Diana was really Daphne and that Daphne was real.

My dose of mescaline had been so small that I stopped tripping within an hour or two of my meeting with Dyer. I still couldn't believe my good luck. I'd spent all those years never stepping a toe out of line, and now, here I was transgressing boundaries and risking my reputation and being rewarded for it. I'd had no idea the world worked like this. I wished someone had told me sooner. If playing the bad boy was really rewarded, I decided to press my luck further. Coming off the enormous high of having en-rolled one hundred students into my Intro to Psych class, I decided to take my daring into my personal life.

I had no idea where things stood between Caroline and Tom, but I felt that it was bullshit to have been edged out of her life like that. I loved her, and I wanted her back. Something as small as my Daphne obsession shouldn't have to separate us forever. Caroline was just being silly. Besides, much to my great sadness, my last meetings with each girl felt like goodbyes. I didn't expect that I'd be see-ing any of them soon. The only Schrödinger girl I longed for and was really waiting to see was Ur-Daphne, whom I hadn't seen in almost a year. I worried that I would never see her again. She and I had not said goodbye.

I knew I would miss the others, but I was getting used to loss, and they seemed to be going about their lives without much need of me. I'd seen the Daphnes so many times on my weekly acid trips that she had become part of me, the memories as vibrant as my memories of my father, and the improbable meetings I'd had with them just as challenging to understanding reality. I still had conviction of their truth, and now this conviction had sent my career soaring! The gifts she'd brought me were boundless.

Each Schrödinger girl resembled a refracted ray of light, part of the entire light spectrum. Ur-Daphne represented a beam of white light, the combined potential of the other Schrödinger girls, the way white light contains all frequencies of light. My acid explorations had allowed me to remember her with such vividness that sometimes it felt as if she had actually appeared—but I was still waiting for her.

I had two small tabs of mescaline to take with me to see Caroline. I decided not to call her. If she was with Tom when I knocked on her door unexpectedly, so be it. We'd all be embarrassed and that would be that. The early-September light along the Hudson was the most beautiful of any time of year, especially in the late afternoon several hours before sunset. An azure-gold miasma seemed to rise from the river.

After Friday-evening congestion on the George Washington Bridge, I was finally in Manhattan and cruising down the West Side Highway to Caroline's apartment. I think I must have been a little manic because I should have been nervous, but I wasn't. I should probably have also realized that I was being boorish by disrespecting her very clearly communicated desire for distance between us, but my success at school had filled me with dreams of glory.

Soon enough I found myself knocking on her door. When she answered, as beautiful and collected as ever, her smart black dress still on from her workday, her hair twisted into a casual bun that enhanced her cheekbones, I knew I still wanted her. When she registered that it was me, conflicting emotions flitted across her face, and I could see her struggle to master them. She was surprised, annoyed, elated, and confused. I watched her compose her features, and she used a composed voice to match.

"To what do I owe this honor?"

"To my love for you and my extreme desire to see you."

"Garrett," she sighed wearily, "I thought we went over all this. Things just don't work between us. We want different things."

"Maybe, but I miss you terribly. Do you miss me?"

"I'm not sure I want to talk about that."

"Can I come in?"

"It's hot. And you know how small the place is."

"Have you eaten?" She shook her head. "How about we share a pizza?"

"Oh, all right," she said, giving in.

We sat at a red plastic booth drinking beer at a table covered with a red-and-white-check paper tablecloth. After the server put a slice of pizza on each plate we began to eat and felt freer to converse.

"How do things stand between you and Tom?" I plunged in.

Her answer was direct: "We're not seeing each other anymore."

"Why not?"

"He was just too normal. I couldn't bear it. I thought I wanted the picket fence and all that, and he's an actor, for god's sake—flighty, right? But no, he's so steady and mundane I thought I'd scream. And you're too crazy. Clearly I'm a girl who can't be pleased. And now I'm thirty-five so it's all over for me anyway. No babies. No marriage. Just art."

"Hm. Maybe you're being just a little melodramatic?"

"Fuck you, Garrett."

"Quite so," I said. "I apologize."

After a longish silence, I took a deep breath and said, "How about we put all that aside for tonight. No mention of touchy topics. How about we have an old fashioned date? Just fun. Holding hands. Getting lucky at the end of the night. We can sort the rest out later."

"You're different. Where did this nonchalant confidence come from?"

"It's a long story that breaks the rules of date night. All I can say is that I had a big win at school, and I'm still high on that. But no more for tonight."

"Okay," she agreed, though I subtly registered some reluctance in the droop of her shoulders and her quizzical raised brow.

Back at her place, I asked her if she wanted to drop the last two tabs of mescaline. Yes, my usage was getting excessive, but I'd had such a tiny dose that morning that I didn't see the harm in doing a little bit more. I had discovered a world of spiritual fulfillment and aesthetic excitement. I thought a new point of view might help Caroline now.

"I know all about your acid experience. Tom told me."

"He was great to me, by the way."

"Yeah. He's a great guy. Don't remind me. I must be crazy to have sent him packing."

"Remember when you said you weren't looking for Prince Charming anymore? That perfection? *That's* Prince Charming."

"I see what you mean."

"It's your choice. Too straight or too crazy. You get to choose."

"Um, too crazy?" She laughed.

"Good answer. I'm sitting right here."

"Why should I take this mescaline? It scares me. I don't even smoke pot."

"I don't either."

"You don't?"

"Once. It's really good if you want to eat a whole plate of brownies. Otherwise, it's not really my thing."

"But mescaline and acid?"

"You see things, Caroline. I'll tell you what. I won't take the mescaline. I'll guide you, like Tom did for me."

"No. I don't want that. I don't want a straight person watching me."

"I won't think anything."

"It's creepy."

In the end we both took the drug. I loved watching Caroline become excited by her visions. She devoured each piece of art hanging on her walls. "I never knew the colors were soooooooo vibrant," she said. "I mean, red is really red. Everything is like van Gogh painted it."

"If you say so, my darling art historian."

We crammed into her tiny shower together for the first time. It had always seemed silly to me to fold ourselves into such a miniscule space, but now it felt just right. The hot water surrounded us like a curtain. Her streaming black hair struck me as primordial, and her laughter came from deep within her flattened belly. The nipples on her breasts were fragrant roses I couldn't get enough of. I entered her while we were both standing in the water, each thrust turning the world rose gold. Caroline exclaimed, "So golden!" so she was there too, in the mist of gold, like in a Klimt, like in the Daphne Klimt. Golden water surrounded us, and we came forever.

When we'd used up all the hot water, we edged ourselves out of that tiny space and toweled each other off. Caroline was lovely, every curve of her body expressive. I had buried myself inside her as deep as I could go, and I felt her accepting me. We watched the stars through the skylight, flaming constellations that no one but us had ever seen before.

The next morning we didn't say much to each other. We didn't want to ruin the afterglow. "I'll be in contact in November," she said. "Forester is sending me back to San Francisco for a while. I'll mail you the keys in case you want to use the apartment while I'm gone."

She'd never offered that before. Something had changed.

"I think you should be careful," she added. "About the acid, I mean. It could get to be a habit. That was beautiful, but I don't think I'd want to trip again. I'll just keep that experience in my treasure box."

"Remember I told you things were going well at school? I'm teaching a course on having psychedelic experiences without drugs. I've got to practice that myself. Blake, Swedenborg, Rimbaud . . ."

"Bosch," she chimed in.

"Sure. And Blake's illustrations. And the amazing shafts of light in Vermeer."

We embraced again, and parted. Daphne hadn't been mentioned. All the ends were being wrapped up in the Schrödinger girls' lives, and they were off on their own adventures.

But where was Ur-Daphne?

CHAPTER TWENTY-SIX

TWO MONTHS LATER I STILL HADN'T HEARD from Ur-Daphne. I reconciled myself to the possibility that she was never coming back. I had stopped my acid trips, staying true to the vision of my course. I still spent time with the time line and listened to all the music she'd given me. I could hear her laughter when I conjured her in my mind. I broke down and called Daphne's house as I had in the past, but just like then, I never reached her that way. The first time, her father answered the phone and I panicked and hung up immediately. The next time, it was her mother who kindly told me that Daphne wasn't home. I could tell that she thought I was just a teenage friend. Her voice was casual and helpful. "Sure, I'll tell her you called," she said. "Do you want to leave a number?" I assured her that Daphne knew how to reach me, but she never called.

But happily, Caroline, true to her word, called me in the middle of November. I was in the doldrums from Nixon's election.

"I have a big favor," she began.

"Shoot," I said.

"I want you to spend Thanksgiving with me. Just us."

That wasn't so much a favor as a blessing. This year

I had planned on going to Florida to my mom's, but the flights were expensive and very crowded. I had been waiting until the last minute to book my flight, hoping for some deliverance, and now it had come. "I can do that," I said.

"I'm still away, so you make the arrangements."

I booked dinner in one of New York's fanciest eateries. I chose the three o'clock sitting. I've always been in favor of an afternoon Thanksgiving meal, and the parade would be over by then, so traffic would not be a problem, although it would cost a month's salary—only a bit of an exaggeration. The restaurant was housed in a brownstone on the Upper East Side. Although I usually eschewed fancy New York City venues, I had read that this restaurant was filled with flowers, and I wanted to celebrate the occasion of Caroline and my Thanksgiving together. I felt true gratitude. Jerry had once raved about the food. I had hoped he'd come home to spend Thanksgiving with his parents so we could get together, but they were having a big hippie Thanksgiving in California, and he wanted to be there.

I may have given up tripping, but I'd kept my beard. Thanksgiving morning, I groomed it carefully and wore my best shirt and the gray pinstripe suit. Caroline and I decided to meet up at the restaurant, and she was already seated when I arrived. She seemed different, softer. And a small smile played about her mouth.

"Hello, kid," she said, sounding like Jerry. Why not? She knew him too. She wore a fitted dress in mauve, if I'm thinking of the right color. The tone suited her black hair, and it was a treat to see her out of black.

I took my seat across from her and we each ordered a glass of champagne.

"I have some news," she said.

"I hope it's not that you're moving to San Francisco permanently."

"No, it's not that. It's something quite different. I'm pregnant."

"You are? How? When? Is it mine?"

"You are definitely the father, and as to how and when, all I can say is that some people don't remember to use birth control when they're taking mescaline. Our baby was conceived in the shower. Like Zeus and Danaë conceived Perseus in a mist of gold. Rembrandt, Titian, and Klimt all painted it."

"Oh wow," I said. I was happy; no, I was beyond happy, because Caroline had so longed for this, but I was also feeling déjà vu. Was it my fate to always get my women pregnant by accident before any true commitments had been made? A shiver went down my spine as I fervently hoped this baby would not meet Amy's fate.

"Are you happy, Caroline?"

"Beyond measure. I am giving thanks."

"What about all my flaws and vagaries? They have been very important to you."

"A trifle," she said.

"Are you sure?"

"How about this," she ventured. "We have until June, until the baby's born, to decide if we'll be loving friends raising our baby or if we'll bow to convention and maybe even get married."

"That sounds fine, providing I can go to doctors' appointments and get to be part of the pregnancy."

"I agree. We'll see how it goes."

"How are you feeling?"

"So good. No morning sickness."

"Do you show?"

She got up out of her chair, and sure enough, there was just the tiniest mound of fullness where the flattest stomach had been.

"Did you know that Galen Green is in Florence for a year?" she asked once she was seated.

I allowed that I had.

"He shipped back another Daphne portrait. It's magnificent. Really. In this portrait she has become the tree, roots and all, but it's not sad. I don't know how he did it. Do you want to wander over to visit the gallery after we eat? It's open. We just wanted an excuse to have mulled wine and pumpkin bread for regulars."

She searched my face. I was being tested, and I didn't know which answer she wanted. She had described the painting so admiringly that only a churl would elect not to see it. And yet, if I was too enthusiastic the delicate détente between us might just dissolve. I told the truth.

"No, I think I've seen enough of the portraits," I said.

"You're sure?"

"I am."

I left out the part about being desperate to see the actual Daphne, Ur-Daphne. A portrait of Galen's Daphne would only make the longing more acute.

I enjoyed watching Caroline eat so much food. And then eat both of our slices of pumpkin pie as well. By tacit consent, although I saw her home, I did not go in. We were going to be friends, or we were going to be spouses. We were not going to occupy the gray zone in between, and it was months until this decision would be made.

* * *

The time flew by in a whirl. Do pregnancies always speed up time? There were trips to the city for doctors' appointments. There was a day spent enjoying all the shower gifts, and there was a day going to a store to watch Caroline try on maternity clothes, proclaiming whether or not each item made her look fat. All the outfits were the same—concealing. You knew there was a swelling stomach in there somewhere, but the clothes weren't volunteering anything.

Things continued to be equally frenetic at school. I had never taught a hundred students before. Why was this enrollment supposed to be a good thing? I didn't get paid more, and the workload had tripled! On the other hand, it was great fun to hear excitement in my students' voices.

We were working our way through an analysis of the Beatles' *White Album*, which had come out right around Thanksgiving. The psychology of the album was one of the choices for the final exam, as was Hesse's *Damian*, and the Diana Project was the subject of their final paper. It had become a massive set of notes our class had put together based on our investigations into personality— the imaginary personalities of the hypothetical Dianas. I felt as if for the first time my students were doing analysis they cared about instead of learning an experimental method that might be accurate but had no practical meaning for them unless they became researchers.

By Christmas my longing for Daphne was so acute that I went into an antique shop and bought her a Christmas present. I found the perfect thing: a vintage pin of a branching tree made of antique gold. Each leaf had a tiny emerald chip. I asked the shop to convert it into a pendant—pins were for old ladies. Of course, I found something for Caroline too, and I trotted along beside her as she chose Christmas gifts for the baby she was carrying, all practical things she would need once the child was born.

Having had a stillborn infant, I found her optimism unsettling, but heroic. When we got around to picking out the crib, I wanted to run out of the store. I was shocked at the depth of my feelings. I'd never allowed myself to feel the sadness of Amy's death before. Emotional doors were opening; my life was like the ecstatic day at Coney Island when Caroline and I had ridden the Cyclone, the day I had also carelessly promised to take her and our future daughter on the teacup ride.

I felt like I was on a roller coaster at school too. I'd become so popular on campus that I was assigned two sections of our introductory class, each with the New Age emphasis I had pioneered the previous semester. The Diana Project name stuck, and it became a staple of the course. Every time we talked about Diana I wanted to talk about Daphne. I wanted to celebrate her. I wanted to capture her essence in the classroom, but most of all I still wanted her to return.

By late winter, Caroline's pregnancy really showed. She delighted in wearing her new maternity clothes. I loved watching her happiness, though I felt disloyal in keeping my longing for Daphne from her. She was an intuitive woman, and I'm sure she suspected my feelings. However, the rules of our agreement allowed me to keep them to myself until the day of reckoning. When the birth of our child was still a few months off, I felt that we needed a game plan in place for when the baby came.

On a temperate March day, Caroline took the train to Poughkeepsie to decide if she'd be bringing the baby home to New Paltz after giving birth in Manhattan. Although the vernal equinox was still a few weeks away, I noticed the first snowdrops, the earliest stirring of spring, when I picked her up at the station. We drove straight home to my clapboard house, and she immediately marched upstairs to the space she had made so cozy with the quilt she had chosen.

"I think the guest room would be perfect for the baby," she said, "but if we're not a couple, then I'd have to sleep in there." She seemed to assume that she would be leaving Manhattan. That was fine with me. I wanted to watch my child grow up.

"I guess I could give up my study," I said. To be honest, it felt like a deserted space without the Daphne time line, which I had removed soon after learning about Caroline's pregnancy. I wanted her to feel safe in every room of my house.

"Weren't you talking about taking over Jerry's apartment?" she asked.

"Yeah, but that was a silly pipe dream. And now with a baby, I don't think I'd want to spend four hours commuting."

"Do we have enough money if I decide to stay home with the baby for a while?"

"We could manage."

"You could take the study downstairs, and the baby and I could live upstairs. Friends, you know?"

"We're not going to make it as a couple?"

"Garrett," she said so softly I could barely hear her as we walked down the stairs to the living room, "have you taken that time line down yet?"

"Actually, I have, but I'm not over Daphne. I still need to understand her."

"We're friends, whatever happens. And whatever happens, it's okay."

"People just keep vanishing," I said. "My dad, Helena, Amy, even Jerry, and now Daphne."

"It's time to learn how to say goodbye, Garrett."

"How are you at that?" I asked her.

"We're not talking about me. Maybe you should visit your dad's headstone."

I had been trying to say goodbye to my father for almost my entire life. They had never recovered his body, so technically speaking he had no real grave. As a behaviorist, a man of science, I had little interest in religion and even less in visiting a headstone placed over an empty grave. Now that I was expecting another baby maybe it was time for me to visit Amy's grave.

Helena was still near Ithaca, and by calling the Ithaca College alumni office I was able to get her phone number. When she answered I heard the laughter of a child in the background, a rich, happy sound. There was laughter in Helena's voice too. "Garrett. It's been a long time. We were just having dinner. My middle son loves to tell jokes, and he was laughing the most at his own. I love that about him."

"Sorry to intrude. Maybe I should call back another time."

"No, it's okay. What can I do for you?"

"I want to visit Amy's grave. Will you come with me?"

"No, I don't think so. I've never felt like we were her parents together. You didn't want to be. I forgave you, but no, I don't think I want to stand over our baby's grave with you."

"I understand," I said.

"Why the sudden interest?"

"I am about to have a child."

"That's wonderful. I'm happy for you."

"Yes, it's great, but I tend to get stuck on things—the past—and . . . well, other things too. I'm trying to clear out some of the cobwebs and scar tissue. Wouldn't it be Amy's eighteenth birthday?"

"You remember."

"This is embarrassing, but I was only there that one time . . . and I haven't been back since. I have no idea where to go."

She gave me the directions and wished me luck with the new baby, and I wished her luck too. I wondered if I'd ever hear her voice again. I wasn't sure I liked thawing out and all these emotions.

Helena's parents had arranged everything all those years ago. They had bought a plot near Ithaca because their daughter was still in school, and they wanted her to be able to visit the grave as much as she needed to.

I drove up on the first true weekend of spring, right around Amy's birthday. Her grave was in a lovely spot, on a high escarpment. There were only a few graves up there, presided over by a stand of birches that hadn't yet come into leaf. I stared at the headstone with her dates. Born and died the same day, though we couldn't be sure she didn't die the day before. The doctors had been cagey. Her gravestone said, *Amy Adams*. I hadn't expected that, though I should have. There were those few months when Helena was an Adams herself. Still, I hadn't expected it, and I found that it made me unaccountably sad, and ashamed. I sat down on the grass near the marker and reflected on how self-absorbed I'd been. It's true that I was only twenty-one, but I didn't think that should have given me a free pass. I had had a daughter. I had had a pregnant wife. But I hadn't acted like it. Helena had only her parents to turn to. I had deserted my wife and daughter, and I didn't want that happening again.

In that moment I saw that I would have to give up Daphne. That's just the way it was. If I wanted to be a mensch, as Jerry would say, I could only live in one reality. I had to be all in. I was almost forty now, and it was time for me to do the hard thing. It seemed that Daphne was out of my life by her own choice. I would have to stop longing for her. If I could.

The baby came right on schedule in the middle of June, the perfect time, when my semester was over, so I could be with Caroline. The infant was strong, with a full head of dark hair like her mother. Caroline had a pretty easy time of it considering her age. She wanted me in the delivery room like so many couples were doing, but I was a crotchety almost-forty-year-old father, a relic, and I wanted to pace in the waiting room like my father had. I loved his story about smoking during my birth. He told me that he'd said, "Some son of a bitch burned a hole in my tie," meaning himself. I wished he were there to celebrate with me. I missed giving Jerry a cigar too. He had already sent a huge giraffe.

The next morning I entered Caroline's room as a shock of sunlight poured through the window. "Hello, you," I said. Our daughter was learning to nurse, and I swelled with an inexplicable pride, watching the rosy baby suckle on her mother's nipple. There were over 3.5

billion people in the world, so why was I proud? It was
just a dumb but universal feeling.

Caroline's face looked like a Renaissance Madonna
as the sunlight refracted off her opalescent skin. I could
see that she'd been waiting a long time for motherhood.
In preparation for the birth I had read some articles discussing postpartum depression, a syndrome that was just
being discovered. I could see that I needn't have, but I
wasn't used to such happiness.

I hadn't looked at the mail from the last few days to
sort through all the good wishes from friends and relatives who hadn't been able to make the shower. In my
mind, I was going over the instructions I'd received about
holding a baby. People kept insisting that I needed to support her head, and I was nervous just thinking about it. I
could hurt her, or even worse, drop her, but she was my
daughter, and I was going to have to hold her after I emp-
tied my arms of the mail. However, she had fallen asleep
nursing, so Caroline put her in the basinette, and I laid
the mail next to her on the bed. As it scattered, I glimpsed
a postcard in the familiar purple-flair writing and caught
the word *graduation,* which had been set off by an ex-
clamation point. My pulse quickened, and I wanted to
snatch it back, but I restrained myself. Instead I said, "I
have to pee," to buy time.

Once in the bathroom I turned on the faucets full blast
and sat down on the lidded toilet. I could feel each beat of
my heart and a constriction in my chest. I was imagining
Caroline reading Daphne's postcard and frowning. We'd
both been holding our breaths, waiting for the baby to
be born, avoiding the big unanswered question of our
future. After seeing Amy's grave I foolishly thought it

would be easy to give up Daphne once I saw my baby, but it wasn't. Not at all.

"Garrett," Caroline called from the other room. With the bathroom door closed and the noise of the rushing jets, I couldn't gauge her mood. I felt like I was about to face a firing squad.

As I walked back in, I stole a glance at Caroline, but her face wasn't giving anything away. She'd moved all the mail, and she gestured for me to sit down beside her.

"Did you see Daphne's postcard?" Her coal-black hair was twisted in back in a casual knot secured by her favorite silver holder. One of us sighed, but I honestly couldn't say which one of us it was.

"I don't get it," she said. "High school graduation? Daphne is studying art history at Sarah Lawrence. Her bio at the gallery says so."

I didn't know what to say. I didn't want to start our familiar argument so I just waited.

"But here's this postcard," she said, thinking out loud. Then she ordered, "Say something!"

"I love you. I love our baby. I don't want to screw it up."

"You have to say something."

So I did: "I believe the four Daphnes are real. I do. But I decided that I'm going to give up all the Schrödinger thinking so I can be a real dad, though I haven't the faintest idea of how to do that. Especially with a daughter. Do you think she'll like baseball?" Then I remembered our day at Coney Island. "We can take her on the teacup ride."

"Yeah, that makes a dad," Caroline said tartly. But

she wasn't really angry. "You're going to give up all that crazy stuff? The time line? The meetings?"

I couldn't get my voice to work right then, so I nodded heavily. I knew it was true.

"Maybe I don't want you to," she said. "Sacrifice for us, I mean."

"Yes, you do. You're afraid it's crazy."

"I still can't tell if it's crazy or true."

"I know." I didn't have a clue about what she was thinking. Other people are always mysteries. "I am going to see her, though," I told her. "To celebrate her graduation."

"Of course. I want you to," she offered.

Neither of us said any more about Daphne. We didn't want to jinx it by talking about craziness, or truth, or other universes, or myths, or physics. We just held hands and watched our daughter sleep.

"What are we going to call her?" I inquired. We'd already decided on Garrett for a boy, but Caroline was evasive whenever I asked her ideas about girls' names.

"Remember when I told you I was named after my father's grandmother, Caroline, and my mother's mother, Tanya? What I didn't mention was that I promised my parents I would name my own daughter after my father's mother."

"At the Russian Tea Room," I remembered. "What was her name?" I asked with an odd feeling of anticipation.

"Daphne," Caroline whispered. "Her name was Daphne."

"Oh my god! Daphne?" I yelped, my voice rising an octave. I felt the same excitement as when I'd stood in the bookstore and the Schrödinger girl had lifted the hood of her rain slicker. I couldn't wait to see the color my daughter's eyes would be. "Yes," I said, leaning over to kiss the mother of my child, "that's our daughter's name."

CHAPTER TWENTY-SEVEN

DAPHNE'S NOTE SPECIFIED THAT I MEET HER in her hometown on Long Island at the very fancy Villa Victor at seven p.m. on June 29. She wanted to drive herself to show off her new license. I got to the restaurant first. Patrons chose this romantic venue for the pond in the front of the restaurant where actual swans floated gracefully, impervious to the traffic on the main thoroughfare in front. I thought of Daphne in Boston posing with the swan boats. It's funny the way motifs recur in people's lives. I left my car to be parked by an attendant and squatted by the swans, watching their reflections in the water. Two swans became four; simulacra fill our universe.

I waited at the reservation desk for Daphne to arrive so we could be seated together. She swept in, small and vibrant as always, dressed in a simple black sheath, her cloud of curly auburn hair swirling about her, making her into a pre-Raphaelite princess.

"Garrett," she said, meeting my eyes with a steady gaze, "you look different. You got contact lenses." Her voice was neutral—I couldn't tell whether or not she liked them. And there was a spark missing from her emerald eyes. I wondered if something was wrong.

We were seated, and I gazed around, noticing other

recent graduates about the room, their families beaming with pride. We were at one of those places reserved for special occasions. The tables were a generous distance apart, and the ambiance was hushed and elegant, yet I felt stifled. Apart from my date with Caroline at the Russian Tea Room, and then our recent joyous Thanksgiving, I had never appreciated the pretension of fancy restaurants.

I had resigned myself to talking to Daphne in this mausoleum when I caught her eye, and she said, "This isn't a good place to talk. I have an idea." She asked a passing busboy if she could to speak to the maître d'. I was surprised at how effortlessly she took control. She really had grown up.

"Is there any way we could sit outside? The swans are so enchanting. Do you have any tables where we could eat alfresco?"

"No, miss. Sorry. We have some small tables out back, but they're just for cocktails. We use them at weddings."

"I'm sorry too," she said. "Could you arrange to get our car?"

"As you wish. May I have your ticket?"

I gave him the chit. "I thought you were driving yourself. Don't you have a car to retrieve?"

"No, at the last minute I decided to be dropped off in case I wanted to drink."

I left a one-dollar bill, generous since we hadn't ordered anything, on the table, and we went to wait by the swans. Their metamorphosis from small gray birds to these elegant creatures was the stuff of myth and fairy tale.

"Where shall we go?" I asked.

"Let's go to Cold Spring Harbor and sit at a clam joint by the water."

That sounded perfect to me. I put the top down on my convertible. She gave me directions, and soon we found ourselves traveling along the shore. The ambient sounds of waves and the patterns of the changing sky were my only distractions as I drove. Daphne was quiet so I was quiet too. I thought it very unlike her.

We stopped at the first clam joint we found. She went ahead and sat on a gray bench at the weathered table closest to the water while I lingered at the trunk of the car trying to decide if I should bring the new sturdy leather satchel I had brought packed with all my notes from the Schrödinger mystery—even the time line I had taped to the wall and the postcard in front of the swan boats Galen's Daphne had given me. I knew that Caroline expected me to discard it all. I remembered what she had said, that our baby Daphne would have to be the only Daphne in our lives. I was considering another idea—giving all my clues to my magical Ur-Daphne so she could pursue the mystery for both of us. That would satisfy Caroline's conditions, but I would not have to destroy two years of work. Unbidden, a memory of tossing my rat research into the trash the day I met Daphne came to mind. That's how all this started.

As I sat down I said, "Now this is more like it." She gave me an artificial smile, the kind when someone's mouth smiles but not her eyes. This was supposed to be a celebratory dinner. I wondered again if something was wrong, and then a wisp of a suspicion took shape—that this girl was a new Daphne. This was not how the evening was supposed to go. I had so looked forward to being with my original Daphne, but nothing felt the way I had thought it would.

I went to the little shack and got us a bucket of steamers, some stuffed clams, more french fries than we could possibly eat, and two sodas. The table was arranged so we could face each other but also turn our heads to see the surf. All ten tables were filled, yet the great outdoors absorbed all the chatter, so it felt like we were alone with the waves of the Long Island Sound. The day had been in the eighties, but I felt comfortable with the small breeze off the water. When I got back to the table with the food, paper plates, and plastic utensils, I noticed that Daphne wore the pearls she had hated when she was sixteen; now they suited her. I still loved her unruly red mane and impossibly green eyes.

First she asked about me.

"Really? You had a baby? I mean your girlfriend did? Really?" I almost saw the old enthusiasm in my young friend.

When she asked the baby's name I was evasive and simply said, "She's named for Caroline's grandmother." I'm not sure why I did that. I tried to ask her about her plans, but she was being evasive too, and offered only that she would be attending the University of Chicago.

"It has a great physics department," I replied evenly. The wide sky over the water was gradually turning rosy as the sun began to set. I had brought a paper bag from the car with me. By this time we had finished the clams and I had gotten us each a second soda.

"I've brought gifts for you," I said.

"That wasn't necessary."

"Don't be silly. After all the gifts you've given me?" I began listing all the things she'd sent me.

"Stop," she said.

But I continued: "Without you, I'd still be a stick-in-the-mud, stuck back in the 1950s. You gave me Dylan and the Beatles. Through you I reconnected with Caroline. I can't bear to think about how different things would be if I hadn't met you. You have been like a pied piper to me." But now that I'd had the idea that I wasn't with Ur-Daphne, I couldn't let go of it. Maybe this girl hadn't been the bestower of all those gifts.

"I have something for you," she said. I had noticed her oversized purse. She reached inside and handed me a baseball cap.

"But this is a Mets cap," I said with true dismay. "I can't wear that. I'm a Yankees fan." This felt more like a punishment than a gift.

"Oh really? You are?" she asked in mock surprise. "I know that, Garrett."

"You're a Mets fan?" I asked. They were a newfangled team, born just seven years earlier, a team that lost a lot, belonged to the folks in the suburbs, and would never be the Yankees.

"Long Island girl, Long Island team," she said. "Besides, I'm sure you've been following their season. They're going to go all the way this year. They're going to win the World Series."

"Ha ha ha. That's impossible. The Mets are never going to win the World Series."

"Put on the cap," she said, so I did, feeling disloyal. "It's okay. It's a different league. You're not rooting against the Yankees. You're just rooting for someone else too. And don't laugh at the Mets."

The sky was a riot of color—golds, salmons, and pinks all streaked across the horizon as if from Galen's brush. Daphne's dark-red hair formed a natural part of the sunset. It was her turn to open a present. The bag held the box with the pendant. Her eyes matched the emerald chips that decorated the leaves.

"A laurel tree! How thoughtful. Trees have such sturdy identities." Then she opened the envelope also inside the bag. "What's this? Tickets?"

I had purchased two three-day passes at seven dollars apiece for the upcoming Woodstock music festival, six weeks away. The tickets were about to go on sale to the general public, but I had run into the promoters at the coffee shop in Woodstock. The festival was going to be three days of continuous music. I expected her to be excited, but she had the same flat affect she'd had all evening.

"I've heard about this," she allowed. "I'm afraid I can't go, although it does sound like fun. The festival is August 15–17. I'll already be on my way to Chicago. We're driving. U Chicago starts at the end of August, but there's orientation first."

I felt a true pang. I had imagined her at the music festival, over and over again, her red hair blazing through the crowd, just as I imagined her staring up at the sky in a few weeks when Neil Armstrong walked on the moon. No history would ever be complete now without Daphne. I had seen them all at Woodstock, together, the Schrödinger girls finally meeting. In some alternate universe they might be there together, but in this reality they were all dispersing.

She had put the pendant back in its little box. "Don't you want to put it on?" I asked. "I could help you take off the pearls." Then I queried, "When did you get those pearls? When did I see them first? Do you remember the day?"

"Of course I do," she said. "I was having family pictures taken. You were afraid that I had suddenly become a Junior League miss. And no, Garrett. I am not another Daphne. I am the exact same girl you met in the bookstore." Now I saw her eyes flash, and I had to remind myself to breathe. My scalp tingled. She'd been reining in this anger, and now her voice had taken on a bitter edge.

"What do you mean?" Now it was my voice that was oddly neutral.

"Just that I know there are other Daphnes and you knew and kept it from me."

It was pointless to deny it. It was clear that we were going to talk as equals.

Daphne continued, "I suspected at the gallery. So I did some research, the same as you did, I suppose. I found articles and pictures of Galen Green and his new muse, Daphne. I even saw a picture of her in an art magazine. She was me in a chignon! Then other kids started telling me that I had a double at a school nearby, and the weird thing was that her name was Daphne too! I saw you looking for her at the march. When we talked about Borges on the bus, you asked me if I suspected that there were other realities. You were quizzing me to see if I suspected. I've been thinking about this as long as you have."

"Why didn't you tell me?" I asked. "And if you were so angry with me, why did you give me a present?"

"Why didn't *you* tell *me*?" she replied. The questions just hung there between us. In a weird way Jerry and Caroline had been right. She really was a good actress. "I gave you a present because even though you were keeping this from me, we are profoundly connected. Don't you think? And because I knew you'd hate it."

"I wanted to protect you," I explained, but it occurred to me that perhaps I hadn't seen her for so long because acting this part felt too burdensome to her. It was time to tell her everything I knew about each Daphne. "Wait a minute," I said.

I sprinted to my car and retrieved all the notes. Daphne was still sitting there when I returned to the table. I removed *Reviews of Modern Physics,* the 1957 issue of the scientific journal with Everett's article, and showed it to her, but she said she'd already read it. I told her about Everett's negative reception in Copenhagen that had forced him to give up physics, but she knew about that too. Then I told her how he had dismissed me.

"It's why I'm going to Chicago to study physics," she admitted. "I want to get to the bottom of this too. As for acting like I didn't know? Maybe I was doing my own experiment, to see how long you'd keep everything from me." Her cheeks were turning red with anger, but her throat was choking back a sob. Her beautiful green eyes were misty. She'd been keeping her feelings to herself for so long. Reality was swimming around me.

The desserts I'd brought sat uneaten on our table, but we sipped our coffees. The tables were emptying, though a few new patrons kept arriving. The sign said the Shell Shack was open until eleven p.m. By then the sky had faded into a nacreous gray, radiant like pearls. The sound of the waves punctuated the quiet that followed my story. An employee came around lighting the hurricane lamps on the tables, and the flames lit Daphne's face. She stayed silent for several very uncomfortable minutes.

"You can have all these notes," I said as an emptiness opened up in my solar plexus.

"I don't need them," she responded. "I have my own notes."

"Take them anyway," I urged, trying to restore something of our old camaraderie. I couldn't lose her.

"I trusted you, and the whole time you were keeping the most important things you knew, and the most important people you knew, to yourself."

"You were keeping what you knew to yourself too. At least I wasn't pretending what I felt."

"That's not the same thing, and you know it."

I had never imagined her angry with me. I had been stupid and misguided, and I had underestimated her. I granted myself permission to be a sole observer. Maybe she was right to call it an experiment.

"I can tell that you were actually considering not telling me tonight," she sullenly remarked, not letting her anger go, letting it flare again. "I can't even look at you," she sputtered, and she jumped up and stormed off in the direction of the surf.

The night was lit by a brilliant full moon, but I didn't take my eyes off her. I watched Daphne sit down in the sand, pull her legs up to her chest, and encircle them with her arms. She sat there for several minutes while the sky grew inky, punctuated by only a few stray stars—the moon was so bright. Finally, I saw her walk slowly back along the beach and take her seat opposite me.

"I forgive you," she said. "I want to meet the other Schrödinger girls. Do any of the others know?"

"Before tonight I would have said no. Now? How do I know?"

"Maybe you should tell them."

"Maybe *you* should," I said stiffly. "The case with my notes has contact information."

"You can relax, Garrett. I said I forgive you."

She assumed that my stiffness was contrition, and that was part of it, but I could also feel grief taking up residence in my hollow chest. We were going to say goodbye.

"People find these ideas crazy, Daphne," I warned.

"No shit, Sherlock," she said. "We have to find out why these worlds penetrated each other." She was thinking out loud. "They should have stayed separate."

I told her of my day at the Met with Caroline. "I investigated the paintings of the Daphne myth, looking for clues—you know, the tree created by the river god, a Daphne tree with branching realities, a laurel tree."

"My pendant," she said. "But it doesn't explain anything, right? Though I love myths. Like Zeus coming as a swan in Yeats's 'Leda and the Swan,'" and she began to recite, "*Did she put on his knowledge,*" but then stopped. "Oh, never mind, Garrett."

I asked her to recite the entire Yeats poem and explain her train of thought, but she insisted it wasn't important, that science was the better tool. I didn't remind her that science said our experience was impossible.

Then she asked for another coffee. I grew tired of wearing the Mets cap in the heat, so I took it off and went to get us both another cup, though we certainly didn't need them to warm up on that summer night. I peered right at her when I returned to the table and handed her the coffee.

"I have a confession to make," she said, her green eyes looking right into mine, which were no longer hidden behind the thick lenses I used to wear.

I just waited.

"I took the pendant and buried it in the sand. I'd like to put it on now. Could you go down to the surf to get it? It's so difficult walking in the sand in these heels. I left it right over there." She pointed to the spot a hundred yards away where I'd watched her sit.

"Sure," I replied, "be glad to."

The moment was bright with moonlight and the warm light cast by the hurricane lamps of the little café. As I walked toward the surf, I turned around once and waved to my Schrödinger girl with a big-armed gesture to express all the things I couldn't say. She lifted her arm in salute.

I turned back, facing the silver waves, and found the spot. I lowered myself to the rocky shore and began searching through the seaweed and beach for the golden tree pendant I'd given her. For a while it felt like a fool's errand, but finally I glimpsed something bright. Eureka! As I gently dug through the sand, links of the buried necklace appeared.

Then a startling sound, like a fluttering out on the water, attracted my attention, and I glanced out to sea in time to glimpse the briefest flash of large white wings, but when I looked again nothing broke the calm surface of the water. The water was serene, the moon a brilliant orange orb climbing higher in the sky. I turned back to give a thumbs-up sign to Daphne to show I had found her necklace, but even from that distance I could see that her place was empty. Jogging back, I was thinking that she must have gone to the ladies' room. We'd had so many coffees. But the minutes ticked on, and she didn't reappear.

A woman made her way back to a table near ours.

"Excuse me," I called out to her, trying to appear nonchalant. "Was there anyone in the bathroom with you? A young woman? I seem to have lost her," I added, trying to make a joke of it.

"No. Empty except for me," she said before turning back to her date.

I returned to the counter, pretending to feel confident that I'd find her there, but there were only two teenage guys buying themselves fries. I walked to the parking lot, but she wasn't in the car. She wasn't anywhere. I circled back to our table to wait for her, but her purse was gone and so was all the Schrödinger material. She had left the Woodstock tickets and the Mets cap primly on the table. I felt for the pendant I was still holding in my pocket. When I lifted the tickets from the table, I noticed a scrap of napkin with words written in her fancy script: *I'm fine, Garrett. No need to worry.*

That ended my plan to notify the authorities. I stashed the little note in my wallet. Then I looked carefully at her bench and saw a shape in the sand next to it. She'd left the satchel behind after all—the Daphne satchel. I almost sobbed in relief. I knew I couldn't take the leather case home if I didn't want Caroline to know that I'd kept it; I could stash it in my office at school. I wanted her and baby Daphne to stay. I lingered at the table in the moonlight, sipping coffee until it was closing time at the Shell Shack, and then I began the long ride home.

THE END

Acknowledgments

My deepest love and appreciation go to Kaylie Jones, my ambassador of quan. Kaylie is the fairy godmother who made my dream of writing a novel that people might want to read come true. She encouraged me to believe in my story and find my narrator, and rescued me with the perfect metaphor when I was in the tall grass, one that showed how to keep my plot afloat. I am honored to be published by Kaylie Jones Books.

To Johnny Temple, my admiration and gratitude. I admire your dedication to literature and your devotion to independent publishing, and my thanks are boundless for your willingness to publish an unknown writer.

I can't calculate Tram Neill's contributions. He has been a friend and inspiration since high school, and he brought his psychologist's eye to the project, making sure the science and psychology were accurate. He also very graciously edited the manuscript and corrected more mistakes than I can admit to making.

Elizabeth Wheeler has been stalwart in reading early drafts of almost everything I write. There is no way to thank a friend enough for that kind of generosity. A writer could not ask for a more sensitive or articulate reader. Lainie Learnard read the finished novel and complained that I had kept her up all night. I can't imagine sweeter encouragement, and I am so grateful. Gina Dubussion and Dan Herbatschek generously read early versions of the novel and encouraged me to continue.

Kevin Heisler read the manuscript and sent me the most beautifully detailed e-mail that raised important questions and urged me to go further and spice things up. Laurie Loewenstein brought her insight and vision to my novel and reminded me to look carefully at each and every word. I offer her my sincere thanks.

I want to thank the students of Kaylie Jones's advanced writing seminar in the fall of 2015, particularly Jean Ende, Dorothy Hom, and Rachel Wong, who always showed me where I was going wrong. That's invaluable feedback. I thank Minna Barrett, Tanya Lowenstein, and Cindy Rinaldi for always listening. Their support gave me the courage to keep writing. The members of the Vigilante Lounge were always there to hear about my progress and urge me to continue.

To Dutchy Brett I offer sincere thanks for so many things. She gave me a "mother grant." When I unexpectedly lost a sabbatical I was counting on, she replaced the lost funds herself so I could miss a semester of teaching to concentrate on my writing. She always shows interest in my work. Beyond that, she introduced me to *Little Women* and other classics, read Shakespeare with me, and showed me the joys of language.

There is no way I can ever thank my husband, Mark Kauffman, enough for his cheerful attention to the more quotidian details of life so I would be free to write. He also read every word of this novel, almost as I wrote them, and was endlessly encouraging and engaged, even at two in the morning. He edited and proofread, listened to my insecurities, and was the best cheerleader imaginable.

David Brett, my beloved son, was involved with every aspect of this story. He thrashed out plot points with me, made suggestions, considered the science, debated all aspects of the story, and attended to every word. He also did more formatting and computer work than either of us want to remember. His support and suggestions made the completion of this book possible.

Mia Brett, my beloved daughter, is a constant inspiration to me. She listened to all my ideas and brought her understanding of history and literature to my beginning efforts. I couldn't have done this without her.

To all my friends and family who encouraged, supported, and inspired me, thank you so much.